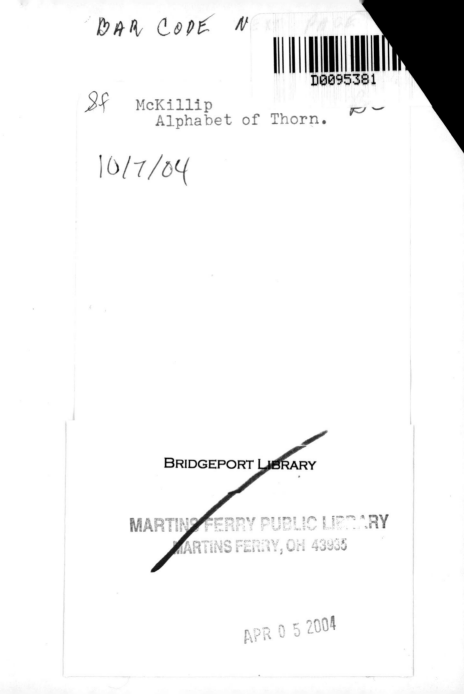

*Alphabet of Thorn*

# Alphabet of Thorn

### PATRICIA A. McKILLIP

ACE BOOKS, NEW YORK

An Ace Book
Published by The Berkley Publishing Group
A division of Penguin Group (USA) Inc.
375 Hudson Street
New York, New York 10014

This book is an original publication of The Berkley Publishing Group.

First edition: February 2004

Library of Congress Cataloging-in-Publication Data

McKillip, Patricia A.
    Alphabet of thorn / Patricia A. McKillip.— 1st ed.
        p.   cm.
    ISBN 0-441-01130-6
    1. Teenage girls—Fiction.   2. Translators—Fiction.
3. Orphans—Fiction.   I. Title.
PS3563.C38A78 2004
813'.54—dc22                                    2003062912

PRINTED IN THE UNITED STATES OF AMERICA

10 9 8 7 6 5 4 3 2 1

# ONE

On Dreamer's Plain, the gathering of delegations from the Twelve Crowns of Raine for the coronation of the Queen of Raine looked like an invading army. So the young transcriptor thought, gazing out a window as she awaited a visiting scholar. She had never been so high in the palace library, and rarely so warm. Usually at this time of the morning she was buried in the stones below, blowing on her fingers to warm them so they could write. Outside, wind gusted across the vast plain, pulling banners taut, shaking the pavilions thrown up for the various delegations' entourages of troops and servants. A spring squall had blown in from the sea and crossed the plain. The drying pavilions, huffing like bellows in the wind, were brilliant with color. The transcriptor, who had only seen invading armies in the epics she translated, narrowed her eyes at this gathering and imagined possibilities. She was counting the horses penned near each pavilion, pelts

lustrous even at a distance after the rain, and as clear, silhou-
etted against one another's whites and grays and chestnuts, as
figures pricked on a tapestry, when the scholar finally arrived.

A beary man, he shed a fur cloak that smelled of damp and
an unusual scent of tobacco. He carried a manuscript
wrapped in leather that he laid upon the librarian's desk as
gently as a newborn. As he unswaddled the manuscript, the
transcriptor standing silently at the window caught his eye.
His hands stilled. He stared at her. Then his head, big, dark,
and very hairy, jerked toward the librarian who had shown
him in.

"Who is this?"

"We called her Nepenthe," the librarian said in his austere
voice. His name was Daimon; Nepenthe had known him all
her life, for he had found her and named her. Of the child she
had been before she became Nepenthe, neither of them knew
a thing. In sixteen years since then, she had changed beyond
recognition, and he had not changed by a moment, being the
same dispassionate, thin-haired wraith who had picked her up
with his bony hands and tucked her into a book bag to add to
the acquisitions of the royal library. "She is one of our most
skilled and creative translators. She has a gift for unusual alphabets. Such as you say you have, Master Croysus?"

"I've never seen anything like it in my life," Master Croysus
said. He continued unwrapping the manuscript, still tossing
glances at Nepenthe. She stood quietly, her long fingers
tucked into her broad black sleeves, trying to look skilled and
creative, while wondering what the scholar found wrong with

her face. "It looks like an alphabet of fish. Where did you come from?"

"Don't let her youth deceive you," Daimon murmured. The scholar shook his head absently, squinting at Nepenthe until she opened her mouth and answered.

"Nowhere, Master Croysus. I was abandoned on the cliff edge outside the palace and found by librarians. The last foundling they took in was named Merle. N was the next available letter."

Master Croysus made an incredulous trumpet sound through his nostrils. "I've seen that face," he said abruptly, "on a parchment older than Raine. I don't remember what it was, except that the ancient kingdom it came from lay far beyond the Twelve Crowns and it no longer exists except on paper."

The librarian looked curiously at Nepenthe; she wished she could take off her head and look at herself.

"A clan of wanderers," he suggested, "remnants of the forgotten kingdom. Perhaps they were passing through Raine when Nepenthe was born."

"There was no one—?"

"No one," Daimon said simply, "came looking for her." He paused, added to clarify and end the subject, "It was assumed that whoever left her in that precarious spot—her mother, most likely—flung herself for her own reasons into the sea. The child was left in hope, we also assumed, of a less difficult life, since she was left alive and wailing with great energy when we found her."

The scholar grunted, which seemed his last word on the

subject. He laid the manuscript bare and gestured to Nepenthe.

She stepped to the desk. They all gazed at the strange, elongated ovals neatly imprinted on something that Nepenthe did not recognize.

She brushed it with her fingertips. It was supple and tough at once. Some kind of pelt, it seemed, though it was white as birch and strangely unwrinkled.

"What is this?" she asked puzzledly.

The scholar regarded her with more than fantastic interest. "Good question. No one knows. I'm hoping that the contents may indicate the tools." He was silent a moment, his bushy brows raised inquiringly at her, and then at the librarian. "I can stay only as long as the delegation from the Ninth Crown stays after the coronation. I'm traveling in the company of Lord Birnum, who will pay his respects and go home to civilization as soon as he can. It is a powerful gesture and a stirring custom for rulers to be crowned in the palace of the first King of Raine, but not even he, with all his ambitions, imagined the rulers of Twelve Crowns under his ancient roof at the same time."

"Are you with Lord Birnum in the palace?" Daimon asked delicately.

"No," Master Croysus sighed. "In a leaky pavilion."

"We can offer a bed of sorts among the books."

The scholar sighed again, this time with relief. "I would be immensely grateful."

"I'll see to that, while Nepenthe takes you down to show

you where she will be working on your manuscript. Transcriptors dwell in the depths. As well, I must warn you, as do visiting scholars."

"I trust the depths don't leak."

"No."

"Then I'll sleep happily buried in stone." He wrapped his manuscript again in leather and himself in fur, and followed Nepenthe.

She led him down and down until mortared stone became solid stone, until they left even the green plain above them and the only light came from windows staring across the sea. Until then, he questioned her; she answered absently, wondering about the fish wrapped in his arms.

"You don't remember anything of your life before the librarians found you?"

"How could I? I had no teeth; I didn't know words for anything. I don't even remember—" She stopped to light a taper, for the stairways had begun to plunge into hand-hewn burrowings. "I do remember one thing. But I don't know what it is."

"What is it?"

She shrugged. "Just a face, I think."

"Whose?" he demanded.

"I don't know. I'm an orphan, Master Croysus," she reminded him patiently. "A foundling. The librarians have always taken us in; they train us to become scribes and translators. We get accustomed early to living and working in stone suspended between sky and sea."

"So you're content here?"

She flung him an uncertain glance, wondering what he meant. "I don't think about it," she answered. "I have nothing of my own, nothing that's not on loan from the librarians. Not even my name. I don't know what else I could choose."

"Do you like the work?"

She smiled, smelling books now, leather bindings, musty parchments, flaking scrolls that lived with her underground. "Here," she told him, "there is no time. No past, no future; no place I can't go, no lost realm I can't travel to, as long as I can decipher its fish."

She showed him where she worked. It was a doorless cell lined with books, a cell in a hive that was itself a cell in the huge hive that clung by walls and pillars and towers of stone to the immense, steep cliff rising straight out of the sea. The palace of the rulers of Raine had grown from a seedling through the centuries. Long ago, it had been little more than a fortress on the edge of the world, guarding its portion of thick wood and plain against other princelings. Through the centuries, the palace had become a small country itself, existing between sea and air, burrowed deep into the cliffs, piled above the earth so high that on a clear day, from the highest tower, the new Queen of Raine could see all but three of the Twelve Crowns she ruled. The first king had taken the first Crown: lands as far as he could see from his single tower. Before he died, he had added two linked Crowns to his own. Now there were twelve, and they flew on a tower higher than the king could ever imagine, even in his wildest dreams, as he guarded

Raine in his sleep in the secret cave within the cliff below the palace.

So many lands had produced so many words. During the centuries they found their way, in one collection or another, to the royal library. The library was a city carved into the cliffs beneath the palace. Parts of it were so old that scrolls and manuscripts got lost for entire reigns and were discovered again in the next. Languages transmuted constantly as they wandered in and out of the Twelve Crowns. Such mysteries required flexible minds. A librarian had found the baby sitting abandoned on the sheer edge of the world; the librarians kept her. That proved shrewd. Nepenthe had drooled on words, talked at them, and tried to eat them until she learned to take them into her eyes instead of her mouth. Surrounded by that rich hoard into which chance and death had brought her, she had not yet imagined any other kingdom.

Within those stones she had grown her weedy way into a young woman, long-boned and strong, able to reach high shelves without a stool. Her hair, which was waist-long and crow-feather dark, she kept bundled at her neck with leather ties; during the course of the day she would inevitably pull them out to use as book marks. In that sunless place, her skin stayed brown as hazelnut. The eyes that gazed absently back at her in the mornings from her wash-basin were sometimes green and sometimes brown. What Master Croysus had seen in her face, she had no idea. She was curious about it, as she was about nearly everything, but that would have to wait.

He examined her tiny space, a shallow cave so full of shelves that her table barely fit among the books, and she had to sit with her stool in the hallway. He looked at work she had done, the fat jars of ink colored variously and stamped with her initial, her carefully sharpened nibs. Finally, reassured, he unrolled his manuscript again. They discussed the oval, finny letters with an eye here, a gill there at random. He told her his ideas; she pulled down previous alphabets she had deciphered, one seemingly of twigs, another of bird-claw impressions in wax. By the time Daimon came to show him his bed-chamber, Master Croysus seemed content to leave his treasure with her.

She dreamed that night about fish, bright flashing schools of them whose whirls and darts and turnings this way and that meant something vital in a language of fish. But what? She struggled with it, trying to persuade her unwieldy human body to move gracefully among the little butterfly flittings, until finally in her dream she swam with them, wheeling and shining, at ease in the water, speaking the invisible language of fish.

Deep in the stones, playing among the fish, she was scarcely aware of the coronation above her head. Master Croysus vanished for most of a day or two, then came to her late in the morning, reeking of smoke, his hair standing on end, to see how far she had gotten into the mystery. He seemed pleased with her work, and less pleased with what was going on in the complex and incomprehensible palace above ground.

"She's very young," he muttered of the new queen. "Younger than you, and with far less — far less — "

Less what he could not find a word for. Nepenthe, oblivious of most of what went on beyond the library, assumed that the world would take care of itself, and got on with her fish.

That night she woke with a start to the sound of her name.

She answered instantly, pulling herself upright out of a stupor of dreams: "Yes."

Then she opened her eyes, puzzled. The world was so still that it might have vanished, swallowed by its own past or future. The name was already fading; she could only hear the backwashed eddies and echoes of it in her head. Outside her door, the stone corridors were silent; no one had called Nepenthe. Neither the drowsing embers in her brazier nor the single star hanging in the high narrow window shed any light upon the matter. Yet someone had dropped a word like a weight on a plumb line straight into her heart and she had recognized her name.

She dropped back down, still listening, hearing only her slowing heartbeat. Nothing spoke again out of the dark. A visiting mage from the Floating School, she decided finally, celebrating the coronation too heartily, had flung a word carelessly into the night, heedless of where it landed. She closed her eyes, burrowed toward sleep, and reached the memory on the borders of dream, the one thing that she could claim as her own, that she had in her possession before the librarians found her.

The memory was of a face, misty, ill-defined. It seemed to shape itself out of the sky, displacing the blue, flowing endlessly above green, racing far into the distance to meet it. She didn't know the names for colors then, nor could she name the force that blew across the green so that it roared and glittered and seemed to stream wildly away from her. The face came close, as close to her as her own face, tried to meld itself with her bones, her eyes. Then she was falling slowly, the face growing farther and farther away from her. She felt the distance between them like something physical, a coldness that refused to end. A word came wailing out of her then, but what it meant had vanished into the blue.

And after that, everything was gone.

She woke to another reverberating sound: the enormous gong in the refectory. Confused, remembering the strange word in the middle of the night, she moved too abruptly and fell out of bed. She untangled herself, muttering, pulled on a patched linen shift, and stumbled down the hall to the baths. There, in that steamy warmth, she closed her eyes again and let herself fall into a chorus of laughter and protest, flat and stiff as a tome into a tank, causing a wave at both ends that submerged more than one floating head.

Someone spread a hand on her head and dunked her again as she surfaced. "Nepenthe!" she heard as she sputtered soap bubbles. "Must you fling yourself into the water like a whale falling out of the sky?"

"It's the only way I could wake up this morning," she answered. Her eyes were finally open. She floated a little, trying to remember when she had begun to comprehend that her mother must have done just that: flung herself like a strange fish off the edge of the world into a sea so far below that until she was halfway there, she would not have heard the waves break against the cliff.

But why? she wondered, as always when she had fallen asleep in the realm of memory.

She felt water weltering around her. A head appeared, slick and white as a shell. It was Oriel, whom the librarians had acquired shortly after Nepenthe. She had been discovered by a scholar on the track of some obscure detail, surrounded by books in a forgotten chamber and bawling furiously. Fine-boned and comely, she could well have been the embarrassing afterthought of a highborn lady-in-waiting in the court above. Her pale hair, which she kept short with a nib sharpener, floated around her face like a peony's petals. Her fingers, pale as well, and impossibly delicate, closed with unexpected strength on Nepenthe's wrist.

"You have to come with me."

"It's amazing," Nepenthe marveled, "how your hands can feel like they're sweating even in bath water."

"They always sweat when I'm frightened."

Nepenthe peered at her, wondering if it was important. Everything agitated Oriel. "What's the matter?" A coming storm, she guessed; the phase of the moon; a translation about to be reviewed by the head of librarians. But she was thrice wrong.

"I have to get a book from the Floating School. I don't want to go alone; that place terrifies me. Come with me."

Nepenthe ran soap through her hair, tempted by the prospect: a ride across the plain through the brilliant pavilions, into the mysterious wood in which anything was said to happen. Then she wondered: what book?

"Why can't they bring it here?"

"Everyone is here," Oriel said vaguely, "and the students are involved in some magic or another. A trader brought a book to the mages that they can't read. The trader told them he thought it might be magic since no one he had ever met could read it. A mage told the librarians last night, and now they can't wait to see it and I must go and fetch it because everyone else is working or celebrating—"

"I am, too," Nepenthe remembered. "Working, for a visiting scholar."

Oriel gazed at her despairingly. "Is it important?"

"Well, he thinks it is."

"What is it?"

"It seems to be turning into a supply list."

"A supply list!"

"For a caravan of traders about to cross—"

"Not an epic," Oriel interrupted pointedly. "You can finish that with your eyes closed."

"It's thousands of years old! And written upon the hide of an animal unknown anywhere in the Twelve Crowns."

"Maybe it was a fish," Oriel suggested grumpily.

"Maybe it was," Nepenthe said, intrigued. "Or maybe some kind of a seal—"

"Nepenthe! Please come with me. Your scholar can wait

half a day. He's probably sleeping off yesterday's celebration anyway. He'll never know you're gone. Please." She added cunningly as Nepenthe hesitated, "I'll let you see the book before I give it to the librarians."

Nepenthe submerged herself to get the soap out of her hair. She shook her head, sending her dark hair swirling around her while she thought. Books sent to the librarians from the Floating School were extremely rare; the mages had their own ways of recognizing words. And Oriel was right about Master Croysus: he might not appear until late afternoon if he found his way down at all from the heady business of celebration.

She straightened abruptly, sent her long hair whirling back with a toss of her head, nearly smacking someone behind her. "All right." She stopped, snorting water as Oriel splashed extravagantly with relief. "Meet me," she added stuffily, "at the library stables after breakfast."

In her tiny, shadowy chamber, she dressed quickly and simply for the ride in a long woolen tunic and boots. It was still early spring, and bound to be brisk on the plain. Then she went to breakfast. The refectory was so high and broad that swallows sometimes nested along the walls. There she could step beyond the arches into light; she could pace above the sea. Dawn mists were shredding above the water, tatters and plumes of purple and gray. The hilly island that was the Third Crown lay clearly visible in the distance, its white cliffs gleaming like bone in the morning sun. She filled a bowl from the huge cauldron full of inevitable boiled oats, and added nuts and dried fruit to it. She took it with her through the arched outer doors to the balcony beyond. It was made of marble from one of the southern Crowns; its fat, pillared walls and railings were high and very thick. There, if she listened hard on a fine, still day, sometimes she thought she could hear the breaking waves.

Not that morning: she only heard the voice of Master Croysus, oddly energetic at that hour. He was standing at one corner of the balcony, talking to a couple of librarians. One glance at his face told Nepenthe he had not been to bed yet. His eyes were red-rimmed and shadowed at the same time; his face was so pale it might have been kin to the glacial, ravaged face of the moon.

"They say she can't keep a thought in her head. She's scarcely there, behind her eyes. Yet she is her father's daughter. She has his eyes, his hair, everything. Everything but his ability to understand what will hold twelve restless Crowns under her rule." He shook his wild head and scooped another spoonful of oats. "It's disturbing."

"She has Vevay to counsel her," a librarian reminded him.

"She has the entire Floating School, but she does not seem to realize that she might need all the help she can get."

Nepenthe, hovering in the doorway, took a discreet step back out of eyesight and stepped on someone's foot. She turned. It was only Laidley, who seemed to have been following her.

His head bobbed diffidently as she apologized. His lank, straw-pale hair hung in his eyes, which were too close together and a pallid gray. Intent on Nepenthe's face, they seemed slightly crossed. He was a stoop-shouldered young man whose hair had already begun to thin, revealing the bulge of the well-filled skull beneath. He knew more languages than most of the transcriptors. Around Nepenthe he could barely find words in any of them.

But he spoke that morning as she began eating her porridge. "Oriel says you are riding with her to the Floating School to bring back a manuscript the mages can't translate."

She nodded, feeling guilty about the scholar, awake and oblivious, just on the other side of the wall. "Why? Do you want to go instead of me?"

He shifted, disconcerted. "I was thinking: with."

"But then I wouldn't have to go."

"But then—" He paused. She read the rest in his eyes, in the slant of his mouth: then I wouldn't go with you.

She swallowed oats wordlessly, then made an effort to change his expression, which seemed to be bleak, lately, whenever he looked at her. "Do you want to see the book before we give it to the librarians? They might keep it to themselves for months while they decipher it."

His eyes looked crossed again, this time with avidity. "Yes. Very much."

"Then work near the south stairs in the library and watch for us to come back."

His head bobbed again; he swallowed a word. Then he smiled, a generous and surprisingly sweet smile that made her stare. "Thank you, Nepenthe."

It took half the morning, it seemed, for the two transcriptors to find their way up and out of stone onto earth. They took horses from the library stables, a pair of gentle nags that could not frighten even Oriel. Once outside the palace walls, as they made their way along the cliff road to skirt the pavilions and paddocks, servants, wagons, the assorted paraphernalia of travel, Nepenthe turned to look back. The immense and complex maze of stone with its spiraling walls and towers built upon towers clung like a small mountain to the cliff, spilled halfway down it, a crust of angles, burrows, parapets between more towers, balconies and bridges thrust out of the face of the cliff, windows in the stone like a thousand watching eyes. The east gate in the outermost palace wall opened as she paused. A troop of guards or warriors in sky blue and silver rode out. Against the massive sprawl they seemed as tiny as insects. Riding away from it among the pavilions, they regained human stature. Nepenthe sent windblown hair out of her eyes and caught up with Oriel, who had turned away from the sea toward the wood.

It seemed a dark, impenetrable tangle, a smudge along one edge of Dreamer's Plain. The school, which occasionally and inexplicably floated above the trees, was nowhere to be seen that morning. Its history was as nebulous as the wood. The school was either younger or older than the royal library, or it had once been the library, during the rule of the first King of Raine. Legend said that as the palace grew more complex through the centuries, the school broke free of it and floated away, searching for some peace and quiet in the wood. Another tale had it hidden within the wood for safekeeping during a war. Yet another said that the wood was not a wood at all, but the cumulative magic of centuries spun around the school, and that the magic itself could take any shape it chose. As far as Nepenthe knew, it generally looked like trees. But they were thick, shadowy, strange. No one hunted there. The animals, tales said, had a human turn of thought and talked too much.

As they rode toward it, the dark wood began to leak color like paint spilling between stones. Oriel pulled her horse to a halt and reached out to Nepenthe at the sight. Light shimmered from between the trees, great swaths of dazzling hues that Nepenthe only glimpsed from a distance when a parade of courtiers rode to hunt beyond the plain. Such silks they wore then, such rich golds and reds, purples and summer blues that they looked like flowers blown across the plain. As the transcriptors stared, bolts of flame and sun unrolled like rippling satin into the air above the trees, shook across the grass, and seeped away.

"I'm not going in there," Oriel said flatly. Her damp fingers were icy around Nepenthe's wrist.

"It's nothing," Nepenthe murmured, entranced. "Magic. Illusion. They made it out of nothing."

"They can kill each other with it!"

"They're students," Nepenthe argued unconvincingly. "They don't practice that on each other."

"If it doesn't kill you, it can transform you into something loathsome."

"They can probably see us coming. They wouldn't turn a pair of transcriptors into maggots."

Oriel balked. "No. Anyway, how do you know what it is or who is making it? They could be having a war in there for all we know, and we'd ride into the middle of something deadly just looking for a book."

"All right," Nepenthe said. "All right. I'll go."

"No."

Nepenthe coaxed her placid mount forward a step or two. "My horse doesn't even see it," she said, but Oriel sat obstinately still.

"I'll wait," she said tersely. "Just hurry."

The mages must have seen them coming some time ago, Nepenthe realized when she saw the robed figure come out of the trees to meet her. The young man was carrying something in one hand. His hair, Nepenthe noted idly, was the same gold-leaf hue that had splashed so profligately out of the mysterious wood. As she rode up to him, he gave her a smile somewhere between amusement and rue.

He nodded at the figure in the distance, then said to Nepenthe as she turned her mount to rein beside him, "We frightened her, then."

"She's easily frightened."

"There was no need." He looked up at Nepenthe, mouth open to continue, then did not, for a moment; only the wind spoke, racing exuberantly between them. He finished his thought finally. "You aren't. Easily frightened."

"No." The word snagged oddly. She cleared her throat, then for once in her life could find nothing coherent to say.

"What color are they?" she heard.

"What?"

"Your eyes. They were brown. Then when you turned your horse to face the sea they became as green as water."

"They do," she answered. "They do that." His own eyes seemed the color of his hair, full of morning light. Rich, she thought dazedly, rich, though he wore the plain brown wool of a student, and that was none too clean.

"What is your name?"

"Nepenthe. I am a ward of the royal library." From mute to babbling, she had suddenly gone. "They were up to N when they found me on the cliff edge."

"Nepenthe." His eyes had narrowed slightly; they seemed to pull at her, doing a mage's work. In some magical world, she dismounted; she stood on the grass in front of him; his hands, graceful and strong, something crusted and glittering beneath the nails, moved to touch her . . .

But no: they still held the book. She blinked, still mounted. He remembered it, too, in that moment.

"Oh. Here." He held the book up to her; she took it. It was very plain, worn, undistinguished by gold ink or jewels; the binding smelled of wax and old leather. "It came to us in a trader's wagon. He said it had been passing from hand to hand across the Twelve Crowns and more than likely beyond them. Nobody can read it, so he gave it to the mages for nothing. If the librarians find it deals with magic, the mages want it back. Otherwise, they'll settle for some explanation of it."

"I'll tell them." Idly, because she had been surrounded by books since she had been found, she opened it, glanced at the odd letters.

"My name is Bourne," she heard him say, "of Seale. If I come to the library, will they let me see you?"

They looked like thorns, the strange letters: brambles curling and twisting around one another, linked by their sharp spurs. "Yes," she said to him. And then a word spoke out of the book, a deep, sudden sound she recognized, swift as an adder biting into her heart and clinging.

She looked at the young man, Bourne, dazed by the unexpected wealth: his gold eyes, his name, the book coming to life in her hands. "Yes," she said again, holding those eyes while she slipped the book into a deep pocket in her tunic, beneath her cloak. "Come to me."

She had forgotten Oriel, the isolated rider stopped in the middle of the plain while it ran hither and yon beneath her. Riding back, she hardly saw the grass. Speaking, Oriel startled her, as though one of them had appeared out of nowhere.

"Well?" she asked. "Did you get it?"

Nepenthe scarcely thought; the answer came out of her as easily as truth. "Oh. The mages didn't send it after all. The student said that they had finally learned its secret language."

Oriel turned her horse, matched Nepenthe's distracted pace. "Then we came for nothing. Oh, well, we had a ride on the plain in the sun. Was it magic? The book?"

Nepenthe lifted her face to all the gold flowing down from the sky. "Someone's secret recipes," she answered vaguely.

"We came all the way out here for a cookbook?"

"So it seems."

She urged her horse forward, racing for the cliff road, wanting to run herself all the way back to the labyrinth of the library, where she could hide and find a way through the brambles. She heard Oriel shouting behind her, but it was nothing, only fear, only beware of falling off the edge of the world, and Nepenthe had been balanced there before she had a name.

# TWO

Bourne lay on earth, in silence, somewhere within the
Floating School. On those days, which were as timeless
and dark as nights, the Floating School seemed to bury itself
underground. The place was silent as a grave. It smelled like
one, Bourne supposed, if the dead could smell earth and stone
and roots and tell about it. The students could and did. They
woke on what felt like pebbles instead of pallets. Forewarned
and given challenges the day before, Bourne was still surprised. Straw turned to stone, light to night, the daily genial
pulse of life within the school with its scholarly murmurings
and colorful mishaps was suddenly, utterly stilled. Illusion, he
knew, all illusion. If he cried out, someone would answer instantly. If he battered at the blinding dark, tried to run from it,
then what seemed a tiny cell of unmortared stone and earth
would suddenly expand around him; a hand would draw him
into light. So he had heard. So far he had been patient in the

dark, more curious than afraid. So far, he had been able to concentrate on the challenge, the test they must pass through to find the day.

So far. He lay on his back, feeling a mass quite close to his face, as though he were in a box. If he sat up, nothing would stop him. But the illusion hung there, persistent and subtle: nothing there, but something. There. They had been instructed, that day, to listen for the sound of the sea and to interpret what it said. Buried in earth and stone and dark halfway across the plain, he could not imagine such a thing was possible. Even standing on the edge of the cliff, staring down at the foaming, churning waters, Bourne had never heard the sea.

But the mages expected the impossible, and Bourne had learned that he could occasionally surprise himself.

He had surprised himself simply by staying at the school since autumn, after his brothers and cousins had made bets that he wouldn't last the season. He would send the Floating School tumbling into the sea, they warned. He would turn himself into a donkey and forget how to change himself back. The mages would lock him out sooner or later. Sooner became later; autumn became winter. In early spring, the Lord of Seale rode to the door of the school and demanded to speak to his youngest nephew about a neighbor's daughter who was waning and weeping and writing poetry about Bourne's golden hair. Find him, the mages had suggested. If he chooses. If you can. Bourne, buried in dark on that silent day, could not be found. He had been given a word he had never encoun-

tered before to interpret. Hearing, from very far away, his uncle's voice, he mingled the sound of it into his interpretation of
the word and produced a very apt description of the fiery,
puissant, bellowing beast the word named.

This time, he heard nothing but his own breathing, his
heartbeat, his blood. Hard enough to concentrate on the sea,
which he could neither see nor hear, let alone imagine the
sound that might come from it. What he kept seeing was a
face. For the first time, he grew impatient in the charged and
magical silence. He wanted to get up, walk until he found a
door, then walk out of the wood toward the cliff road until he
saw again the rider coming toward him, her long hair shining
and crisp as a blackbird's feathers, her shoulders as straight as
any hunter's, her skin like sun-drenched earth.

His breath broke explosively out of him. He held it a moment, then lay quietly, drawing and loosing air, drawing and
loosing slowly in long, measured cadences, until the dark was
filled with the soft rhythm of it and he recognized, his eyes
widening suddenly and his breath heaving and breaking
again, the ceaseless patterns of the tide.

He smiled in the dark, charmed. So the sea breathed like
some great, restless, dreaming animal. So it spoke. But what
did it say? An ancient and untranslatable language, like the
voices of trees, the voice of wind. It was enough that he had
heard it; the mages could expect no more.

But it was still dark; he had nothing else to do but listen.
Blood in his ears sang like water; his breath weltered like
spume. He heard her voice again: Nepenthe. The orphan N,

reared by librarians. Her voice, low and slightly husky, dredging words out of the strange silence that had encircled them both like a spell. A little world. The air that they both breathed. He heard his breath again at the memory of her eyes, that moment when they changed. Chestnut, then leaf. Opaque, and then luminous as she turned toward the sea.

Come to the library.

He had been to the palace with his uncle, Ermin of Seale, Lord in the realm of Raine and ruler of the Second Crown. Lord over three sons of his own, as well as three of his dead brother's, all of whom were either safely and appropriately married, or wealthily betrothed. He had different plans for Bourne, whom he sent to the Floating School. Not, Bourne knew, for any great gifts he possessed; his uncle had no illusions about that. What he had were ambitions, which the young and inexperienced queen, ascending to her perilous place in the world, had sharpened immeasurably. A mage's powers, he made Bourne see clearly, would be a great asset to the family. The more power Bourne acquired from the Floating School, the better. His uncle would hardly approve of an orphaned transcriptor distracting him from his studies. The librarians' foundlings came from everywhere, like blown leaves, and no telling from what tree she might have fallen. Let alone what far-flung language she had been born to speak.

Where had she come from? he wondered, shifting a little to rearrange a pebble under his shoulder blade. She with those long bones, those eyes?

What does the sea say?

He breathed an answer; the word washed over him, through him, fanning out, separating into pale, delicate fingers of spume. He stared back at the changeless dark, trying to see through illusion into light.

"Nepenthe," the mage Felan repeated curiously when Bourne explained what the sea had said to him. There was a muffled snicker amid the unwashed, hungry students clustered together at the end of the silent day. Some had heard poetry; one or two had heard spells, which they attempted then and there, but which came to nothing in the light of day. They lacked an element, Felan suggested. Perhaps the true sea, cold, dangerous, and indifferent, might have fed the magic, rather than their imaginary seas. Others had heard nothing, not even their own breathing.

"You told us to listen for the sea," one said bewilderedly. "Why should I listen to myself?"

"Everything connects," Felan said mildly. He smiled at the fretting student. "Don't worry. There will be other days." He was a huge, gentle man, bald as a stone, with astonishing power. He could hold the Floating School in the air by himself, if the students lost faith in their powers and threatened to drop it. "You hold it with your heart," he would tell them, "not with your hands. It has nothing to do with strength."

Felan taught the beginning students and ran the school. He was responsible only to the ruler of the Twelve Crowns and to the aging mage Vevay, who had headed the school for a century or so, by some accounts. Others said she had founded it, she was that old. She lived in the palace now and rarely visited the school. Bourne had never seen her, only the imaginary Vevay, made timeless and immortal by legend, whose beauty and powers would never change.

"A transcriptor," he told Felan when questioned further. "She gave me permission to visit her."

"Then you had better do so," Felan said, without a smile hidden anywhere on his broad, calm face. "If that is what the sea said."

So Bourne did that on his next free day, walking through the wood to the plain. The trees were quiet that day, and not quite so thickly tangled as they had been the day he had passed through them on his way to the queen's coronation ceremony. Then he kept tripping; he heard rustlings in the brush; things dropped on his head, including some yellowish slime from an invisible bird. It seemed the wood's opinion of his intentions toward the new queen. He ignored it. Brilliant he was not, but anyone with half a brain could learn how to blow apart a wall with a thought. And like his uncle, Bourne did not see why the young queen should possess so many Crowns. By all accounts she was hardly capable of ruling one.

The wood seemed to approve his intention to see Nepenthe. The thought of her in his head seemed to open a path through the trees, as though the wood guided him. The palace was more complex: he spent an hour or two passed from guard to guard through a system of gates and stairs and hallways that challenged his memory. When he finally passed through the palace to the library, he wandered a long time through the maze of stones and manuscripts, listening within its silence, its thick ancient shadows and sudden spills of torch fire, for the word from the sea.

He picked up the thread of her finally. Someone had glimpsed her this way. She might have gone that way. She was usually to be found here. Or if not here, then probably there. So he was passed from librarian to scribe, deeper and deeper into stone. When he came upon her finally, it was not where he had been told to expect her. He had simply gotten lost. He turned a corner into a quiet corridor and saw a transcriptor alone at a desk in an alcove of books, poring over another, open on the desk.

"Please," he said, and there they were, those eyes, vague with words still clinging to them from the page, and so dark now they seemed to have shifted from brown to black. Then she recognized him. She smiled, and the breath he hadn't realized he was holding ran out of him swiftly. A flow of color like firelight ran beneath her burnished skin. She started to close the book she studied, then didn't.

She said instead, a little breathlessly, "You see, the librarians gave it to me to translate. I'm good with odd alphabets. Notches on twigs, such things . . ."

He said, "Oh," without comprehending. Then he glanced at the book beneath her hand, saw the tangles of thorn like winter-stripped canes winding across the page. He said, "Oh," again indifferently, then remembered that it might be magic.

"How did you find me?"

"Only by accident," he answered wryly. "I have no idea where I am, or how I will ever get out of here." He paused. "I wanted—I had to—"

"Yes," she said softly and studied him, her eyes filling with him now, instead of thorns. "Bourne. Bourne who? What? From where?"

"Odd questions," he commented, "coming from an orphan."

"You might have fallen out of the sky, for all I know." She gestured. "There will be a stool at the next desk down the hall. Sit with me. No one comes down this far during the day, except the occasional visiting scholar searching for something obscure. So we can talk."

"Am I interrupting work?"

She looked down at it. "No. I am. I should be translating something else entirely. But I was too curious about this."

He stepped down the hall, brought a stool back, and sat beside the desk, half of himself still in the hallway, for the alcove was tiny. The vast stone ceiling, high above the books and barely illuminated by the torches, had been formed by some unimaginable burrowing, centuries before, into the solid heart of the cliff. He was under the earth again, he thought, and still listening for magic.

"Bourne of Seale," he answered her. "My father is the younger brother of the Lord of Seale, in the Second Crown. He died several years ago. My uncle Ermin sent me to the mages' school."

She raised a brow, tapping lightly and idly on the pages with a quill. Her eyes grew opaque for a moment; he waited, while she laid his name on her scales and weighed it against all kinds of things. Trouble, for one, he guessed. Heartache, he hoped, for that was on his scale as well. Then she stopped weighing, yielded to whatever it was that outweighed everything.

"You are right," she said abruptly. "I don't want to know. My heart saw you before you had a name. That never happened to me before."

"No," he breathed. "Yes."

"Especially not twice in one moment."

"Twice?"

She touched the book again with the pen. "Twice," she said, and he saw the wonder in her eyes. "There was you — all that richness in your hair and eyes, all that gold — and there was the book you gave me. It seemed in that moment that my heart recognized the language. And until that moment, I hardly knew I had one."

"One what?" he asked dazedly, thinking of all that glowing dark she carried with her, all that mystery.

"A heart."

"Nepenthe," he said, the word out of the sea. "Can you — Is there a place — Must we sit here with all these books listening?"

"For a while. If we go up, we will be seen, and I should be working. Can you stay?"

"How can I possibly find my way back through this labyrinth?" he asked her. "I am at your mercy."

She smiled at that. "I don't know if I possess such a thing. Nobody ever asked me for it before. Except maybe Laidley."

"What is Laidley?"

"Just someone. No one." The pen flicked again between her fingers; her attention strayed, was caught on thorn. "This book—"

"Never mind the book," he said huskily. "You saw me first."

"Let me talk," she pleaded. "I have no one else to tell."

"The librarians."

She shook her head, the swift blood running into her face again, so that he wanted to open his hand to that fiery warmth. "I lied," she said, her voice catching; she cleared her throat. "I lied to you."

"We hardly know each other," he said, astonished. "What could you have found to lie about so soon?"

"The book. The librarians don't know I have it. I told the transcriptor who rode with me that the mages had puzzled it out for themselves; they didn't need to send it after all."

He stared at it with sudden interest. "Why? Is it magic? It must be, for it to have possessed you like that."

"Is that it? Is that what magic does?"

"It charms; it transfixes; it binds. Have you understood any of it?"

"I think so. The letters are like thorns: they cling to each other to make words, but like thorn branches they can be sep-arated—look." She drew the book toward him, her voice eager now, unafraid. He moved close to her, so close he could feel the scented dark of her long hair against his lips. "The thorns make a circle around a center."

"Like a hub. Or an axle."

"Axis," she suggested. "It is repeated, on nearly every page. I think it might be a name. And here—this must be the writer's name, this branching of thorns on the first page. No other word but that, and not centered like a title, but—"

"Sprawled all over the page," Bourne murmured, "like a warning. You should tell the librarians."

"I will," she said absently. "I will. But not yet. The book spoke to me. I want to keep it just a little longer."

"Promise," he insisted, his eyes on the thick, spiky canes of thorn rising between his eyes and the book's inner secrets.

"I promise."

He looked at her, not knowing her at all, he realized, even as he recognized the perfunctory tone in her voice. If she would not tell them, then he must, he realized. Soon. After she showed him what kind of magic compelled the book, for he might learn something from it, beyond what the mages thought he should know.

But not that day. She closed it and showed him something else, a kind of alphabet of fish on an ancient pelt, whiling away the time until she could put the fish away and draw him deeper into the labyrinth.

# THREE

"And so," Vevay said to Gavin as the candles guttered around them and the embers murmured dreamily, "there they were, then: Axis and Kane. King and mage. Rulers of the entire known world. No one born who didn't learn their names. And where are they now? Vanished like rain."

"Raine?" Gavin asked through a yawn.

"Rain. Underground. A pair of names chiseled into a broken sandstone tablet in a language so old no one remembers it anymore."

"You remember."

"Well," she said lightly, "I'm so old I'm sure I was alive back then."

She heard him yawn again, and looked down at him affectionately. She sat up in their bed among linens and furs, clothed for the night in pearl-gray silk, her hair, a paler shade of pearl, falling around her like a cloak. Her blue-gray eyes, hooded with age, had once inspired poetry; her hands had inspired epics. Her deeds had inspired a great many different passions; she had managed to survive them all. Now, at home, at rest within the mighty palace of the rulers of Raine, she occasionally wondered, with amazement and rue, how she had survived her younger self.

She dropped a slender, age-rumpled hand on Gavin's bare chest, stroked the white fur there. Once it had been black; once her own hair had been the color of polished bronze. Once he had commanded armies; once she had counseled the mages of warrior-kings.

Now, she thought, it was enough to try to keep a step ahead of one young and inexperienced queen who had inherited the Twelve Crowns of Raine.

"Is that the end of the story?" Gavin asked. His eyes were closed.

"How could it be anything but the end? They lived, they died, they were forgotten."

"How did they die? Honored and beloved, with funerals that lasted days and tombs overflowing with treasure? Or in a final, ignominious battle with some bastard son or another upstart?"

She folded her arms, rested them on her upraised knees, and dropped her chin upon them, watching the embers, lying open like broken hearts, pulsing and dying at once. "I don't remember," she said absently, losing interest in her own tale. She felt his fingers drifting down her backbone.

"Heroes die a hero's death. Always. In tales if not in truth."

"Do they?"

"Make up something."

"All right. Axis, the ruler of the world, had so many children he couldn't keep their names straight, and he died contented in his nightcap, so old and shrunken that he was buried in a child's coffin, which is why no one ever found his tomb. No one believed that such a magnificent and indomitable emperor would rattle like a seed in a pod in his own coffin."

"Unconvincing," he murmured, his eyes flickering behind the closed lids, seeing himself, she guessed, his own unfinished story. "And the mage? Can you do better for him?"

"Kane lived so long that he forgot who he was. He died in some ruler's palace, where for decades he had been useful, so that in his decline he was well treated even when nobody else could remember who he was, either."

"You are not kind to heroes."

"No," she said, her eyes mirroring a cold reflection of the burning hearts. "Nor were they, Axis and Kane, the brothers who ruled the world. Nor were they kind."

His hand opened on her back, warm against silk and skin. "You've laid them to rest. And me as well. Now come to sleep. Meet me in my dreams."

"Where?" she asked him, settling into his arms, and he told her a briefer, gentler tale that lured her into sleep before he finished it.

They lived, as befitted a great mage and a great warrior, in a high central tower from which they had the wind's view of everything: the waves, the broad island across the channel that was the Third Crown, the archipelago beyond it that was the Fifth Crown, the misty northern forests and slopes, the southern fields, and the great green plain that flowed like a second sea over the cliffs above the sea. From there, Gavin watched for trouble; Vevay kept an eye on the Floating School and other anomalies. When he wasn't summoned to the king's company, so weighted with mail and leather and jewel-crusted weapons that he could barely mount his horse, Gavin wrote poetry and studied the accounts of early battles in the long history of Raine. Vevay toyed with an account of her own very long life, ignoring those events that might be embarrassing to the living, including herself.

Now the shrewd and vigorous king was dead from falling off his horse during a hunt, leaving his rabbity daughter Tessera to rule the Twelve Crowns of Raine. Vevay, not certain that the girl could even name them all, had tutored her ruthlessly before her coronation. She had learned everything obediently, but with a distinct lack of interest, her mind occupied by other matters. What matters these were eluded Vevay completely. In desperation, Vevay consulted the queen's mother, who was no help whatsoever.

The lady Xantia, who had loved the dead king dearly, was in deep mourning and had no patience for anything but her grief.

"You must help her," she said brokenly to Vevay. She wore dark purple and black, even to her daughter's coronation. Since then she had appeared in court only rarely, blinking bewilderedly like something seldom exposed to light. "Of course she is lacking in experience; what do you expect? No one expected her to rule so soon, and under such circumstances."

"She's fourteen," Vevay said grimly. "Your husband the king was crowned not two years older than that. And he faced the first challenge to his reign from the Fifth Crown three months later. And won."

Xantia closed her eyes and applied black linen to them. "You teach her," she said faintly. She leaned back in her chair, summoned her ladies-in-waiting with a gesture. "Teach her, Vevay. As you taught the king to rule. I place all our hope in you."

"Thank you," Vevay said dourly. The queen's mother shifted a corner of the silk over one eye to glance at her.

"You're a mage, Vevay. Do some magic."

Baffled, Vevay went in search of the queen. The days after the coronation were scarcely less hectic than the preparations had been. The palace had never held so many noble guests, all with their families and entourages; the people camped on the plain, celebrating night and day, showed no signs of going home. A few days of rain might dampen their spirits, Vevay thought. Perhaps the students at the Floating School could practice conjuring with the weather. The queen, who should have been holding audiences with various rulers that morning, meeting with ambassadors, accepting gifts and giving them, becoming acquainted with possible suitors, was doing none of those things. She was, Vevay realized after coming across any number of bewildered courtiers, nowhere to be found.

She roused Gavin from his poetry with a silent call; he

knew how to search without causing alarm. Then she took the shortest way to the top of her tower and began her own silent search through the palace, among the throng on the plain, even in the depths of that most unlikely place, the library. Trawling the busy palace and plain with a single line of thought baited with the queen's name, she felt no response to it anywhere. In desperation she searched wildly improbable places, like the kitchens and the stables. Finally she flung a question into the Floating School, catching Felan's attention.

Is the queen in the wood?

Forever passed, it seemed, before he answered. She paced the tower roof, waiting, while banners from the Twelve Crowns whipped around her like snakes. What would Tessera be doing in the wood? she asked herself impatiently. She had never shown any interest in it. But if not there, then where?

The answer from the Floating School came finally in the form of Felan, who fashioned himself out of cloud and light to stand with Vevay on the tower.

"No," he said, his habitual calm shaken, though his face did not show it. Vevay could feel the perturbed air between them. "The queen is not in the wood. You don't know where she is."

"I don't," Vevay agreed grimly. Then she saw the tiny figure, far down on the face of the cliff, as far as the ancient outermost stairs led, which was, to all but the most knowledgeable eye, nowhere. She sighed. "Yes. I do. Thank you, Felan."

He rubbed a hairless eyebrow, gazing down. She saw his expression before he vanished, and she thought darkly: you can laugh.

She met the queen halfway down the steps, as Tessera made her painstaking way back up. The queen reeled at the unexpected sight of a body on her next step, but Vevay had expected that. A solid, invisible wall of magic protected the young queen from any danger, including an errant wind or her own clumsy steps. Vevay sat down on the weathered, crumbled stairs; Tessera stood still, gazing at her perplexedly.

She was slight, with lank hair, pale gold like her father's but lacking its exuberant curls. She had his almond eyes, too, though hers were a more watery blue, especially now after her trek in the raw wind. A quiet, seemingly unimaginative child, she was growing into a pallid young woman, with powdery skin and uncertain expressions. She looked apprehensive now, thin lines appearing and fraying above her colorless brows.

"What," Vevay asked, trying for calm on the deadly face of the cliff, with the wind roaring around them and the sea wrinkling and snarling below, "are you doing here?"

"Just—I was just—" She shrugged slightly, shivering at the same time, for she had come without a cloak. "It was something I always wanted to do."

"What?"

"Go down far enough to hear the sea."

"She is utterly exasperating," Vevay told Gavin that night while he laughed. "And what's so funny? She has no direct heir. If she had fallen into the sea, the Twelve Crowns of Raine would be spending the next century bickering over who should inherit the realm."

"She didn't fall."

"She's not a child anymore; she can't just go off looking for seashells whenever—"

"She is grieving, too," he reminded her gently. "She'll learn. I have faith in you."

"I don't," Vevay said bleakly. "I don't understand her at all."

"What were you like at that age?"

"How should I know? I barely remember the last century." She stiffened then, pulled away from him. "I shouldn't say such things to you. You're still a child."

He dropped an arm over her shoulders, pulled her back. "Don't be absurd. You enchant me."

"Still?"

"Always."

Content in his hold, she didn't pursue the matter, though she knew she would never be entirely secure. "You could help," she suggested. "You were her father's greatest general; he always looked to you for advice."

"I'm an old man," he reminded her. "I could fight and die for her sake, but I can't protect her from whatever Crowns might conspire against her."

"She doesn't even understand such threats yet. The kingdom of Raine is very old, but she hasn't learned that it is not immortal. She has no idea what brute forces and subtleties hold a realm together. Maybe you could explain more clearly than I can."

Gavin was silent a moment, savoring some memory of the dead king; Vevay felt him sigh noiselessly. "Her father spent his life eluding rebellion and war precisely because he constantly anticipated them. He understood how precariously this palace sits on the edge of the world. How do I begin to explain that?"

"I don't know," Vevay said tautly. "Someone must."

"She needs to study the history of her realm."

"She needs—" She shook her head helplessly. "So much. I don't even know where to begin."

He drank wine, set his cup down. "Tomorrow," he suggested. "You're tired now. Begin again tomorrow."

He eased his long body beside her, one arm loosely across her, the other crooked beneath his head. He had held her lightly through the years, she knew, because he had never been entirely secure either, during the long, busy, unpredictable life they had made together. She seemed, he had complained more than once, always at the point of vanishing.

But I am here, she thought. Now. This is what we have now, this moment of peace. Humans die, mages vanish . . .

"You've gone somewhere," she heard. "I am holding you in my arms, but you have disappeared."

She came back, glanced up at his strong, craggy face, with its grizzled brows and slackened skin, the faded scar on one cheekbone from when he had turned his head during battle and an arrow had skimmed across his skin instead of striking him. He met her eyes. His own were light blue. She had seen that blue blaze like sun-struck ice; they were mild now, quizzical.

"Where were you?"

"I wandered off into a tale," she answered. "The tale I told you last night. Human and mage . . ."

"Axis and Kane."

"I was putting a different ending on it. Only slightly different," she amended. "In the end, all endings are the same. Even for those two."

"Are they?" he murmured, as though there could be some question about the matter. He settled himself to listen. "Then tell me the different story."

# FOUR

He fought his first battle at the age of seven. He fashioned his army out of river mud and spit, causing the poets of Lower Eben to write later:

> *Out of earth and water he made them,*
> *Out of his breath,*
> *They rose up from the mud in endless multitudes,*
> *His killing army,*
> *There on the bank of the Serpent that rings the world.*

He fought his father. Centuries later, the poets would say that he slaughtered his father's army, that the Serpent turned red with death, that when he faced the last man alive on the riverbank, it was his father.

> *They fought under the full moon rising out of the water*
> *Under the Serpent's eye.*

*Axis slew his father,*
*The good, the just.*
*The Serpent swallowed his bones,*
*And the bloody-handed child became king.*

It was actually a tranquil afternoon beside the river. Axis's father, hiding from his own kingdom for a couple of hours, helped his son daub the minute heads of his foot soldiers blue and attach plumes of milkweed seed to the heads of the horsemen, whose horses were left to the imagination. The child who called herself Kane in their secret language made the blue dye out of the brilliant wings of dragonflies she captured with her hands. She whispered to them through her fingers, and their twig-bodies vanished, leaving behind their glittering cobalt wings. Axis did not notice then how Kane did what she did; that came later.

"My army is numberless as the grass in the fields," the king said to his son. "As grains of sand. How will you defeat me?"

Axis considered. Even then he was a burly child, snub-nosed and fair; he had his father's heavy-lidded eyes, as green as the Serpent on a lazy afternoon. Light could glance off them, as off the river water, without penetrating their secrets. The king waited, gazing fondly at his son, twirling his coronet of gold and bronze idly on one forefinger. His sandaled feet were muddy; so were his hands and the hem of his short tunic. He wore a light shirt of metal scales and a gold sheath for his knife in his belt. These things were magnificently transformed later into elaborate armor and a sword that had drunk the blood of thousands. The knife, lying on a sacrificial stone, had drunk the blood of one small hare: a gift, the king explained gravely to the children, for the Serpent, who long ago had acquired a taste for things of the land and needed to be fed now and then so it would not crawl out of its path to come looking for them.

Axis opened a hand above his cavalry. "I will fight grass with fire. These will ring your army with torches and set you ablaze."

The king grunted. "And your foot soldiers? What will they be doing?"

"They will stand along the riverbank and kill everyone who tries to escape the fire by water."

"Show me."

Axis lifted one of the stubby, blue-capped soldiers, who were barely the size of his thumb and mostly resembled a standing army of cocoons with heads. He set it at the water's edge. The Serpent, a muscle rippling beneath its glassy surface, sent a wavelet rolling over it. The soldier melted into a lump of mud. Axis stared at it, his eyes round. The king laughed.

"Remember that whatever weapons you possess may also be used against you. And that it was I who gave the Serpent a gift."

Axis considered again, then gathered foot soldiers in both hands and stood up. Ankle-deep in drying nubbins of plumed and dragon-scaled warriors, he sent handsful of mud-men plopping into the water. They dissolved as they fell, leaving a tiny floating memorial of seed-plumes and crushed wings.

"This is my gift to the Serpent," he called to it. "Life to make death. Take my living and send me death to fight my battle."

The king cocked an eyebrow at the odd request and gave another spin to the crown dangling on his forefinger. "The Serpent is both," he reminded his son. "It gives life as well as—"

The water bubbled up in a mighty wave and a hissing bellow. Kane screamed, dancing away from it. Axis, ankle-deep in water now, was stunned motionless. Death, attracted perhaps by the glint of light from the king's hand, opened a great, green maw and heaved itself out of the water at the gold. Blood spattered over the army. Most of the king vanished instantly. The remainder—a muddy hand relinquishing the crown, a sandaled foot—left an imprint on the memory as they were dragged through Axis's army. Then they disappeared into the churning Serpent. Axis shouted then, a sharp, wordless cry, wading deeper into the water, which frothed red around his knees. Kane splashed to him, dragged him back to shore, both of them trampling his army underfoot. Axis, trying to speak, seemed stricken dumb; he could only hiss like the river-beast that had eaten his father. The circlet of gold caught his eye. He picked it out of the mud, turned it mutely in his hands, looking, Kane thought, bewilderedly within it for his father.

Thus they were found a moment later by alarmed guards left by the king to idle out of eyesight.

The knife on the stone, the bloody water, the heir holding his father's crown in his hands: all became, in the confusion of the moment, shadowed with ambiguity.

"We were fighting," Axis told his mother, when he could finally speak. "I called death out of the water, and the Serpent ate him."

Kane, questioned thoroughly, gave a detailed version of events that made more sense than the impression Axis left. But while events were sorted in a haphazard fashion to a coherent conclusion, impressions lingered and turned, long past memory, into myth.

Kane remembered.

> *He was born speaking the language of stars*
> *The Emperor of Night,*
> *The language of thorns,*
> *The language of the fiery serpents of the sky,*
> *And of the thunderbolt.*

It was Kane who devised the alphabet for that language, when they were old enough to learn to write. The daughter of one of the queen's many sisters, she had been born and raised in the royal palace in Great Eben. Thrown together with her teething, wailing, babbling cousins, she and Axis performed the ancient ritual of flinging their toys at one another's heads, and in that moment recognized a common destiny. They became inseparable. The language they spoke before they learned their common tongue was their way of keeping secrets in front of the horde of curious, chattering cousins. We are one, each private word said. We alone understand. Later, when Kane learned to write, she formed their language into brambles, perhaps anticipating their secret life together in that script of warning and protection. In her riddling way, she placed herself in each cane of thorns; every letter said her secret name.

At the time of the king's abrupt and peculiar demise, Kane was a slight, quiet, observant child who followed Axis everywhere. Like her own mother, she was dark-haired and delicate, with great eyes the color of smoke. She followed Axis because he wanted her with him; when he did not see her, he searched for her or sent for her. Their childish friendship seemed harmless; it was assumed that they would grow out of each other eventually. They never did.

> *At his side the Hooded One*
> *At his side always*
> *The One who walks in shadow*
> *Whose face is never seen,*
> *Kane, who opens doors between stars,*
> *Who points the way.*

Axis's father had spent most of his life extending the borders of his kingdom; he was a great general himself, worthy of poetry. He taught Axis to play war-games at an early age. The concept of battle interested Kane only because it interested Axis. The king became the first to die on Axis's battlefield. The event shocked and grieved the boy enormously. But instead of giving him a horror of violence, it turned his interest in war into an obsession. He had had a stunning glimpse of power on many levels, which he examined in dozens of half-coherent messages written to Kane in their private language. It had become what he wanted above all else: that power, that mystery.

And so, whatever this nebulous thing was that had its bloody birth at the river's edge, she wanted it for him.

The dead king's brother became regent for Axis. For a while, until it came time for him to relinquish power, all was peaceful in Eben. While Axis learned how to rule, Kane educated herself in other ways. They were secret, like the language, like her letters, full of riddles, odd juxtapositions, ambiguities, correlatives. She came to her knowledge, her power, in odd places: in a line of poetry, in a tale the gardener told, in musty scrolls that made her sneeze and always began with dire warnings to the uninitiated. A bird in flight taught her many things: about air, time, coincidence, the nature of movement, the moment when the breath indrawn at the beauty of flight becomes the spellbinding moment of human flight. She did not tell Axis everything she learned, for she did not know then why she wanted such knowledge, or even what it was. She recognized it long before she knew its name.

> *The Sorcerer,*
> *The Magician,*
> *The Hooded One whose eye is magic,*
> *Whose spoken word becomes the word:*
> *Kane, the left hand of the Emperor*
> *Whose right hand was war.*

The second moment in Axis's life that came out of nowhere to stun him to the heart was when he learned he must marry.

Not only must he marry, and then and there, he must marry the daughter of the king of a neighboring land, whom he had never met. This would ensure the loyalty of that kingdom, whose younger generation was getting restless, and provide Eben with a wealth of goods and warriors, which would otherwise go elsewhere if Axis did not marry or conquer it.

"I'll conquer it," Axis offered immediately.

To which his mother replied, "I am tired of war. Your father fought enough of them. I hardly saw him; it's a wonder he stayed in bed long enough to produce you. Stay off the battlefield and give me some grandchildren first. Then you can conquer the entire world if you must."

"But Kane—" Axis began blankly, catching his first glimpse of life without her. His mother, who was embroidering something, snapped a thread between her teeth, then studied him silently.

"Did you think," she asked, not without compassion, "that you could marry her?"

"No. I never thought—I never thought about marriage at all. But if I must—"

"There would be no advantage to marrying your cousin. Think, Axis. You are King of Eben. Kings marry to the advantage of their realm."

"But—"

"No. You cannot marry with her beside you. She cannot sleep under your bed. You must leave her outside of your marriage. She will have her own life to lead."

"I am king," Axis said mutinously. "I say what she will do with her life."

His mother rifled through her thread box, chose a different color. "Perhaps you should talk to her," she suggested. "Before you make choices for her."

"She wants what I want. She always has."

"Tell her," his mother said. "Then ask her what she wants. Young women see far more clearly than young men. I doubt that this will be the surprise to her that it is to you."

It was not, for Kane had already recognized the patterns of life around her, and what they might mean for her and for Axis. She saw the messengers from Cribex coming before anyone else did. Hers was the shadow mingling with the shadow cast by the half-drawn tapestry across the window while Axis spoke to his mother. So she had time to think before she permitted Axis to find her.

Still, there were tears on her face, for his mother was right: there would be places in his life where she could not come.

She took him to the most private place she knew, a tiny garden full of weird, thorny succulents that loved the sun. There she sat on a sandstone bench, while Axis knelt on the hard ground, his arms across her knees, his face buried in them. They had not yet become lovers, which is why legend was silent about their early relationship. Until she masked herself, Kane remained simply unseen. Until the cousin vanished, presumed lost in an unremarkable life between the lines of history, the magician, the lover, the Hooded One, could not exist.

"You must marry," she told Axis. "You will need that army from Cribex to fight the regent."

He raised his head, stared at her. Later during his life he was known as the Lion, because of his broad, golden face, his wide-set eyes, his tawny hair. He never doubted her; he only wondered, "How do you know such things?"

"I listen," she said.

"Do you become invisible?"

"No. I'm there, if you know how to look. I stand between the place you look at and the place you see. Behind what you expect to see. If you expect to see me, you do. I listen in places where no one expects me to be."

He nodded, becoming calmer; he wiped at his face with his forearm and sat back on his haunches, his hands on her knees. He asked her what his mother told him to ask.

"What do you want?"

"What you want," she said.

"I want you. With me. Forever."

She put her hands on his, her own eyes dry now, seeing them both where no one would expect them to be, ever; always they would be the last thing anyone would expect to see.

"So it will be," she said, and made it so.

# FIVE

The queen was in the wood.

A week had passed since her coronation, and her guests showed no signs of going home. Elaborate feasts still came up from the kitchens, endless slabs of meat big enough to flag a floor, loaves of bread the size of cartwheels, tiered cakes she might have worn as skirts festooned with ribbons and scrolls and invariably topped with crowns shaped of beaten egg whites and gold leaf. Her guests had drunk small ponds of wine and roaring rivers of ale. They had drunk to the name of everyone who had ever ruled the Crowns of Raine, including a pair of twins who had killed each other in a brawl over which should be king in the middle of the coronation ceremony. Outside, the broad plain was littered with empty barrels and feathers and bones; it was turning into a midden. Late at night when the winds were still it smelled like one.

"I'll send them all away soon," Vevay promised. "But not

until you know your ruling nobles' names, and their faces, and you can remember one striking opinion from each one of them. Dance with them. That's the easiest way to begin a conversation."

Tessera could only gaze at her, amazed, wondering who the mage thought she was talking to. One of Tessera's ladies-in-waiting, perhaps, those poised and smiling creatures who could drop an eyelid and unsettle a kingdom.

Vevay was beginning to look cross-eyed back at her, something that happened when Tessera had seemed particularly obtuse.

"Dance. You know. Movement of the feet in an orderly pattern in time to music—"

"I know," Tessera said hollowly. "I did it with my father."

By which she meant she knew how. But Vevay heard something else, apparently; she closed her eyes and pinched the bridge of her nose a moment.

"Your father. You are no longer a child, and your father is dead."

"Yes." She had to stop and swallow what felt like a hard little turtle lodged in her throat. "I guessed as much when he got buried."

Vevay closed her eyes again. The lines of her face shifted subtly, turning her somehow very old and very beautiful at the same time.

"I am sorry, Tessera. I only want—I want for you everything your father had."

Tessera looked past her, out the open window of the council-chamber where she met every hour with Vevay to be told whom she would speak to next, and of what, and what she had to gain or lose by it. A gull, hovering in the wind, looked back at her in her tower room, then caught a shifting angle of air and slid with dizzying grace to freedom.

"I am not my father," she said, while her heart swooped and fell and soared through that airy nothing above the sea.

"Don't judge yourself harshly," Vevay answered, regaining her composure and misunderstanding Tessera entirely. "That's what I'm here for. To help you, I mean."

"Yes," Tessera said indifferently; dancing would help nothing. But there it was: she must move her feet and talk at the same time. And remember, as well, so that they could all be sent home and she could hear herself think again.

She tried very hard to remember their words; after a while everything they said all sounded alike. What she remembered most was their eyes as they took her hand and turned her, drew her close and relinquished her, according to the instructions of the pipes and the viols after supper that evening. Alien as birds they were, watching her, waiting for her to shift her shape to something grublike, helpless and possibly edible. So she felt, as she tried to make civilized noises. Even those came out oddly, in whispers and squeaks. Vevay watched from a corner, her face a remote mask. Around Tessera, other young women laughed and chattered amiably as though there were no danger, as though they had all the power.

The younger men, some would-be suitors, spoke of her beauty, which she knew was negligible, and of her charm, which was nonexistent. She peered at them anxiously, trying to see what they really meant. The older nobles and courtiers spoke to her of their worthy and eligible sons, or, lacking them, made reference to difficulties in their Crowns to which, they said, her father had been on the verge of attending just before his tragic accident. These she promised earnestly to keep in mind, while she tried to match the problem with the shape of a mustache or a sagging eyelid to remind her. Only one man, the uncle of the Prince of Chessery, the Ninth Crown of Raine, attached himself instantly to her memory.

He was a compact, gray-haired man whose composure she found calming. He said to her simply, as she turned under his upraised arm, "I miss your father. I liked him better than my own sons. He could be very kind, when he thought about it."

She stared at him, until she had to turn again. When she faced him, she asked abruptly, "Are you allowed to say such things? Nobody else says what they think."

"If you have nothing to lose," he answered, "you can say whatever you want."

She was silent a moment; when she tripped over his foot, they both ignored it. "I may not say what I think," she told him, "and I am Queen of Raine."

"That's because you have everything to lose."

She barely saw anyone else that evening; when Vevay questioned her later, his was the only face she could remember clearly.

"His expressions were kind," she said. "He made me remember why I loved my father. He told me the difference between everything and nothing."

"Which is?" Vevay prompted, looking baffled.

"Words."

Vevay was still baffled. But she had taken a word as a suggestion; her voice seemed kinder than usual when she finally spoke. "It is enormously difficult to lose so much and gain so much at the same moment."

"Oh, yes," Tessera whispered. She walked out of her dancing shoes with a sigh, went to the window, which framed black now, above the sea, starless and roiling like the beginning or the end of time.

"Tomorrow," Vevay said behind her. "The first thing after breakfast, you must meet the delegation from the King of Almorania. It is an ancient kingdom, along the southern borders of the Fourth Crown, mountainous and harsh. Each time rule changes hands in either of our lands, treaties are renewed to keep peace between us. They pay certain tributes; we leave them alone. The delegation missed the coronation, but that is not an issue: traveling through their mountain passes in early spring is difficult for them. They will offer coronation gifts of bowls lacquered with the crushed wings of butterflies, and necklaces of gold and amber for which they are renowned. In a day or two, you will sit with your council while the treaty is renewed. After meeting them tomorrow, you will . . ."

"Yes," Tessera said, and "yes" and "yes" whenever it seemed required.

———

In the morning, before breakfast, she went to the wood.

It was not a conscious decision. She found herself awake early, and restless. The dawn sun spilled gold across the stones around her bed. She dressed herself; no one was awake to stop her. She wandered through side corridors, down narrow, winding stairways no one had used for a century or two, where every arrow-shaped window overflowed with light. That was not far enough. Light drew her farther, past stables, through gardens where she breathed the scents of brine and early roses. The plain, she knew, would be a great, gilded, shining thing where winds like wild stallions raced from the sea to the end of the world. But when she went through the last of many gates in the maze of walls around the palace, she saw the flapping pavilions, dogs chewing on last night's bones, servants sleepily poking up their fires and trying to quiet children running half-naked and laughing through the light.

Tessera passed around them, not noticing how wide a berth she had to give her well-wishers just to try to find some place where no one would want anything from her, not a smile, not a word, where the people ended and the empty plain began again.

The wood suddenly filled her eyes, crouching like some dark feral thing on the horizon. She had forgotten that, too, along with the pavilions. It hid itself occasionally, she guessed, which must be why she always seemed to come across it un-expectedly. Lured by light, she had already walked a long way around the pavilions. Now dark, silence, secrecy tempted her, all the mysteries hidden within the wild wood.

The mages' school was somewhere in the trees, she knew; she looked for it as soon as she crossed from grass into bracken and shadow. She had only seen it once, on a summer afternoon when she went riding with her father. Then it had floated above the trees like something sunning itself: a strange stone puzzle of walls with too many angles, blind towers, and no gates anywhere in sight. It cast its own reflection in the air, a mirror image of itself. The reflection had windows and doors and gates everywhere. She remembered her father's surprised, delighted laugh at the vision, and how one of the eyeless towers grew a window to flick a glance at him. Then it sank with a stately, lumbering grace to hide itself again within the trees.

Now, the wood in early morning was utterly silent. She walked carefully through damp leaves, around tangles of bramble and vine, trying not to disturb the stillness. She could not see the sky, only green and shadow woven thickly above her, yielding not a scrap of blue. She breathed soundlessly. So did the wood around her, she felt; it seemed a live thing, alert and watching her, trees trailing wisps of morning mist, their faces hidden, their thoughts seeping into the air like scent. It was, she thought, like being surrounded by unspoken words.

She stopped moving, stood as silently, listening to them, trying to understand their silent language. Their words lay all around her, she realized slowly; each fallen, moldering leaf, each twist of ivy along a branch, each outstretched twig in a thicket made a shape in the air, in the eye. What did they say?

she wondered, entranced, and tried to breathe in the language of the wood, tried to take it in through her skin, as though she too were hidden within leaves, within bark.

Leaves crackled suddenly; branches whipped. The wood spoke, describing something imminent and, from the sound of it, fairly big. Tessera tensed, then spun, searching. The wood looked the same from every direction: trees and thickets, bushes and brambles and great veils of ivy twining up to cover the heads of huge old trees. Nothing pointed out. She chose a direction at random and ran.

Tessera? she heard from very far away, as though someone had thought her name. Vevay, most likely, she guessed, and remembered the morning's work: breakfast with her guests, the delegation from Almorania, the bowls painted with crushed butterfly wings . . . She ran faster, through endless silent trees, wondering if she were heading deeper into the wood, so deep into its magic that not even Vevay could find her.

And then she crossed the border between shadow and light. She was on the sunlit plain again, the wood only a tangled memory behind her. She could see the ragged smoke from the distant campfires; she could feel the exuberant wind again, which had not stirred a single leaf within the wood.

She stopped, panting, turning to look back incredulously at the self-contained, secret world. For the second time in her life, she saw the Floating School, another secret world, hanging between sky and tree, its blind towers sunlit, even the reflection it cast of itself catching light, throwing glints of crystal and brass from windows and doors.

There were shouts of wonder behind her. The giant who had stalked her in the wood parted branches at the edge of it to look at her. She glimpsed his great bald pate, his massive shoulders, before she turned and ran again. One of the guards keeping watch over the plain, sitting on his horse and gawking at the school, saw the girl running out of the wood and rode over to her. He recognized the flying, spider-web hair and the pale, unfinished face, with its white eyebrows and startled eyes.

"I went for a walk," she told him in response to his astonished questions. "I must get back quickly."

He gave her his horse; she reached the palace in time to dress for breakfast.

maybe, or two oxen. Something to do with transporting all the fish lined up over here."

He made an appreciative noise or two through his nose, then extended an inky finger out of the fur. "What do you make of this grouping? It's repeated often."

"There are several repeated groupings, positioned like that. They might turn out to be people's names. The merchants, or drivers in the caravan, perhaps."

He grunted again, then remarked, "Lord Birnum seems in no hurry to leave. You might have time to solve this puzzle before I have to go."

"I hope so," she replied absently, not willing to abandon the thorns for the scholar's kettle of fish. He jingled something in the fur; a coin or two spoke.

"I can't pay much," he said, "but you deserve something for all this work."

She shrugged, surprised. "I don't expect much. I'm still an apprentice. We go for months without seeing money."

"It helps, in the world beyond this stone." He dropped a coin among the fish. "There's your newly-minted queen. I can give you a few more of those if you finish before I leave. If she's still on her throne."

Nepenthe picked the coin up, studied it curiously. It was a round of copper, big, but what she had learned about money was that the bigger it was, the less it was worth. The young queen's profile, stamped on the coin, was likely to be as close as a transcriptor ever got to seeing her. The impression made

# SIX

By sheer chance, Nepenthe was swimming with the fish when next she saw the visiting scholar's hairy face.

He put his head into her alcove, looking over her shoulder to read her translations. She started. His head was worse for wear, his eyes hollows of dark, his hair plastered to his scalp as though he had dunked himself into a barrel of ale. She wondered if he would survive the queen's coronation.

But he seemed cheerful enough, wrapped in smelly fur against the afternoon chill and paying close attention to her reasoning as her finger moved from fish to fish.

"This one has two small lines here, like two mouths. Two little hooks, or smiles. I think it's a method of counting. The counting fish have varying numbers of smiles, and they always come at the beginning of a line. So that kind of fish is both a number and the beginning letter of a word. Two wagons, was of an abundance of hair, a rounded, determined jaw, and an enormous crown; other details seemed imprecise.

"It's more like," Master Croysus said heavily, "what we wish than what we see. I don't remember much of a jaw-line at all, and her hair is rather limp."

"Maybe she'll turn into herself," Nepenthe murmured, feeling some pity for the defenseless young woman who had the weight of twelve Crowns and all those centuries of history on her head. The possibility of war occurred to her; the scholar's musings seemed to suggest it. In the epics she had read, war usually came to a bad end. "Will the Crowns fight her, Master Croysus?"

His head ducked down into his fur, as though hiding from the listening stones. "Don't talk so loudly —"

"You always do."

"I speculate." He lowered his own voice nearly to a whisper. "I think many are. It's why everyone is lingering."

"Why —"

"Speculations, conspiracies, alliances — nobles testing her, testing one another before they make decisions."

"Really?" Nepenthe flicked her pen against the desk, gazing raptly upward at solid stone, trying to envision the complex, restless world beyond it. "What of the library? What do we do if they go to war?"

Master Croysus shook his untidy head. "Who knows? Words do not always survive war." He tapped the fish. "Entire languages disappear. Librarians?" He shrugged and said again,

"Who knows? Epics are never written about libraries. They exist on whim; it depends if the conquering army likes to read."

Nepenthe mulled over that, sitting safely on her stool, surrounded by stone as old as the world. She came to no satisfactory conclusions about anything, except to realize that her head was filling with thorns now, instead of fish. The thorny alphabet, far from keeping her out, was proving oddly accessible. One thorn led to another; the very shapes of the flowing, graceful brambles suggested the words they formed. Warfare, battles, seemed a constant, underlying theme. War and poetry. War and love. Though neither battle nor passion had emerged yet from the brambles, both were hidden among them, she was certain. Stumbling among the strange letters like a child learning to read, she had come to recognize those words first.

She rolled up the fish, since Master Croysus would not return that day, and took the thorns out of their hiding place behind a pyramid of scrolls on a shelf.

She was surrounded by brambles, trying to unravel some twining canes arranged in brief lines that suggested poetry, when she became aware of a looming something breathing over her shoulder.

She jumped, nearly spilling her ink, as she threw an arm across the books. It was Laidley behind her, his mouth open, his close-set eyes snagged on thorns.

"What is that? I've never seen anything like it."

She hunched over the thorns protectively. "It's mine," she

heard herself say sharply. Then she lifted one hand, touched his arm. "Laidley," she pleaded. "It's just something I'm doing."

He dragged his attention from the thorns finally, looked at her. She was reminded then of what intelligence he carried behind his vapid expressions. "It's that book, isn't it," he said shrewdly. "The one from the Floating School that you said the mages had already translated. You've had it all along. You didn't give it to the librarians, and you didn't show it to me."

She opened her mouth, but nothing came out. There were no excuses, she realized; she had deceived and stolen and lied again. All for a tangle of thorns, for a language she had never seen in her life.

But it spoke to my heart, she thought confusedly. It said my name.

Laidley was still gazing at her, waiting. She nodded finally, wordlessly, and shifted so that he could see.

He studied it silently; she heard him swallow. He touched a thorny letter tentatively, as though it might prick.

"What made you take it?" he asked with wonder. "What compelled you?"

"I don't know," she whispered. "I just wanted it. Laidley. Don't tell anyone. I need to do this. I don't know why yet, but I need to know. Bourne says it might be magic."

"Bourne?"

"The student from the Floating School who gave it to me."

"Magic? As in spells?"

"It doesn't seem to be."

"Well, what does it seem to be?"

"It seems to be—I don't know yet. A story, maybe. About two people. If I'm right, then the language is very old, and they died so long ago no one really knows when."

"Who were they?"

"Axis and Kane."

He stared, brushing at a straw-colored strand sliding over one eyebrow. "Axis and Kane," he said incredulously, "compelled this fervor in you? They've been dust for thousands of years."

"We don't choose our passions," she said meekly, hoping the subject would compel him to lose interest in it. But he lingered, trying to comprehend what drew her to the thorny matter. He saw no way into the brier; stubbornly, she did not enlighten him.

"I'm only guessing at their names," she said evasively. "It might not be about them at all; it may be a different history entirely."

He took himself away at last, casting a final, baffled glance at her. Alone with the story, she continued her painstaking path through the thorns, shifting a cane here and there just enough to glimpse what might be behind it, if it shaped this letter, or what might not, if it shaped that.

She did not see Bourne again for days after he first came. She refused to think about him; he was dangerous, a chimera. Lords' sons took penniless foundlings lightly, infatuated as they might be with a dark fall of hair, eyes that changed color in a shift of light. And the library, burrowed into solid stone, buried as deeply underground as a catacomb, its entry ringed by the labyrinth of palace walls, was barely less difficult to breach than a wall of thorns.

He came when she least expected him, one early evening when she sat at one of the long tables in the refectory, eating a briny bowl of stew and trying to hear the librarians speaking at the next table. Beside her, Laidley ate silently, wordless as usual except when they spoke about words. There was some kind of gossip that had worked its way down from the palace; Nepenthe was straining to piece it together, chewing as quietly as possible. Waves of chattering and laughter, some story that Oriel was telling farther down the table kept rolling over the interesting glints and shapes tumbling from the librarians' table.

"She just vanished—they say she went to hear the sea."

"He got lost in ancient mathematical scrolls—"

"She was found on the very last—"

"And found his way out among the sandstone tablets, which meant—"

"Legend says it is there. But who knows? No one has been there since—Who was the last?"

"He was really lost then, because no one had seen the sandstone tablets since the dead king's father was crowned."

"Did she know?"

"No one knows. The mage Vevay says she couldn't possibly."

"He finally found his way back hours later, but he couldn't remember where he had seen the tablets. So they're lost all over again."

"Knows what?"

Laidley made a sound. Surprised, Nepenthe looked at him. His head had sunk tortoise-fashion between his shoulders; he stared at his stew as though a fish had leaped in it. On the other side of the table someone in a dark robe shifted the hood around his face, and Nepenthe coughed on a mussel. Within the hood Bourne smiled at her. His gold hair was tangled; his eyes seemed not quite human, as though a windblown tree had glanced her way. They cleared slowly, as Nepenthe, spoon suspended, stared at him.

She rose abruptly, walked without looking back across the refectory to the outer doors, which were open to the evening winds. Torches on either side of the doors shivered and flared, revealing and concealing sporadically. Bourne appeared after a moment, but whether he had walked or flown through the refectory, Nepenthe was suddenly uncertain.

They were alone on the massive balcony, but for the night winds and a gull or two. Still Nepenthe kept her voice low, for the hooded man had a wild, secretive look about him, as though he might vanish at the wrong word.

"How did you get here?"

"We're practicing movements through time and space." His own voice sounded on the verge of laughter. "I didn't think it would work."

"What?"

"You were on my mind. So I envisioned you in the library among the books. Something happened. I took a step toward my heart's desire and there you were, with a spoon in your mouth, and a man with a face like a pike beside you gawking at me."

"Laidley," she said breathlessly.

"Yes. I thought it would be a Laidley."

"Tell me again," she begged. "I don't understand. You walked across space? You folded up time?"

"I suppose it was something like that. I didn't think that there was the remotest chance that I could do such a thing, so I wasn't listening very well when Felan explained it. I did hear him say something about a place I really wanted to be, so I thought of you."

"What was it like? What did you see?"

"Your face," he answered, "coming more and more clear, as though you were rising up out of water. I kept moving toward it . . ." He did so as he spoke; she felt his hand slide across her neck beneath her hair. The torches blew his direction; she saw his eyes again, dark and full of wonder, at his own magic, or at hers. "It was like crossing some immense, black chasm in one step . . . And then I heard all these voices, and smelled fish. It was much easier than finding my way down here—that takes days."

"How will you—"

"Get back?" He laughed. "I don't know. I'd need your face at my journey's end. I'm sure," he added, his own face drifting closer, "that I'm not the first student to lose his way and not find it again until morning." She stood very still, while his lips brushed hers. "Onions," he whispered. "And celery root. And something out of the sea."

"Mussels."

"Mussels," he agreed, shaping the word as he kissed her. "They have to go very far down to get them, don't they?" he murmured between tastes. "So far down you could actually hear the sea. You could taste it . . ."

She drew a sudden breath. "That's it—That's what they were talking about."

He opened one eye, squinted at her. "What are you thinking of, at a time like this?"

"The steps on the cliff—that's where she was. The last step. You might hear the sea from there. And it is a place of great antiquity; there is a legend—"

"There always are," he said bemusedly. "They gather on places of great antiquity like barnacles. Who was where?"

"I think they were talking about the queen." She linked her fingers around his neck, banged her head against his lightly. "But what was the legend? I can't remember."

"The queen went down those winding slippery old steps?" he said incredulously. "What for?"

"I don't know. I didn't hear."

"She might have killed herself."

"She didn't."

"She might have." He was silent briefly, considering the notion curiously. "How strange. This legend you can't remember—might it be in a book?"

"It might."

"Might you look it up?"

"I might." She peered at him, her face inside the hood with his. "Now?"

"No. Now, I want you to think of your heart's desire and take a step toward it."

She slid her hand down his arm, took his hand, and said simply, "We'll get there faster if we walk."

However he left her chamber, on foot or folding back into his thoughts, he was gone by morning. Nepenthe woke in the early dawn. Bourne had set the coals burning in her brazier. Love? she wondered. Or just cold? Whichever it was, she was grateful for the unexpected warmth. She lay empty-headed, watching the single star in her slit of a window swallowed by billowing morning mist. At any moment the gong would thunder, pulling them all into day; anticipating it, the still world seemed to be holding its breath. She listened for the sea in that pent silence, knowing she could not possibly hear it, but trying anyway, for some of the night's magic might have lingered into day.

She saw the queen then, in her mind's eye: a tiny figure with a coin's profile standing on the final, terrifying step into nothingness carved into the face of the cliff. Halfway there at that point, she must have heard the sea. A word popped into Nepenthe's head. Legend, she thought. And then the great, deep voice of the gong splashed through the world like a stone into water. Doors began to open; voices called sleepily to one another down the corridors. Legend, she thought again as she swung her bare feet to the stones. She was halfway to the baths before her drowsing thoughts caught up with themselves and she remembered why the word was in her head.

She glimpsed it now and then swimming behind the fish, a glint of color and shape that didn't belong with them. Later, after she had done enough work to satisfy Master Croysus should he find his way out of the revelries, she wandered among the thorns. Her mind snagged on the word; she gave it half a thought. Half a thought turned into Bourne, which was why, she realized, the word persisted. For some reason he was curious about this legend involving the cliff and the steps and the queen's journey down them. He could appear out of nowhere again; he would ask; she could give him that small thing to watch him smile . . .

The word, having been given attention, vanished out of her head again as she worked her way, bramble by bramble, into legends far older than Raine. Canes suggested letters; letters suggested words; she was surrounding herself with briars when she saw Laidley again, trying to find his way through them to her.

She blinked; the thorns dwindled back down onto the page. He hovered beside her stool; she waited, without discernible patience, for him to collect his thoughts.

"Who was that?" he asked finally. "Last night?"

He looked sullen; so did she, she felt, at the sight of his bleak face. "A student from the mages' school," she said shortly. "Why?"

"He looked arrogant. Spoiled. I didn't like his expression."

"I don't suppose he liked yours."

"Who is he? Some noble's son taking up with a transcriptor, who will break your heart?"

She looked at him silently until he shifted, and blood rose under his sallow skin. "Maybe," she answered evenly. "But I don't want to think about that now. I'm busy."

"You're obsessed."

"Did you just find me to pick a quarrel over everything I'm doing?"

He swallowed. "No. I didn't." He put a small, leather-bound book on her desk. "I found this. It's a translation of an eyewitness account of the defeat of the armies of the ancient city Denub by the Emperor of Night, and his triumphal entry into the city, accompanied by the Masked One."

"The Masked One?"

"Kane. I thought it might help you, knowing some background. Be careful," he added, as she picked it up. "The binding crumbles."

She opened it gently, glanced at the neat, measured lines. "The Emperor of Night," she murmured, "being Axis?"

"Yes."

"Yes." She drew breath. "That will help. Thank you, Laidley. Why did they call him that?"

"I don't know. He had the name before he conquered Denub. Something to do with the moon? The stars?"

"He always came at night?" she guessed. "Do armies war at night?"

"I don't think so. It's dark. How could you know if you were killing your friend or your foe?" The glumness was easing out of his face, she saw with relief; the scholar, curious and greedy for knowledge, asserted himself. "I can find out for you," he offered.

She hesitated, reluctant for some incomprehensible reason to share her thorns, a moldering epic by the sound of it, with anyone. But if she refused, the dejected Laidley would return, and she had no idea what to do with him. "Don't get obsessed," she warned him.

"I already am," he breathed ruefully; the unexpected crook in his mouth made her smile.

"Laidley," she said, remembering the odd word wandering in and out of her head as he turned. "Do you know the legend attached to the steps in the cliff?"

He nodded. "I ran across it once," he answered vaguely.

"What is it?"

"That the steps were carved in the cliff face so that the body of Mermion, the first ruler of Raine, could be carried down for burial."

"He was buried at sea?"

"No. We were all taught that part of it," he reminded her. "He is not dead, but sleeping in a hollow in the cliff beneath the palace. The steps are how they got him into the hollow. In a time of grave crisis and peril to his kingdom he will wake and ascend the steps again to defend the Crowns of Raine."

She chewed on the end of her pen, trying to imagine his

burial. "Is he really in there? A skeleton in a cave somewhere at the end of the steps?"

"An armed skeleton," he amended. "With a crown on its head and a great sword at its side. He will hear the cries of terror and despair from his land and rouse himself from his dreams to rescue it. Why?"

She thought of the living queen again, young, vulnerable, and ignorant, standing a step above oblivion. She looked at Laidley, feeling suddenly, oddly vulnerable herself, though like Mermion of Raine they were all buried in stone.

"We might need him."

# SEVEN

Kane gave herself to Axis for his wedding.
Poets of the time paid their tribute to the young king's marriage to the Princess of Cribex with flowery and forgettable verse. Theirs was not the matter of romance or epic; hearts were not crushed in the making, nor were kings slain.

> *A thousand peacocks*
> *A hundred white stallions*
> *Ten coffers of gold*
> *And her heart*
> *The beautiful Princess of Cribex,*
> *The daughter of swans,*
> *The daughter of willow trees,*
> *Brought to the golden Lion of Eben.*

All princesses were beautiful, all kings were lions for the occasion. In truth, the princess, while comely, was plump, stood barely as high as Axis's armpit, and looked more like a sparrow than a swan. Kane had behaved badly since the announcement of the wedding, weeping all day and refusing to eat. On the morning of the ceremony, which took place in the great palace beside the Serpent, she locked herself alone in her room and would not come out. Her mother and all her aunts threatened; she refused to open the door. Axis's mother told them to leave her alone; she would come out when she was ready. And so she did. She left a note upon her pillow and ran away. Later, various stories surfaced. She joined a sect of women dedicated to the Serpent. She changed her name and became a shrewd and very prosperous merchant. She flung herself into a well over her unrequited passion and drowned. History loses sight of Axis's young cousin on the day of his wedding. It was assumed through the centuries, by anyone taking note of her disappearance, that it was brief, and that, during the blink of history's eye, an inadvertent glance away, she was found or chose to return home. Whereupon she would have been hastily bound in a marriage suitable for a highborn woman of Eben, to become a mother and live a life otherwise devoid of significant detail.

But she did none of those things. She did not even run away. She simply wrapped herself up so well that not even Axis recognized her and came to his wedding as a gift.

She appeared at the door of a room along the courtyard where the gifts of nobles and rulers were displayed. The sight of a tall, dark figure in a hooded cloak, its face shrouded behind black silk, carrying a staff of ebony and gold, startled the guards watching over the gifts.

"What do you want?" one asked sharply.

The figure said nothing, only proffered a letter with oddly bulky fingers. The message was open, signed, bore a seal with flowing ribbons and the wax emblem of a distant kingdom. The guard squinted at it.

"What does it say?" a second guard demanded.

"I don't know. I can't read."

The other snatched it from him, perused it while the same puckered expression grew on his own face. Kane waited motionlessly.

"What does it say?"

"I can't—I think it's in some strange language." He raised his head, glanced around vaguely for help.

"Everyone's at the wedding," the first observed.

"Well, what should we do with this—this—"

"Is it armed?"

Kane gestured quickly, indicated the wedding gifts, and then the vicinity of her heart several times, until one guard, hands raised to search her, drew back and scratched his chin.

"What's it saying? It's a wedding gift?"

"Seems to be . . . Go and ask—No. She's at the wedding, too."

"I'll ask outside, see if anyone can understand this."

The guard took the letter, went into the courtyard. Kane watched a ring of heads gather about him. The remaining guard watched her narrowly. She bobbed her head several times, indicated her heart and then the tables full of gifts.

"Yes, yes," the guard muttered at the eerie, hidden face, "I know. You're a present."

The first guard returned finally, said to him, "The captain recognized the seal. It's from Ilicia, over the southern mountains. He's sending for a friend of his, a scholar. Somebody who didn't get invited to the wedding."

"What should I do with it? Are we at peace with Ilicia?"

"We're at peace with everyone today." He gave the message back to the mute figure. "Put the gift over there in the corner, and if it does anything suspicious, arrest it."

"It already looks suspicious," the guard grumbled.

But he led Kane into the room and positioned her against the wall, where she waited for the scholar to arrive. The wedding gifts shone dimly on the other side of the black silk over her eyes: jeweled saddles, tapestries, fine mirrors, sumptuous robes, swords, alabaster vases, and birds with brilliant plumage pecking at the bars of gilded cages. She gave them scant attention, just stood stiffly, watching birds flick in and out of the sunny courtyard, listening to the tranquil fountains and hearing, now and then, within chambers on the other side of the courtyard, the ceremonial music of tabors and trumpets.

The scholar arrived finally, a chubby, sweating man who looked as though he had run all the way to the palace in the dust. The captain of the guards led him to the silent figure. He grunted at it in surprise, then said something in what Kane vaguely recognized as the language of Ilicia. She did not speak, only offered him the letter. He carried it to a table, shifted a gold tray and a birdcage out of the way, and took his tools out of a leather case: pens, paper, ink. There were no chairs. He unfolded one of a pair of stools of ivory and red leather embroidered with gold thread, and sat down to write.

The guards watched over his shoulder; he explained, erratically, as he translated, "In Ilicia it's not uncommon for servants who have special talents to be given as gifts. Cooking, for instance, or a way with horses . . . If they aren't freeborn . . . The hidden face is explained . . . So is the muteness. There is a suggestion of occult power in the staff. Not a great deal, I would guess—no ruler would give much of that to another. But enough perhaps to amuse the children . . . It ends with an odd symbol, but the rest is clear." He blew on his hastily scrawled translation and handed it to the captain. "Give that to the king. It is definitely a gift, and probably valuable."

He wrapped up his tools, folded the stool, and returned the sealed letter to the wedding gift. Smiling, he suggested his payment.

"A glance, perhaps, at the wedding feast?"

"I'd like one myself," the captain said fervently. "I've been smelling it for three days." He handed the translation to one of the guards and nodded at the other. "Take him down to the kitchens."

Kane, left alone in the corner, heard the triumphal march of the king and the new queen of Eben. She bowed her head against the staff in her hands and prepared to wait through the endless wedding feast.

She had bought the staff from a peddler weeks before the wedding. A shaft of ebony higher than her head, it was intricately carved with long-jawed, lozenge-backed lizards that spiraled up the length of it. To Kane, they looked not unlike what had eaten Axis's father. The object of their sharp-toothed smiles was the crown on top of the staff, which Kane had had fashioned out of a bracelet of garnets and gold that her mother had given her. The black, voluminously hooded cloak, which covered her from head to foot, she had found at the bottom of a clothes chest; judging from the musty smell it had been there for decades. Her hands were hidden within great leather gauntlets that kept threatening to fall off. The oversized hands coupled with her height and slenderness made the faceless figure look bony, awkward, unthreatening, perhaps not quite human. So the guards must have thought, for they didn't give the peculiar gift another glance, not even when platters were sent up from the kitchens of meats and savory pastries from the wedding, and they lounged, munching, in front of her.

Finally, the sky turned a tender lavender above the palace walls, and in the gardens the night birds began to sing. The wedding couple arrived to pay due attention to their gifts before they retired. Kane, her mouth suddenly dry, clung more tightly to the staff. The bride entered, twittering and chirping over the riches even before she got through the door. The groom followed, hardly seeing anything. He looked, Kane thought with sympathy, as though he had been clubbed. A river of aunts and cousins from both families followed them, headed by Axis's mother and her own. Kane stared numbly ahead. All the bright silks spilled through the room, rivulets of color, murmuring and cresting over one gift, then another.

Axis moved silently among them, borne hither and yon, the young Lion in his white and gold silks uninterested in anything he saw, including his placidly chattering bride.

Axis's mother saw the dark figure first.

"What is that?" she demanded, gripping the nearest arm, which belonged to Kane's mother. Kane's lips tightened behind her silk; she felt her face grow taut and chill. But not even her own mother recognized her; she only fanned herself with gilded feathers, staring speechlessly. Around them, little pools of silence grew, as guest after guest turned at the sound of it. Finally, even the bride noticed it.

"What is what?" she asked. Axis, glancing toward his mother, saw the hooded figure.

He blinked, finally interested in something. Beside him, his bride grew suddenly inarticulate. Axis's mother, closest to the apparition, examined it with amazement.

"What—Who—Is it a gift?"

Mutely, Kane proffered her letter. Axis's mother looked at it bewilderedly, then at the guards.

"From Ilicia," one explained.

"I recognize the seal," she said, at which Kane loosed a shallow breath. The crowned and coiled serpent had been mercifully easy to duplicate. "But what kind of gift is it?"

"Let me see," Axis said, stepping to her side. Belatedly, the guard remembered the scholar's translation. But not before Kane saw Axis's eyes find the little familiar twining of thorns, barely noticeable among the unfamiliar words.

She saw his eyes close briefly; the flat lion's face gave nothing away. Without looking at her, still gazing at the canes at the end of the letter, he held out his hand for the scholar's translation. By then his wife had made her way to his side, and was looking in blank astonishment at the wedding gift. She gripped her husband's wrist for reassurance.

"My lord, whatever is it? And who has sent it to us?"

Kane began to read the translation. It was hurried and somewhat clumsy, but then Kane's message from the ruler of Ilicia was not exactly polished, either.

"'To Axis, Ruler of Eben, on his wedding day:

'I am a gift to you from Marsyas, Ruler of Ilicia. I cannot speak, nor will you wish to look upon my face, for I am grievously deformed from birth. My powers lie in my heart and my staff. Both I pledge you, as the king commands me: To serve you and yours faithfully and well all the days of my life. Say my name and I will show you what I can do. My name is Kane.'"

Such was her name in their secret language: no one else knew this. Her given name vanished with the young woman who had erased herself from history. Only Kane was left now, a curve of brambles on the king's letter, an exact translation on the scholar's. She held her breath, the silk motionless above her lips. Axis, his face expressionless and oddly colorless in that gold-laden room, seemed also to be holding his breath. His bride, regaining composure, tugged at his arm.

"My lord, what does it do? Does it do tricks? Magic?" When there was no response from her bridegroom, she spoke the word herself: "Kane."

The ebony lizard curling around the top of the staff came to life and seized the gold crown in its jaws. Axis, recognizing his own history, gave a startled cry. His queen clapped her hands and laughed with delight.

"It is a human toy!"

The faceless figure knelt on both knees and bowed its head. There Kane remained, staring blindly at Axis's sandals, feeling the weight of his gaze, while the queen laughed again and whispered above her.

"Make it show its face. How dreadful could it be?"

But the young queen's own mother came to Kane's rescue, nipping the notion in the bud. "You must not look upon such things. If it frightens you, your unborn children might come to resemble it."

"Oh," the queen cried, stifling the sound in her horror. She recovered quickly. "But it must show us what else it can do. Do another trick for us, Kane."

Still on her knees, Kane pointed the staff; the cluster of guests shifted out of its aim until a wedding gift appeared in front of it. By then the lizard was lifeless wood, and the crown, disgorged, was back on top of the ebony. The staff trembled only slightly in Kane's hold. The gift, wrapped in tapestry and tied with braided ribbons of gold, unraveled itself to reveal a matched pair of goblets carved from solid amethyst. The bride clapped again. Kane bowed her head again.

Axis spoke.

"Rise, Kane. And welcome." Like the staff, his voice trembled only a little. "We will explore the extent of your talents later, at our leisure."

> *The Shadow of the Emperor*
> *The Hooded One*
> *Who unmasked night*
> *Who laid the stars like paving stones*
> *Who rode the Thunderbolt*
> *Down the star-cobbled path into day*
> *Was Kane,*
> *The Emperor's twin*
> *Silent, as lightning is silent,*
> *Before the thunder speaks.*

# EIGHT

Bourne sat alone in the wood, trying to lift the Floating School.

The students had been sent outside the school for no particular reason that he could see. To learn something, Felan had indicated, though exactly what seemed nebulous.

"You will find your way back when the wood has revealed its nature to you," he told them. "In revealing its nature, it will also reveal yours. You will not see the school once you have left it. The wood will become the world; it will become your vision; you will not see your way beyond it. If you need help or become frightened, I will find you."

They had all looked back at the school once the outer gate had closed behind them. Green wood was all they saw: the tangled weave of ivy and ancient, twisted branch, shrub and brush and flowering bramble growing around and into and through one another, moist and sweet, and so still that the briny wind churning the grasses on the plain might well have been in some distant country.

"Will the wood feed us?" one of the dozen students wondered wistfully. No one laughed. They had all been at the school too long to expect anything predictable or comfortable.

For a few moments they stood aimlessly, talking and waiting for something to happen. Gradually, in boredom or curiosity, or for less obvious motives, they began wandering away in no particular direction, just wanting, Bourne thought, to begin the exercise so that it would come to an end.

He began walking, determined to find his way out of the wood. It might be futile, he thought, but at least it was a purpose, a goal. The wood, after all, was small; he could have ridden around it in an hour. Later, he sat sweating on an old stump, watching a dank little pool overgrown with water lilies for a frog, a fly, a minnow, anything to disturb the utter stillness around him. He felt he had walked all morning. It might be any hour of the day. The damp, shadowy mistiness of a wood not yet found by sunlight remained unchanged; he might have just left the Floating School.

Thinking of it, for he was beginning to be hungry, he remembered the task they were given a week ago: to lift the Floating School above the trees while sitting within it. It seemed beyond impossible. "You will," Felan had promised them. "It is simple. A child could do it with one finger." They had strained their brains to the utmost; none of the students could lift so much as a brick.

Maybe, Bourne thought, it would be easier to do it outside.

It was something to do, at any rate. He settled himself cross-legged on the stump, let the silence of the wood seep into him, like an old toad drowsing in the moss, until his thoughts were formless and pellucid as air. After a time, he let the image of the school drift into them, a floating island of walls and towers, a dream, an airy construct of space and light, weighing nothing, no more than a memory, no more than an imaginary world. It hung there, suspended in his mind above the trees, immense and serene, the old stones butter-colored in the sunlight, as solid and as insubstantial as cloud, there and not—

"Bourne!" his uncle exclaimed. He jumped like a frog, then wondered with horror if he had truly heard what he thought: the sound of something unimaginably massive shaking the earth as it dropped.

But the wood, except for his uncle, was still soundless. No birds scattered, crying, out of the trees; he heard no human shouts.

I dreamed it, he thought confusedly. His bones felt surprisingly stiff as he straightened, sliding off the damp stump.

"Uncle Ermin," he said, feeling less than his usual composure. "What are you doing here?"

"I rode over from the palace to see what you are learning," his uncle said. "They told me you were out here." He dismounted, leaving his horse to snort suspiciously at the bracken. "What were you doing sitting on a stump and doing nothing?"

Ermin of Seale was a big man, like Bourne's father had been, his yellow hair graying, his eyes restless and piercing, a predator trying to run down his prey before time ran him down. There were many like him, Bourne knew, in the palace above the sea. But no one else had thought to place a nephew in the Floating School to make a warrior mage of himself to aid his uncle's ambitions.

"We were sent out here to perform a task," Bourne explained. "I've been waiting for mine to come along."

"What kind of task?"

Bourne shrugged. "Something the wood dreams up. I don't suppose you have anything to eat."

"I've just sat through another endless meal," his uncle said pitilessly. "This one to honor a delegation from Almorania. They all wear beads in their hair and smell like sheep. They only want to be left alone; no help to us there. Show me what you've learned lately."

Bourne turned away from the Lord of Seale, shifting his thoughts with an effort out of the tranquil nothingness in which they had been drifting. He had to kindle fire from cloud, from the quiet wood around him, from his own toad-stupor. When it came finally, the sudden, vivid red-gold flash did little more than leave a blackened scar across a hoary tree trunk. But his uncle was impressed.

"I saw that," he said, "in your eyes before it came out. That'll be useful. Can you take down a wall with it?"

"It should be possible," Bourne said. He felt suddenly weary, something damp and smoldering, without true heat or warmth, just a lot of smoke pretending to be fire. The effects of twiddling his thumbs in the wood for hours on end, he thought. He added, with an effort, "I learned something even more interesting, though I can't show it to you now. I traveled from the Floating School to the library in a single step, the other evening."

"The library?" His uncle took a step toward him, astounded. "You don't mean the royal library?"

"Yes. I was here in one breath, there the next, in the refectory where the librarians were eating supper."

His uncle thought for a breath, color mottling his face. "Can you make yourself invisible and do that?" he demanded sharply.

"I thought you'd see where it might lead," Bourne said evenly. "Not yet. I haven't been taught to make myself invisible, and I can't control the traveling. It—" He paused; his uncle watched him narrowly. "It still depends."

"On what?"

"On what I travel toward. It depends on what—on how much I want to get there."

"And what book did you want that much in the palace library?" the Lord of Seale asked shrewdly.

"It wasn't exactly a book."

"I imagined that it wasn't exactly a book." His uncle sighed. "You're doing well with this. But be careful. Don't get yourself into trouble with anyone I'll have to fight or pay to get you out of."

Bourne shook his head. "It's no one like that. She's an orphan. A transcriptor."

"An orphan." The Lord of Seale touched his eyes. "Well, at

least she inspired you to make use of your talents. Just guard your words around her."

"Why? Do we have anything to keep secret?"

His uncle glanced around them, as though wondering if the trees were listening. Probably, Bourne guessed, but they seemed to guard their words quite well.

"Not here," the Lord of Seale said abruptly, "not in a wood full of mages. It'll wait. Just keep working. Be ready when I need you."

He mounted. Bourne watched him ride away, but not far. The trees and brush closed around him quickly; even his horse's steps faded soon in the underbrush. Bourne sat down to wait again. Some time passed, only a moment or two, perhaps, but who knew in that timeless place? Then he felt his entire body prickle eerily. He raised his head, the breath flashing out of him, to stare at the place where the shifting branches had hidden his uncle as he rode away from Bourne.

His uncle, Bourne remembered clearly, had already returned home to Seale. He had taken his heir with him, and left his other sons and nephews to celebrate the event and make what they could of the political winds pounding across the plain. "I've seen the young queen," he had said grimly to Bourne, visiting the school before he left. "And I've seen the gathering of wolves around her. I'll leave them here to howl at one another, while their own Crowns lie unguarded. I have work to do in Seale. And you have yours here. Do well for me, Bourne. We'll use all you can learn."

"It was only a dream," he whispered. "Only a dream. The

wood revealed my own thoughts to me. That's all. But I knew them already."

Then he felt his heart floating again, sunlit and serene, impossibly heavy, impossibly light; he felt the earth itself balanced on his outstretched finger.

The wood will reveal your nature, he heard Felan say, and his skin prickled again, this time with wonder.

Which? he asked it. Which?

He rose again, turned aimlessly this way and that, hoping to see the walls of the school and finding only trees everywhere, interminable walls of green. He stood uncertainly, restless and disturbed for some reason, and suddenly tired of looking at himself. He heard a few twigs snap and tensed. Then one of the other students emerged on the far side of the tiny pool, and he sighed with relief at the company.

She looked only vaguely familiar. One of the newer, younger students who had entered the school at the beginning of spring, he guessed. He hardly knew them. She was flushed; her long hair, a lank white-gold, had snagged a leaf or two, a bit of moss. She nearly walked into the pond before he spoke.

"Watch your step," he advised. She stopped dead, staring at him as though he were one of the wood's portents. "I'm Bourne," he added quickly. "Another student." She was still looking at him in a kind of bewildered horror; he wondered if he had grown horns or if his face had turned green from proximity to all the trees. "There's a pool," he explained gently, "in front of you. It looks very shallow, and I think it's uninhabited by monsters, but you will get your feet wet if you take another step."

She glanced down finally. "Oh," she said, and stepped backward carefully, as though she were practicing a dance step. When she looked at him again, her face seemed calmer. "Thank you." Her voice was soft, very shy; she might bolt like a deer, he guessed, if he sneezed. She was oddly dressed for a student, wearing an oversized homespun cloak over what looked like pink silk worse for the mud, and a pair of black riding boots. She studied him silently, for a disconcertingly long moment, before she spoke again. "The wood," she said hesitantly. "It's odd today. Not like the last time I was here."

"It is very odd," he agreed fervently, and watched her begin a path around the pond. All her steps were cautious, precise; there might have been monsters sleeping all around her she was trying not to waken.

"It seems full of things," she continued. "Last time it seemed empty."

"What kinds of things?" he asked, settling back against the stump, curious about someone else's visions.

"Except for the giant," she amended.

"You saw a giant?"

"Last time. This time, I saw birds."

"I haven't seen so much as a mosquito. Not even over this pond, which should have spawned vast numbers of flying things."

"They spoke."

"They—?"

"The birds." She had rounded the pool within a few feet of him; she stopped again. He could see her eyes now, a pale blue beneath her very pale brows. "I could understand them. Don't you think that's strange?"

"Oh, very," he agreed. "What did they say?"

"There was one in particular—a fiery red, every feather, and black, black eyes. It told me to beware what I might meet in the wood. That's why—"

"That's why," he finished, enlightened, "you seemed so frightened of me."

"For a moment," she admitted. "I was expecting something that breathed fire, or had teeth as long as my arms. But it was you."

"All I saw was my uncle," Bourne mused. "Who looked so much as ever that I forgot he had gone back to the Second Crown a week ago. What else did you see?" he asked the odd young woman, who seemed more woodland animal than human. A useful quality in a mage, he thought. *Some of us have a harder time forgetting our humanity.*

"Things," she said vaguely, remembering them. She took an unconscious step toward him. "A tree spoke to me. It looked like a very old man, twisted and slow, with mossy hair down to its ankles and eyes like dead leaves. It did not say much, just my name. I think that's very strange, that a tree I have never met would know my name. And there were the stags with the fire in their antlers. They did not speak. The warrior followed them."

"The warrior."

"Fully armed, on a white war horse. The warrior wore a great sword with a crosspiece inlaid with uncut jewels; it looked too long and heavy for anyone human to wield. The warrior was very tall and broad-shouldered. I could not see the face or hands; the visor was down and of course the hands were covered with mail gauntlets. Anyone could have that gold hair, flowing from underneath the helm."

"Anyone," Bourne echoed, puzzled. "Did he speak?"

"No. The warrior only pointed, and all I saw was a huge thicket of brambles. Perhaps it was meant to be seen by someone else."

"I'm not sure that's the way the wood works," Bourne said slowly, "though we are all out in the wood together today. You've seen a great deal for a beginning student."

She blinked at him; he wondered what word had silenced her. She told him. "Student."

"You are a student, aren't you?"

"At the mages' school?"

He was silent then, wondering. A peculiar expression flitted over her face, as though she had bitten into something unfamiliar. "Is that what you are?"

"Yes," he said. "A student at the Floating School. Our task today was to stay in the wood and let it speak to us."

She gave a little, breathless laugh. "That's what I thought you were," she told him. "Something of the wood speaking to me."

"Then who are you?" he asked, amazed. She backed a step, her face closing. The wrong question, he saw.

"I must go," she said.

Or maybe she really was something magical in the wood that he had failed to recognize. "Go where?" he asked recklessly.

"Back. Before they miss me."

"Are you staying on the plain?"

She hesitated, then gave a little nod. "Yes."

"But you saw so much—the wood spoke to you. You must have a gift for magic; you shouldn't ignore it."

"Is that what it is?" she asked. "I'm never certain. It seems unimportant to anyone." She took another step backward, lingered, studying him, shy again, but this time unafraid. "How will we really know," she asked him, "if either of us is real?"

He opened his mouth to protest, then closed it and smiled ruefully. "Then let us agree to be one another's vision," he said gravely. "Perhaps we will meet again in the wood, if that is the only place where we exist to one another."

"Yes."

"Anyway, thank you."

"For what?" she asked.

"For coming to talk to me. I was getting lonely."

She smiled, a surprised, genuine smile, before she turned. She doesn't smile often, he guessed, watching for a long time, it seemed, before the wood hid her away.

"How strange," he breathed, thinking of her rough wool and fine silk, the contradictions of wildness and power in her uncertain face. Why do I know that face? he wondered, baffled. He straightened, took a step or two away from the stump, then noticed how dark it was getting, even in that perpetual twilight.

I've been out here all day, he realized with surprise, and saw her face again, her hair impeccably braided and bejeweled, her head held very high, very stiffly, so not to dislodge the crown that had been placed on it.

He felt his skin constrict again. "No," he told her finally, hoarsely. "You could not possibly have been real."

When he could see past memory, he found the massive walls of the school a pace or two away across the pool, the outer gate beginning to open as though he had just knocked.

# NINE

Vevay sat high in the tower overlooking the plain, trying to remember her life. It was late at night. Fire murmured in the great hearth beside her, whispering things she had long forgotten. If only I could remember the language of fire before I understood it, she thought absently. The perpetual winds rattled at the thick windows, trying, like memory, to reach her. Once, long ago, she had stood in them for the first time, let her mind and body flow into them, become the dark, singing force beneath the moon. Now she was draped in white fur, listening to them from within stone and glass. If she opened an inner ear she could hear the sea, churning restlessly with some in-coming squall, tearing at the cliffs with silver-white fingers, trying to reach the palace, trying to catch the wind. If she opened an inner eye, she could see into the wild spring night that once, long ago, she would have tried to breathe into her marrow; she would have changed the shape of her bones to enter into its realm.

Easier to understand the wind, she thought. Easier to walk on the surface of the frothing sea, than to remember the hunger to do it. Easier to remember knowledge than ignorance, experience than innocence. Easier to know what you are than remember what you were, so long ago that what you were then lived in an entirely different world . . .

Gavin's reflection, entering the room through a pane of glass, startled her; her thoughts had strayed that deeply into past. She turned, noted his expression, or lack of it.

"Writing?" he asked, making an effort. She shook her head.

"Trying to remember what it was like to be young," she said dourly. His set face eased a little, but not enough, she thought. He poured wine, sat down on the bed to pull off his boots. She smelled smoke on him, and wind, horses, and beer; he had been roaming, she guessed, speaking to guards on the plain, on the walls, picking up threads of rumor, incidents, gossip that might lead somewhere, mean something. Thus he kept watch on the Raine he understood, while she kept watch—or tried to—on the Raine she didn't.

"I wish they would all go home," he sighed.

"Maybe the queen should travel," Vevay mused. "Visit her Crowns. They would have to return to their own lands to prepare for her. And she might learn a few things."

"The size of her realm," Gavin suggested.

"The size of her problems." She crossed the room, sat down on the bed beside him. "Perhaps I'll suggest it."

"You'll have to go with her."

She contemplated that with horror. "No. Would I?"

"Who else? Her mother?"

"A younger and more energetic mage, surely. The thought makes my bones ache."

"You were her father's trusted counselor," he reminded her. "The rulers of the Crowns know you; they wouldn't want to deal with a new queen and an unfamiliar mage at the same time."

She rose again, restively, to pace a little among the tall candle stands and tapestries. "Maybe it's not a good idea. I used to be a mage," she added impatiently. "Once I used my powers. Now I feel like a dancing instructor, reminding the queen whom she is dancing with at this hour and with which foot she should begin."

"Be thankful," Gavin advised with a laugh, "that so far the music is still being played and everyone is trying to dance in harmony."

"It won't last."

The words came out unexpectedly and far too bleakly; she stopped, met Gavin's eyes. He gave a little nod after a moment, acknowledging her deepest fears.

"I feel it, too," he said softly. "Trouble on the wind. But from which direction, I can't guess, and I can't place incidents together to put a pattern to them. Everything troubling seems isolated, random. And if everyone is still here, who would attack?"

"Ermin of Seale went home."

"But it's the Lord of Seale whom I would suspect of insurrection first," Gavin said simply. "Even he is being predictable. That nephew of his in the mages' school—"

"Felan is keeping an eye on him."

"That's so transparent it's ridiculous. Does Bourne have any talent?"

"Felan says yes. He might be disturbing except that he doesn't take anything very seriously, not even his uncle, and he seems to have no ambitions of his own."

"If he did?"

"Felan can't guess. So far he can only watch."

"And all we can do," Gavin said, standing up to loosen his belt. Vevay went to the window again, stared back at the enormity of night pushing an eye against their tiny, bright window, spying on their comfort, their fragile peace.

"I can see into you, too," she whispered.

"What?"

"I think it's time to do what the queen's mother suggested the queen's mage do."

"That being?"

"Some magic."


So she did, the next day, while the queen rode off reluctantly with her guests to go hunting in the great forests east of the plain. Gavin, sighing over his stiff joints, rode among her guards, to ease Vevay's mind. Vevay made herself invisible,

wandered hither and yon through walls and narrow passage-
ways so old that not even the servants knew they existed.
Words drew her here, there, like a feather blown on a breeze;
stray voices, scraps of conversation, soft murmurings from
ladies and maids took her from high airy chambers down to
stony cellars and moldering dungeons, and even deeper than
that, to the weird labyrinth burrowed into stone that was the
royal library. She gave that only cursory attention: even in the
long, tumultuous history of Raine, the rulers had never had to
go to war with their librarians.

She moved unseen through nobles and courtiers who had
chosen not to hunt. Most of the younger ones had gone with
the queen, leaving their elders beside the hearth fires in private rooms and council chambers. She learned a few startling
things about affairs among the rulers of the Crowns, but nothing troublesome to the new queen that Vevay had not already
guessed. Everyone suspected everyone else of plotting; she
caught no one actually doing it.

When twilight fell, she roamed with the wind on the plain,
listened to the soldiers and servants, the poor relations, ped-
dlers, gypsies, the merchants and village folk of the Crowns
who had traveled untold distances for a glimpse of their new
queen. Seeing Tessera meant good luck, she learned. Her youth
meant strength and beauty, her inexperience had been transformed into a kind of wisdom unsullied by reality that would
lead Raine into a perpetual spring of prosperity and hope. She
had been seen in improbable places: riding alone among her

people on a white horse, flying out of the Floating School as it hung suspended among the trees. Along with beauty, strength, and wisdom, she had acquired magical powers.

She would be the last to recognize herself, Vevay thought ruefully. She stopped to talk to a flea-bitten witch who was telling fortunes. The witch cast the fortune of Raine with little carved bones and pieces of crystal onto a gold silk cloth with a black line painted across it.

"Above the line is good fortune," she told Vevay. "Below the line is not."

She closed her eyes and threw her motley tokens. They landed in an arc above the line. The witch clasped her hands in wonder, proclaiming the best of all possible fortunes for the Twelve Crowns of Raine. It was evident in the perfect rainbow's arc above the black, and in the unbroken pattern of crystal alternating with bone. Clearly a great ruler had been crowned; a reign of unprecedented peace and affluence had begun.

"Clearly," Vevay said, and left her a coin stamped with the new queen's profile.

Clearly if that were so, then Vevay would not be wandering around in the dark feeling something amiss and trying to find out what from a handful of knuckle bones.

She caught the wind's current again and flowed with it, half-visible to a mage's eye as a swirl of cloth, a strand of ivory hair, and invisible to anyone else. It took her where she wanted, to the thick, clotted dark that crouched like an animal on the plain, never sleeping and never awake. She felt the wood's awareness as she blew into it. She caught her balance among the trees, amazed as always at their utter stillness, even in the howling winds from the sea.

"Tell me what you see for Raine," she asked the wood. But nothing spoke, not a leaf, not a breaking twig. It only revealed the school after a moment, a denser dark within the leaves. A gate opened; light beckoned. She went into it.

It was not the school that the students saw. That school was an eccentric, drafty puzzle-box of stone that changed shape according to their needs. Sometimes the stone walls would shift to let in the wood, sometimes the sky; any kind of weather was apt to appear. Stairs and corridors were rarely predictable, except for finding meals and beds. Monsters might roam the halls; doors might open to reveal riches, or strange beasts, or nothing at all as far as the eye could see. Through the centuries different mages had worked their spells into the rooms as tests and teaching devices; not even Felan knew anymore what waited behind every door, or how many magically charmed rooms lay unopened, forgotten until chanced upon by some hapless student. The school itself became a student's first test: the inflexible mind that balked at its erratic behavior never stayed long.

The school that opened itself to Vevay was a comfortable, cluttered place, with thick carpets and musty tapestries and many fat candles. Owls queried her passing; in the windows, ravens and kingfishers muttered sleepily. A milk-white snake in a dark corner uncoiled its head and opened a sapphire eye at her. Books lined the walls, lay open on stands; some of them whispered constantly, reading themselves aloud. The hallway she walked opened into a room with an elaborately patterned floor of wood and ivory, and walls of oak and stained glass. In it, she found Felan, who would have been expecting her the moment she set foot in the wood.

He was sitting in moonlight and candlelight, scratching the head of some beast that looked to Vevay a cross between a lion and a bear. It had a black pelt, a flat, broad, fanged face, a powerful, bulky body. It seemed to be purring. It cast a smoldering red glance at Vevay then closed its eyes again, leaned heavily against Felan's knee.

"What on earth is that?" Vevay asked.

"I have no idea," Felan said. "It came out of an old book I was reading once and it never went back in. It seems harmless and it's very obliging: it lets the students practice transformation spells on it. It eats strawberries when it can get them." He stroked the pointed ears a moment, studying Vevay. "What's wrong?"

"I'm afraid," Vevay said tightly.

"Of what?"

"Of what, I don't know. I'm afraid for Raine."

"Sit down," Felan suggested, and she did so on a broad stone bench strewn with cushions and furs and littered for some reason with dried flower petals. The wood, she noted, not for the first time and always with wonder, had made its own moon. It was quite full that night, spilling light into the open casements. Over the rest of Raine, no moon was visible. The odd animal collapsed, sighing, across Felan's feet. He leaned back in his chair, his calm eyes on Vevay. "Are you afraid of the Crowns working against the queen?"

"Well, that, yes. That's always on my mind. But every ruler I have ever counseled in my long life has always had to contend with—contention. The possibility of war if they weren't making it themselves, trying to add another Crown to the kingdom. If that's all I'm afraid of, I should be able to recognize it by now."

Felan was silent again. A single line appeared and frayed across his brow; she had shattered his tranquillity.

"If that's all," he repeated slowly. "There might be something worse than twelve Crowns at war with one another?" He was on his feet so quickly she barely saw him move. The animal gave a guttural whine of protest as he stepped out from under it. "Something at war with the Twelve Crowns?"

She gazed blankly at the possibility. "There have been no rumors. No indications."

"But you're not afraid of nothing."

"Maybe I am. I'm very old and trying to remember my past. Perhaps I'm simply unburying ancient fears. That's why I came to you. You've known me longest; you can tell me if I've roused one of the fretful squalls of old age."

His face had grown still again, watchful now rather than serene. "You've known yourself longest," he reminded her. "Are you afraid of death?"

"I don't have time to think about dying. I'm too worried about Tessera."

"Then perhaps together we can see what it is that's troubling you. Come."

He stepped to the center of the patterned floor; she followed him. A circle of aged ivory lay there like an ancient moon, with many intricate paths raying out from it. Felan stood at the rim of it, facing the wood's moon, so that the light illumined the ivory; his shadow fell behind him. He gestured. Vevay moved to stand opposite him, so that the moonlight fell on her back; her shadow lay across the face of the moon at their feet.

"The wood's moon suggested this to me," he explained. "Perhaps the wood is speaking to us. Or perhaps I am making an entirely random connection between two white circles. We'll see. You must show it what you fear."

"How can I, when I don't know myself?"

He smiled. "Just tell it silently what you told me."

So she told the moon her fears, word by word, until words became unnecessary; it became easier to feel fear than to speak. The ivory at their feet rippled like water, became insubstantial, cloud. It glowed through her shadow like the true moon through night, seeing, revealing. Something began to take shape on its face, a shadowy form, human it seemed, yet faceless and gleaming strangely. Vevay frowned, trying to make sense of it. It seemed to be sitting on a roughly carved stone chair, in a hollow of stone. It held a long streak of white light across its knees and carried a circle of gold on its head.

She gave a sudden hiccup of astonishment.

"What is it?" Felan asked.

"I think—" The figure became clearer, faceless because its helm was down; the long streak of light was a sheathed sword, the circle of gold a crown. "I think it's Mermion."

"Who?"

"The first king of Raine. The Dreamer. Asleep in his cave within the cliff until he is roused to defend his realm. But why in the world—" She stopped abruptly, without knowing why, only that suddenly she did not want to know why, she wanted to close the moon like an eye and creep back into ignorance.

The Dreamer's mailed hand tightened on the sword; light melted down it. The helmed head turned slightly, as though disturbed by some sound from the world above. Vevay stared, frozen, her white brows lifted as high as they could go. She heard Felan's uneven breathing.

Within the moon, the Dreamer woke and rose.

# TEN

*The Thunderbolt*
*The Emperor of Night*
*The Lord of Time*
*With his army the stars*
*Rode out of the Gates of Nowhere,*
*Shook the tall towers of Zirxia*
*To the ground*
*And plundered the ancient graves of its kings.*

Nepenthe paused to study her translation. "Zirxia," she murmured. "Where is Zirxia? Was Zirxia? And was it even Zirxia? Maybe that thorn is not a Z. Tirxia?" She frowned at it, weaving her pen through her hair. "And what are the Gates of Nowhere?" She shook her hair loose, slumped on her stool, sighing. Books surrounded her on all sides; thorns filled her eyes, her thoughts. Here, she thought.

In this library stand the Gates of Nowhere through which the Lord of Time will lead his army . . .

But only Laidley came through them, carrying yet more musty scrolls. She watched him, happy to see another human face after hours of work, yet perversely wishing that the human face belonged to someone else. She envisioned Bourne everywhere, like the thorns, just because once he had appeared out of nowhere when he was the last thing she expected. Maybe that's where the Gates of Nowhere are, she thought, illumined. Anywhere but here.

"I found some old epics about Axis," Laidley said.

Nepenthe straightened instantly, reaching out for the scrolls, forgetting about Bourne. "Laidley, what do you know about Zirxia?"

"What?"

She showed him the fragment of poetry. He studied it, his young face wrinkling like a walnut in concentration.

"Are you sure that's a Z?" he asked finally.

"No. What might it be if it's not a Z?"

"Dirxia. It was a small, very rich kingdom in the south deserts of what is now the Ninth Crown."

"That must be it."

"But."

"But?"

He looked at her without seeing her, the way she usually looked at him; his own eyes were full of thorns, she guessed. "It didn't exist when Axis lived. So he couldn't have conquered it. That must be a later piece of poetry, which means that the book you are translating was written centuries after his death. Which means, of course, that everything in it might be suspect. A compilation of fact and legend and poetry, all jumbled together."

"It doesn't seem like that," she protested. "Kane seems to be trying to separate fact from legend."

"Kane?"

"Well, it's her alphabet. She invented it."

"She?" Laidley was looking fishlike now, goggle-eyed and breathing through his mouth. "Kane was a woman?"

"This book says she was. That's why she was masked."

"That may be, but how could Kane write about a kingdom that didn't exist until centuries after she died?"

Nepenthe mused over that, twirling hair around the wrong end of her pen. "Then," she concluded, "it must not be Dirxia."

"You're getting ink on your cheek. Unless the later kingdom took its name from an earlier one."

"Do kingdoms do that?"

He shrugged. "They could if they wanted to, I suppose. But how could Kane be a woman? He is Axis's brother. His twin, in at least one account."

"And not related at all, in others. Legends change through time. They get tangled up with other legends, names change, events that have nothing whatsoever to do with the legend cling to them and change."

"I know that. But sex is usually constant. Men don't change into women."

"He is she in this book."

"Are you sure you've got the right thorn for her?"

"It's more than just a pronoun," she said patiently. "It's the way she fit into her culture before she became Kane. It's unmistakable. She had to hide her sex to stay with Axis when he married. She became the faceless figure of mystery. The Masked Sorcerer. The Hooded One."

Laidley grunted, not entirely convinced. "Sounds like wishful thinking on the part of a writer enchanted by Axis's legend, and trying to be part of it while making sense of all the unlikely pieces of it."

"Then why is it written in Kane's alphabet of thorns? Who would bother to invent a secret alphabet for that?"

"Someone who could," he said simply. "Anyway, how do we know it was a secret language back then? Maybe all other records of it were obliterated by a conqueror who allowed no language under his rule but his own."

"Axis?" she suggested drily. "Laidley, go away if you can't be more helpful. This was all becoming clear until I told you about it."

"Do you want me to stop bringing you books?" he asked wistfully.

She held her breath, loosed it noisily. "No. And it does help me to be able to talk about it. But you can't see what I'm seeing without—without—"

"Without translating the thorns," he finished for her. She looked down at them; her hands rose protectively, slid over the coiling letters, hiding them. For no reason, she told herself bewilderedly. No reason that either of them could see.

"Kane was a sorceress," she said softly. "Her alphabet was a secret between her and Axis. No one else knew it. Maybe she put some kind of seal on this book that still lingers even after thousands of years."

"Then why does it let you into its secrets?"

"I don't know. But it makes me want to keep it secret."

He tried to peer at it through her fingers, gave up. "Well," he said finally, "if you ever do want me to learn it, tell me. Meanwhile . . ." His voice trailed away as he gazed at her. He reached impulsively toward the smudge on her cheek. She ducked reflexively; he drew his hand back without touching her.

"Meanwhile what?" she asked, to help him regain composure.

He only reddened more deeply, and mumbled, "I'll pay closer attention to Kane's—to the question of—"

"Pronouns."

"Yes," he said tightly and wandered off into the books. Nepenthe stared down at her hands for a moment or three before she saw the thorns they were protecting.

She read late that night in her chamber, trying to find, among the epics Laidley had brought her, some reference to the dubiously named Zirxia. She kept an eye on pronouns, too. But in every different epic, even in the badly translated shards that came out of forgotten kingdoms, the Hooded One was male. Axis's brother, Axis's twin, younger by a breath, Axis's mage, whose age and origins were obscure, Axis's closest companion, whom he trusted as he trusted neither wife nor lover. Regarding either wife or lover, poets rarely commented, except in the flowery conventions of the time. When Bourne appeared, unexpectedly out of nowhere, Nepenthe had fallen asleep face-down on the open pages and was dreaming of herself, hooded and masked in black, telling Laidley her true name.

I am Kane.

She woke with a start, saw the hooded figure stirring the coals in the brazier. She squeaked; it turned, revealing a familiar pronoun.

"You . . ."

Bourne pushed his hood back, smiling. "I'm practicing my movements across distances. It's easier to be private now that I know where you sleep." She rolled over, struggling with clinging bedclothes. "Don't get up."

"I thought you were Kane. No." She rubbed her eyes. "I dreamed I was."

"That sounds like a riddle. What is Kane? Another foundling?"

"No." She looked down at herself. "I'm still dressed."

"So you are."

Their eyes met across the brazier. She smiled then, fully awake. His smile deepened. "There is still some distance," she observed.

"Only a step," he said, and crossed it.

In the morning, he seemed inclined to linger past the awakening splash of the gong's powerful voice, even past the hour when he should have been at the school.

"I'll tell them I got lost last night," he said with a laugh. "Forget your fish, or whatever it is you're working on. We'll take a journey down the cliff steps and look for the Dreaming King in his cave and listen to the sea."

"I can't," she said, thinking guiltily of the scholar's fish. But it was the thorns she wanted. Even more than Bourne, she realized surprisedly, she wanted the ancient, unfinished tale growing under her pen. "And you should go back to the wood before the mages start searching for you and find you here in my bed."

"No one will come," he assured her. "Students get tired or frustrated, wander off for a day. Usually they're back by supper time. So I will be."

"I have to work."

"No, you don't. Not today."

"Yes," she said, taking his face between her hands to hold his eyes. "I do."

He gazed back at her, reminding her of what she was so carelessly tossing out of her bed: all that wealth of gold hair and eyes and skin, that smiling mouth. At her implacable silence, his eyes narrowed; he breathed incredulously, "It's that book. Isn't it?"

She let go of him, rolled out from under him. "I work," she

said doggedly, "for the librarians, to repay them for my up-bringing and education. I may even get a coin or two from the scholar with the fish manuscript. I can't just absent myself for the day for no reason."

He followed her out of bed, caught her shoulders. "You promised me that you would let the librarians know you have it."

"I will," she promised again. "When I'm finished with it."

"Show me what you're doing."

"No," she said adamantly. "It's secret."

"Whose secret?"

"Mine."

"No, it's not." His hands tightened on her shoulders; his eyes looked suddenly unfamiliar, a mage's eyes, she thought, reflecting the magic that they glimpsed. "It's someone else's se-cret, and you've become part of the secret. You're tangled in those brambles. I want to know what they're hiding. Or I'll tell the librarians myself. And the mages."

She stared at him, flushed and angry, wondering why she had ever liked him. "You won't tell," she said finally, "if I show you."

"Unless it's dangerous—"

"It's not dangerous! It's just some very old story that I want to know the ending to before I give the book up and never see it again."

"They'd let you finish it. You've already figured out the al-phabet." He pushed at her disheveled hair, trying to find her eyes again. "Wouldn't they? Or is there some reason why you think they wouldn't let you finish?"

"It's not—" She drew breath, trying to make sense of her

own disorderly thoughts. "I don't understand why I don't want to give it up. Maybe if you let me finish it, I might understand. Maybe then I won't need it anymore, and I can give it to the librarians without a second thought. But you're right: I love that alphabet of thorn; it has worked its way into my heart. I'll show you what it is, but you won't understand. All you'll see is the story of two people who died long before Raine ever existed."

"Perhaps." His own face had lost color, she saw; he looked more serious than she had thought he could be in his facile life. "But the most powerful thing I have learned at the mages' school is that words can have a life of their own. Show me what you're doing. If I see danger in it, I'll tell you. And then, if you don't see it, I will tell the librarians."

She sighed gustily. "All right. Then you will leave me alone?"

He blinked, startled at that. "Alone—"

"For today at least," she said, relenting; her own hands rose to cling to his straight shoulders. He dropped his face against hers; she felt him sigh.

"For today," he promised.

They dressed then, scraped what was left of the porridge out of the bottom of the cauldron in the refectory. She led him deep into the stones, down the long corridor that ended in half-bubbles of chambers carved along it, all of them so full of manuscripts, books, and scrolls that there was barely room for dust. Her desk, half-in, half-out of the cluttered alcove was, as always, undisturbed except for Laidley sitting on it.

He caught sight of Bourne and slid off, stood, wordless and awkward. Nepenthe wished they would both disappear.

She said shortly, "Laidley, this is Bourne of Seale. He gave me the book about Axis and Kane. I told him I'd show him what I was translating."

"Axis and Kane?" Bourne repeated, amazed.

Laidley had flushed. His tongue became unstuck from the roof of his mouth. "You wouldn't show me," he said accusingly.

"You didn't threaten to go to the librarians if I didn't," she said dourly. "Bourne thinks it might be magic, or dangerous."

"That moldy old tale?"

"No," Bourne said precisely. "The language of the moldy old tale."

"Since you're here, too, Laidley, I'll show you both."

Laidley sniffed, but refrained from comment. Nepenthe opened the book and her manuscript paper and, index finger moving from thorn to thorn, began to read.

"'He fought his first battle at the age of seven . . .'"

She broke into her reading now and then to question a troublesome word or explain a choice she had made. They listened silently, their eyes on her face until she finished. Then, unexpectedly, they turned their faces to gaze at one another for enlightenment.

"I don't understand the compulsion," Bourne said finally.

"Neither do I." Laidley went to the desk, studied the coiling and uncoiling letters curiously. "But it is an odd little mystery, who actually wrote it."

"Kane wrote it," Nepenthe said stubbornly.

"How could he—she—have quoted poetry written centuries after her death?" Laidley asked reasonably.

"The scholars are wrong."

"About what?"

"When the poetry was written."

"It was written in countries that didn't exist when Kane—"

"Then they're wrong about when Kane died," Nepenthe argued.

"When did Kane die?" Bourne asked. "I have only the vaguest knowledge of anything to do with Axis and Kane. They lived; Axis conquered the known world; they died. I get lost any time before my great-grandfather getting his head cut off for treason against Raine."

Laidley thought, ruffling at his thin hair. "I remember when Axis ruled, but I don't remember when either of them died."

"Why don't you go and find out?" Nepenthe suggested, sitting on her stool again.

"All right," Laidley said, to her surprise.

She turned pointedly to Bourne. "Unless you think it's dangerous knowing such a thing."

"It doesn't sound so," he admitted. He lingered over the thorns, as though listening for all they did not say, all that they kept hidden behind their words. But he heard nothing. Still troubled, he bent to pull a kiss from Nepenthe's mouth before he left her.

"I wonder what it sounded like," he murmured, "that barbed spiky language they spoke to one another."

"You won't tell the librarians, then?"

He shook his head. "Not yet. Not until I know more."

He stepped away from her; she watched, expecting to see him melt into time, into a distant moment. But instead he caught up with Laidley in his pursuit of history, leaving Nepenthe to stare at both their backs.

"We're all obsessed," she said, astonished, and then picked up her pen and forgot about them.

# ELEVEN

Tessera slid wearily off her horse in the torch-lit courtyard after the endless hunt, thinking of the bloody hare in her saddlebag that her arrow had accidentally hit. It had screamed at the arrow's bite; the memory still made her eyes swell.

I'm sorry, she told it soundlessly. I am sorry.

Much it cared now, on its way to have the fur ripped from it, its bones tossed into the stew pot to feed the hordes at her table. Stablers led her horse away; a torch, looming over her head, made her start.

Her father's aging commander, who lived with Vevay in their airy tower, bowed his head and smiled kindly at her. "A long day, my lady," he observed. "May I escort you inside?"

"Yes," she said unhesitantly; she liked him and trusted him instinctively, as her father had.

"I feel every hour of it in my bones," he commented as he lit her way out of the yard into the palace.

"I'm tired, too," she told him softly. "I never much liked hunting."

"You'd think," he murmured with sympathy, "that being queen meant that you wouldn't have to do the things you disliked."

"Yes, you would think. But I have not found it so at all. Especially not after the hare screamed when I killed it."

"No," he said after a moment. "I never got used to that sound, either, my lady. Not even after years on the battlefield."

"All I killed was a hare," she answered, and felt his flash of surprise at her perception. "I hope I never have to listen to anything worse."

"I hope so," he breathed, "for all our sakes."

Guards opened doors for her; he dropped the torch into a holder as they entered the hall. Her ladies came to meet her, drew off her cloak and her boots, eased her cramped feet into slippers. She watched Gavin unbuckle his heavy sword, yield it with relief to his servant. He rubbed an aching muscle, then caught her glance and smiled again, ruefully, at his aging bones. His smile changed purpose and focus in the moment; she turned her head to see where it was going and found Vevay coming toward them.

Her own smile faded; she felt a sigh she did not express. Vevay wanted more and more, always something, and she seemed never pleased with anything. Vevay had loved and understood the dead king, Tessera knew; the king's daughter left the mage completely baffled. Gavin seemed unafraid of Vevay.

He did not irritate her with his obtuseness, nor inspire in her exaggerated calm, or forced patience. Perhaps I must grow old and gray, Tessera thought, and learn to use a sword and even grow a mustache, and Vevay will finally grow fond of me.

The mage had a peculiar look on her face, Tessera saw when Vevay stopped in front of her. No: it was more of a peculiar emanation, for in public Vevay's unruffled expression rarely changed. She seemed unsettled within, Tessera felt, as she gazed mutely at the mage, her own expression one that usually inspired Vevay with acute exasperation. The mage, Tessera decided finally, felt like someone who had stepped with confidence onto a stair that wasn't there.

"What's wrong?" she asked before Vevay spoke, and Vevay stared at her with utter astonishment.

She recovered herself swiftly, laying a hand on the queen's shoulder and turning her adroitly away from her ladies. "Your mother wishes to see you before she retires," Vevay murmured, pitching her words toward any listening ears. "To assure herself that you are alive and well after the hunt."

"Very well," Tessera said obediently. Her mother, she knew from experience, would not be expecting her at all; it was Vevay's way of assuring privacy for some momentous discussion.

This time, however, Vevay surprised Tessera, leading her directly to her mother's chambers, where Xantia, still prostrate in black, was ignoring the enticing smell of quail stewed in cream and brandy on a tray near her. For some odd reason she seemed to be expecting them; she was entirely alone. Sunk in a chair with her eyes closed and the back of one hand resting on her brow, she lifted her other hand heavily to her daughter. Tessera took it awkwardly. Xantia, opening her eyes at last, drew Tessera to her and examined her anxiously.

"You are well, my child?"

"I killed a hare."

"How clever of you. You take after your unfortunate father in his love of hunting . . ." She turned her wan face restively to the mage. "Now, Vevay. You know I need peace and quiet above all at this time. What is so pressing that you can't deal with it yourself and must disturb me when I can barely lift a scrap of linen to wipe my tears?"

"Raine is going to war," Vevay said succinctly. "You won't have much peace and quiet after that."

Xantia stared at the mage, her eyes, the color of rain-soaked violets, enormous, red-rimmed. They narrowed; she straightened abruptly, sending embroidered velvet pillows flying.

"Who?" she demanded.

"I don't know yet."

"Then how—"

"The Dreaming King has awakened. I want to take Tessera down the cliff to his cave to see if he will tell her what the danger is to Raine."

Tessera felt her face blanch. She tried to speak; words stuck to the roof of her mouth. Her mother, clutching a pillow to her bosom for comfort, was as mute for a moment, her face so icy pale that Tessera thought she might faint.

Instead she rose, flinging the pillow across the room. "Who would dare attack my daughter?"

"We talked about this. Any one of twelve Crowns."

"They're all under her roof!" She paced a step or two, her lips thin; both mage and queen watched her, transfixed. "I've never heard of the Dreamer waking for any ruler. I thought it was just a legend. Vevay, are you sure?"

"Without a doubt."

Xantia whirled, held her daughter's eyes. "Then you must go. Without a doubt."

Tessera unstuck her voice; it shook badly. "I don't want to talk to a skeleton."

"This was your father's realm, and now it belongs to you," Xantia said fiercely. "You will do what you must to keep it."

"I don't know how!"

Vevay closed her eyes. "Exactly what I've been trying to tell you—"

"Vevay, there must be someone you suspect, one Crown above the others. Unless—" Xantia caught a breath, put her hands to her mouth. "Unless it is all of them at once. But the rulers are—"

"All here," Vevay finished. "All but the Lord of Seale. But I don't think that the first King of Raine would rouse his bones in alarm over Ermin of Seale." She stared at the problem silently a moment, her pale eyes nearly colorless and very cold. They moved finally from the problem in midair to Tessera, who felt their cold like a frost in her bones. "At dawn, tomorrow, we will go down."

"Vevay," Tessera pleaded, "can't you talk to him? You're a mage; you —"

"You are the ruler of the Twelve Crowns of Raine. It's you he'll talk to if he's awake."

"He's dead! He doesn't have a tongue!"

"He's sleeping," Xantia said firmly. "Dreaming. You go down there and ask him what you should do. And you —" Her voice faltered as she looked at Vevay, the strength fading visibly again from her face. She groped, found Tessera's shoulder. "You and Gavin —"

"Yes." Vevay moved quickly to help her back to her chair.

"I want whoever it is threatening my daughter found —"

"We will."

"And dropped forthwith over the cliff into the sea."

"Forthwith," Vevay promised grimly.

Xantia, half-falling into her chair, burst into tears again, searched among her skirts for the crumpled linen. Vevay summoned her ladies from the next room. Tessera, rigid with terror, thought: I will run into the wood tonight. The trees will hide me; they know my name. No one will ever find me . . .

Vevay, fixing Tessera with a probing eye as she closed the door on the distraught dowager, said softly, "We will go now."

They left most of the palace at supper, and Gavin to tell those who questioned the queen's absence that she sat that evening with her grieving mother. For Tessera's sake, Vevay brought a torch to light the queen's path down the worn, slippery steps. She might as well not have bothered, for Tessera, her teeth chattering with cold and fear, barely saw anything but the vision behind her eyes. The vision was of a crowned skeleton sitting on a stone, whose armor hung loosely here and there, clanking as the skeleton moved. Its skull was sometimes raw bone, sometimes sagging pleats of flesh and withered, angry eyes that stared incredulously at the waif in front of him.

I dreamed of you and woke, the first king told her, in a voice that boomed and weltered like the waves through his tomb. You puny, helpless, powerless grub, how did you become the ruler of twelve Crowns? You yourself are the threat to Raine . . .

The wind took up his words, growling and whining and worrying at the clouds. Some spell of Vevay's kept it from blowing Tessera off the stairs, though she thought wistfully, once or twice, of jumping. Surely the deep, wild water would be kinder to her than the dreaming warrior wakened to battle. But Vevay would never let her fall. Down and down they went, Tessera mute and trembling and half-blind with terror, the mage following inexorably, holding the torch over her head. Finally, after what seemed a nightmare walk into forever, she heard the first delicate sough of the waves, far below, breaking against the cliff.

She stopped, her eyes closing, her knees almost refusing to hold her up.

Vevay said from some other time where she no longer remembered what fear was, "Don't be afraid. You are Queen of Raine. He will recognize that in you. He will want to help you."

Her voice was as implacable as ever. Tessera opened her eyes again. There was no going back, with the mage behind her, herding her like a sheepdog toward a dead king in a cave. Her hair hung lank with mist; she wiped water out of her eyes with a damp sleeve. I don't feel like a queen, she thought. I am the hare in the wood, trying to run all directions at once to get away . . .

Not bothering to answer Vevay, she forced herself to move again. The boom and break of water grew louder, waves tearing at the cliff, trying with each crash and flight of spume to reach higher, higher, touch the last stone step, flow into the Dreamer's cave. Vevay's hand closed on Tessera's shoulder, and she stopped, staring ahead, not even seeing that she stood on the last step; her next would be into airy nothing.

Vevay said nothing. After a moment, Tessera turned her head, looked at the face of the cliff. The torch light spilled through solid rock, showed her the narrow path she must take into stone to speak to the dead.

She could not go back; she could not go into the sea instead; she could not hang there between earth and sea forever. "Go on," said the streak of wind and fire that was Vevay. "I cannot enter. You must go alone." Nothing to do but face the dead. So she turned her back to the sea and walked into stone.

The armed figure stood waiting for her.

She stopped, frozen, at the open threshold of the tomb. The cave was a hand-hewn bubble of air and dark; the torch light illumined the armed warrior within it. The visor was down; she could not see a face, either skull or ravaged flesh. The warrior was very tall, armed from head to foot, and crowned with a band of gold molded into the helm. The sword slung at its waist looked nearly as tall as Tessera. Uncut jewels glowed darkly in the firelight along the crosspiece, and tiny fire-white stones inset on the backs of the gauntlets glittered fiercely. Long hair flowed from under the helm across the straight shoulders; it was as pale gold as corn-silk.

Tessera felt a lump in her throat. It dissolved, left her voice free again. How long she stared at the tall, armed figure she had no idea. When she finally spoke, she had forgotten Vevay, forgotten the endless, terrifying walk down the cliff in the night. She felt she had, in entering the Dreamer's cave, become part of the dream.

"I don't know what to do," she whispered.

The armed warrior lifted a gauntlet, raised the helm. Tessera, staring at the young, beautiful, powerful face, felt her heart untangle itself then, as though it had been wound in a knot around itself for so long she had stopped noticing. The warrior smiled and unsheathed the great sword.

"Save our realm," she said in her deep, sweet voice, while the hiss and clang of metal echoed through the cave. "Queen of Raine. Save the Crowns of Raine."

Tessera nodded, her heart pounding, her lips dry and bitter with brine. "How?"

"I will fight with you. When you need me, I will be with you in your heart. Beware. Beware."

"Beware what?" Her voice came without sound, but the Dreamer heard it.

"Beware the thorns."

"Thorns?"

"They must be destroyed before they destroy us all."

"What thorns?"

Wind gusted into the cave, howling, laced with spume or rain, and spun Vevay's torch fire into a thin, fluttering thread of light. Emen, Tessera heard, the word melting away in the force of the wind. Eden, Egen . . . When she could see again, the armed figure had slumped onto a rough throne of stone. Its helmed head sagged onto its breast, the face invisible again behind the visor. The long hair, like the parched, golden grasses of summer, looked brittle and sere, as though it would turn to dust at a touch.

Light spilled like tide over the walls as Vevay finally found her way in.

"Did he speak?" she asked, looking doubtfully at the ancient sleeper. "What did he say?"

The Queen of Raine turned away finally from the dead. "She."

"What?"

"She. The first king of Raine was a woman."

Vevay's mouth opened; nothing came out. Her long hair tangled with the torch fire; she twitched it free impatiently, holding Tessera's eyes as though searching for the reflection of the warrior queen within them. "She," she whispered. "What did she say?"

"She said to destroy the thorns before they destroy us all."

"Thorns."

"Yes."

"Are you sure she said—"

"Yes. Thorns." She took a step toward Vevay, feeling the cold again, beginning to tremble. "What does that mean?"

Vevay's fearless and exacting voice wavered suddenly, as erratically as the torch fire in the wind.

"It means we are in very deep trouble, because I have no idea at all what it means."

# TWELVE

Axis fought his second battle with his father's brother, the regent Telmenon, who was lord of a great swath of land in Lower Eben. Having ruled Eben for nine years while Axis grew up, Telmenon resented yielding his power to a boy. When Axis turned sixteen, three days before his wedding, he was crowned King of Great and Lower Eben, and Lord in the Name of the Serpent of all who dwelled within the river that divided the kingdom. Telmenon had seen that day coming for many years and planned for it. A month after the wedding, after the queen's family had gone home, Telmenon rode at the head of the army from Lower Eben to attack the boy-king. Telmenon's army would cross the Serpent by night and be massed around the royal palace by daybreak, giving Axis no time to gather his own forces. So Telmenon planned, and so it might have been but for the wedding gift from Ilicia.

As far as anybody knew, the tall, mute, faceless figure did

nothing besides entertain the young queen and her courtiers on lazy afternoons with his tricks. Kane pulled doves out of empty goblets and pearls out of flowers. He made wine flow out of his staff and danced on the water lilies in the pool in the courtyard. Nobody wondered at the extent of his powers. Even when he walked on water he was only the deformed, gangling, gifted servant who did tricks. If at times his tricks were inexplicable except by magic of a complexity that should have been suspect, no one questioned it. He did always as commanded; if he had a thought of his own he never indicated it; when he was not wanted, he was not seen. Indeed, he might have been invisible, insofar as anyone but Axis remembered his existence then.

Which she actually was: invisible, many times. Kane had been watching the regent for years. Like Axis, she had known him since they were children. After he became regent and Kane learned to seem invisible, she tested her new powers everywhere in the palace, even under her mother's nose. Thus she chanced upon a seedling meeting between Telmenon and one of his generals, and learned that he had no intention of relinquishing his power over Eben. That seedling, encouraged, spread secret roots of rebellion throughout Lower Eben. Kane did not tell Axis until she knew his heart, until she knew by his secret love for her that he could keep a secret. His face, at once beautiful and feral, revealed no more than the lion's face, which says nothing at all as the lion crouches and waits. It speaks only when it springs.

So it was that when Telmenon's army appeared by moon-

light along the southern bank of the Serpent, Axis's army rode
out of the cornfields to meet it. The battle was reminiscent of
that long-ago massacre of his mud-soldiers and his father by
the Serpent. Axis waited silently in the night, while Kane
watched. When most of Telmenon's army was in the river, she
signaled the Lion to attack.

> *The Serpent ran red in the moonlight,*
> *The red moon floated on the water,*
> *The Serpent's eye, open and bloody,*
> *As it fed.*
> *The army of Telmenon*
> *Drank their own blood*
> *As the Serpent dragged them under its waters.*
> *The boy-king*
> *Who would be Emperor of Night*
> *Slew his father's brother*
> *And fed to the Serpent the dying warriors of Telmenon.*

Kane helped the Serpent feed. It was late summer; Telmenon chose a time when the great river would be at its shal-
lowest for his army to cross. As the poets described the scene
later, the river would have had to be swollen with all the rains
and melting snows in Eben to have drowned so many warriors. So Kane worked some illusions into the water, which
drowned the wounded with their fears, and she coaxed a few
streams and field channels that ran out of the river to flow
back up their beds to swell the Serpent's waters. The swirling

floods confused the warriors in the dark. They saw the Serpent moving in waters they could have walked through; they panicked and ran into one another's swords, or splashed blindly across into Axis's army. The bloody eye the poets envisioned was a fair description of the full moon that night, as it was reflected in the reddened waters. Or as it appeared to the eyes of a warrior watching the burning arrows soar out of the sky across the river into the army still struggling on the south bank. At the battle's end, many who fled still had no idea who had attacked them. Axis had dressed his warriors in black; their faces were hidden under hoods and veils not unlike Kane's. They were the first faceless army of the night.

> *The boy-king*
> *Brought his masked army*
> *Out of the dark,*
> *Out of stars and fire,*
> *Out of the Gates of Nowhere*
> *To conquer the enemies of Eben.*

The poets were wrong about one thing: Telmenon did not die that night. Axis's warriors, capturing what fleeing men they could find in the night, recognized the regent among their prisoners. He was wounded, stunned by events, and so exasperated he could barely speak when he was dragged from the dungeons at dawn and confronted by the boy-king he had tried to depose. Kane was there, of course, but only as a stray shadow without a visible source, if anyone had noticed.

The regent, pushed to his knees in front of Axis, dirty, sweating, and bleeding from a slash across one shoulder, looked so like Axis's father that Kane expected the Lion's heart to melt a little with pity. The king showed no anger; his voice remained even. As always, his broad, golden face revealed almost nothing of his thoughts.

"So, uncle," he said, still in battle-black, with the cloth he had worn over his face hanging around his neck, "what shall I do with you? You taught me how to rule. What would you advise?"

His uncle, tasting the unbearable bitterness of his defeat, spat at Axis's feet. Prudently, he missed. The Lion only waited, his tawny eyes unblinking.

"How," Telmenon asked finally, hoarsely, "did you know? Who betrayed me?"

"You betrayed yourself. And you betrayed me."

"Who was it?" Telmenon demanded. "Tell me before you kill me."

"You will never know," Axis said softly, and that was so. No one of Telmenon's warriors ever knew which of them had betrayed them all; everyone suspected everyone. Telmenon's power had broken itself against a fourteen-year-old girl whom he had dismissed long before as something Axis would grow out of. Telmenon had told Axis what to do with him. Axis had his headless body returned to his family in Lower Eben by a small army, who also brought documents that declared Telmenon's lands confiscated and sent his family into exile. Axis let them take what they could, along with their heads. Nobody argued.

Thus he bound Great Eben and Lower Eben, the twin kingdoms of the Serpent, securely under his fledgling rule. Inspired by the incident, he looked for something else to conquer. His mother protested; his wife pleaded. Peace, they craved, though it had been peaceful in Eben all through Telmenon's regency. They wanted to sit in the courtyard among the peacocks, listening to the singing fountains and the cooing of doves while they played with Axis's children, for the young queen was pregnant.

During Axis's long reign she would have many children, not all of them her husband's. But not all of his were hers. They had married one another for reasons of state; they expected certain things of one another, but love and fidelity were not among them. Compromises were reached: he would not bring his battles into Eben, and she would not bring her lovers to his attention. She had to relinquish certain illusions. Kane had seen the soft lights of hope and expectancy in her eyes when she looked up at her young husband. But nothing answered in his eyes. She was an affair of state, his wife and the mother of his heirs; he treated her kindly and with respect. But he would never love her. Having a practical soul, she consoled herself with her status and her right to his company. She grew to become an affectionate mother and a discreet wife. So the poets mentioned her rarely and without interest. Her life was not the stuff of passion or tragedy, at least as far as they could see.

Not even Kane saw much more, though she was very much aware of what could eat at the heart beyond anyone's detection. For a while she could only watch, always masked, always silent, while Axis moved freely through his world. She longed for their childhood, when one was seldom seen without the other, when she could show him her naked face in public and smile, when they hid in the gardens and spoke their secret language. That Axis missed her as much, she could not have guessed. He married, became a father, ruled his kingdom, while Kane could only do her tricks to make the queen laugh, and trail as a shadow after her heart.

*The Lion*
*Fearless, magnificent, unchanging through a thousand years,*
*Casts a glance of desire*
*And takes.*
*Walk in shadows, fear that glance.*
*The Lion sees through time,*
*Through cloud and stars,*
*Into a different day.*
*Beware if that day is yours.*
*Beware his watching eyes.*

Axis's golden glance had fallen on the Serpent. The river bordered another kingdom to Eben's west, and passed through yet another to the east before it ended its journey in the Baltrean Sea. Marrying Cribex, the land to the west, he had secured the headwaters of the Serpent for his own interest. The kingdom between Eben and the sea, containing the rich delta lands the river watered as it fanned into the Baltrean, caught the Lion's interest. He felt a certain kinship with the Serpent; it had consumed any number of his relatives during his uncle Telmenon's ill-fated battle. So, he decided, the world that the Serpent ruled should be his.

He broached the matter in secret with his battle commanders; at his request, Kane listened in the shadow of a potted palm. He met with her at midnight, as was their habit when discussing such things. Invisible to his guards, she followed him into his private chamber, where no one else was permitted and where, it was assumed, he pondered the advice of his counselors, weighed it against history and experience. That he had a secret door to admit lovers and other whims, it was also assumed, though nobody ever found the door. There Kane allowed herself to be seen, only by Axis.

She unwound the thin black veiling around her face with relief, as well as some trepidation. He had not looked at her for a long time, and she had lost sight of herself as well. Nearly sixteen by then, she had been the lonely, misshapen Kane for so long that she felt she must be turning into him. The Lion's expressionless face, gazing silently at her, did not help matters.

He spoke finally. "I am going to war with the sea-kingdom of Kaoldep. You must find a reason to come with me."

She blinked, not understanding. "Why would you bring the child's toy from Ilicia with you to battle?"

"I have no idea." He still gazed at her, his wide-set cat's eyes intent and unreadable. "I mean, I have no idea how to explain you. I want you there with me because I want you."

She closed her eyes, the breath running soundlessly out of her. "Yes."

"Before I married, I only had to turn my head to find you. I only had to say your name."

"Yes."

"And now, day after day, I must see you veiled, hidden, invisible even to me. I cannot see your face, you cannot speak. I can only watch the shadow of you, using your astonishing powers to amuse my wife."

"My lord, I could not think of any other way—"

"Say my name."

"Axis."

"Again."

"Axis."

He gripped her hands, so close to her now that she could feel his heart beat against her fingers. She could not speak; tears spilled down her face. He put his mouth to her cheekbone, caught hot salt between his lips. He slid one hand behind her head, unbound her hair from its tight scarf. It swept down her back; strands caught in her tears. He shifted them away from her face, kissed her again, here, there, wherever he found tears.

"You have grown so beautiful," she heard him say, his voice trembling against her ear. "I am King of Eben and a father, and I have fought for my crown and won my first battle, and always, always, with your voice in my thoughts, your face in my heart. Make yourself part of my life again. I don't care how you explain yourself. I want you with me again. Kane. My first and only love. Make it so."

"Yes," she whispered, feeling herself for the first time all that he said: beautiful, wanted, loved. He spoke those words, and she became them; he had that power over her.

That was the night Axis and Kane became lovers, and of that all poetry is silent.

After that night, she began to make certain, subtle changes in the tricks she played to entertain the court. Kane seemed as astonished as anyone when he accidentally knocked a hole in a wall with power from his staff, or set a tablecloth on fire. He made instant reparations, sending stones flying back into the wall to mend it, directing a stream of water out of a fish pond to put out the fire. Then he curled himself into a ball, in terror of the courtiers' wrath, and tried to beat himself with his own staff. The queen spoke of those mishaps to Axis, worrying that Kane might set her children on fire. The king, intrigued, sent for Kane and tested his powers in front of his counselors and commanders.

Kane, trembling with fear, destroyed three huge flower pots and shot fire out of the window over the courtyard. The peacocks fled, screaming. In the war room, the advisors consulted one another silently.

"My lord, that is no longer a toy," one said finally. "That is a weapon."

Kane's knees hit the floor promptly; he flung the staff away and bowed until his forehead touched the floor.

"He does not know his own powers," someone observed softly.

"What shall I do with him?" Axis wondered. "It would be a pity to kill him. He is innocent of all malice, and his powers are hardly his fault. Yet he would be a danger to my children."

"He would be a danger to more than children," one of his commanders murmured, seeing the future as he stared at Kane.

"I cannot send him back to Ilicia."

"No, my lord, you cannot. That would be foolish, and killing him, as you say, a pity. I suggest you take him with you to Kaoldep and see what he can do on a battlefield."

Axis stood up, stepped to the veiled figure crouching on the carpet. "You have pledged your loyalty to me," he said to Kane. "Will you make your staff into a weapon for the armies of Eben?"

Kane straightened just enough to seize the king's hand and bestow fervent kisses on it. Then he held out one hand; the staff, lying in a corner, flew unerringly back to his hand. He rose, feeling the tension in the sudden silence. He put the staff into Axis's hands, then held both hands over his heart and bowed his head.

And so, for the first time, Axis and Kane rode together into battle.

# THIRTEEN

Bourne stood in a chamber within the mages' school, trying to turn himself invisible. He was alone; the chamber was empty. If he had opened its door a moment earlier than he did, or a moment later, a dragon as pale as snow might have spat blue fire at him. A mage older than the school, sitting alone and patiently waiting to die, might have looked at him and died. A woman so beautiful that his knees melted might have said something in a language he did not recognize. He had found all of these behind doors he had opened in the school at one time or another. They were like random tests that he passed or failed; he was never quite certain. Shutting the door again had seemed the simplest answer to the dragon. He had almost closed the door on the dead mage and gone to find help. But in time he remembered that the door would slide away into some other part of the school, or into some other moment, if he turned his back on it. Instead, he entered the room, stood beside the dead mage, and learned, in that moment, how to send a silent cry for help. He would quite willingly have joined the beautiful woman in her sunlit chamber, except that as he put one foot across the threshold he suddenly understood her incomprehensible words, as though his heart had grown an ear. *Shut the door*, she had said; he withdrew his foot and went away.

The chamber he stood in now held only a few cobwebs and a couple of tarnished mirrors leaning against a wall. Light and the sweet breath of the wood wandered in from an open casement. He glanced out, hoping to glimpse the palace, for the room seemed high, at a level with the treetops. But the wood beyond the window went on forever; he could not even see the plain, just the upper boughs of endless trees. He had been roaming the school with nothing to do that day, and Nepenthe in every thought. But she had made it clear, the night before, that no delight he could suggest would tempt her from her work that day; she would see him at supper time in the refectory, not before.

So he whiled away the time exploring, recklessly opening doors, wanting monsters, warrior-mages, riddles, and tasks. He found little but old furniture and dust. Not even a magical tome to look for trouble in. Finally, seeing his reflection in the mirrors, he had posed himself a task: How could he make himself and his reflection disappear?

All the students wanted to know. But Felan only told them, "You are not ready yet." He would give them no clues. Books that might have answered the question stubbornly refused to open, or revealed blank pages when the subject came up. The students protested; Felan only said, "Be patient." Bourne said nothing at all, not wanting to draw attention to his own keen interest in the matter. Invisible, he could drift at will through the palace, listen to secret meetings, find out what hidden strengths and vulnerabilities the Crowns and the queen might have, and so impress the Lord of Seale with his powers that his uncle would want Bourne to stay in the school forever, which was exactly how long, that day, Bourne wanted to keep seeing Nepenthe.

Invisibility eluded him; he kept seeing his baffled face in the mirror no matter what he tried. He closed his eyes and concentrated on nothing until he felt he must have turned into it. He opened one eye, saw his one-eyed self peering back at him. There must be a potion, he thought, bemused. Words he must say. A cloak made out of threads of thought. Perhaps he should look for the dragon again, put himself in such peril that only invisibility would save him, and in his desperation he would find the way to disappear. Desire, he reminded himself, had precipitated him across the plain in a step. Perhaps terror could inspire a different magic.

He opened both eyes, stood idly scratching his brow with a thumbnail, wondering if scaring himself witless with a dragon would be the best time to find out if he had the power to save himself from it. A breeze trembled under his nose, loosing scents of opening leaves, moist earth, wildflowers scattering their fragrances profligately through the warm spring light. Nepenthe's eyes would turn from brown to green in such light. He saw her turn her head in memory, look at him, her eyes the tender green of young leaves, and he closed his own eyes, felt the hot sweet light on his lips. He gave a stifled groan of longing and exasperation, took a restless step . . .

And there he was, smelling leather and parchment and wax instead of trees, feeling the implacable stone all around him. I should go back, he told himself before he opened his eyes. Shut the door. Before she sees me. Unless she has already and I am already in trouble. Unless I can very quickly turn myself invisible . . .

He opened an eye again, cautiously, saw her desk and her ink jars, her parchments full of fish. He raised his eyes, saw the face looking at him above the fish.

He stared. So did Laidley, who was sitting on Nepenthe's stool and gawking gracelessly. He closed his mouth and cleared his throat; still nothing came out.

"What are you doing here?" Bourne asked. "Where's Nepenthe?"

"What are you doing here?" Laidley managed finally. "She told you not to come until this evening."

"Does she tell you everything?" Bourne marveled, hearing an edge in his voice that nothing about Laidley could explain.

Laidley only shook his head. "No." He hesitated. "That's why I'm here."

"I see." Bourne stepped to the desk, illumined. "And looking as guilty as I am."

"I thought she—she told me she was going to finish the

scholar's manuscript today. I found out more about Axis and Kane, so I came to tell her. But she isn't here, and neither—"

"And neither are the thorns," Bourne finished softly.

"Yes. Neither are the thorns. I searched for them. She's working somewhere else, hiding them from us."

Bourne sighed. "With some reason. That's my fault—I threatened to take them away from her. It didn't occur to me that she could make herself invisible. Where might she be?"

Laidley shrugged. "The library is immense. Entire rooms go forgotten for decades. She could be anywhere."

"It sounds like the Floating School." He brushed aside some fish, sat on the desk, and looked blankly down one end of the silent corridor, then down the other. "Well. I could probably find her if I wished, but she did ask me not to disturb her."

"She'll be waiting for you later," Laidley said. "Not even the thorns will make her forget."

Bourne glanced at him, surprised. "I didn't intend to come here," he explained after a moment. "It was an accident. I was just thinking about her—"

"Yes," Laidley said, studying one of Nepenthe's jars with cross-eyed intensity.

"I'm sorry."

"For what?" Laidley queried the ink. The words came out with unexpected harshness. Laidley swallowed, his eyes finally relinquishing the ink jar. He looked at Bourne. "I'll still be here," he said simply, "when you've forgotten her."

"Fair enough," Bourne breathed. "In that case, we may all

grow very old together . . ." He slid off the desk. "I should go before she finds me."

"How?"

"What?"

"She brings you here," Laidley said. "You think of her and work your magic. What magic in that school is strong enough to draw you back to it?"

Surprised again, Bourne made an effort and thought. "I suppose the magic draws me back. The possibility of doing the impossible. It's harder without Nepenthe. But even the difficulty becomes interesting. A puzzle. A challenge. Also—" He hesitated, added with a laugh, "My uncle would be furious with me if the mages threw me out of the school for my disorderly ways."

"Why does your uncle care that much whether or not you become a mage? You're a noble of the ruling court of Seale. You don't have to be anything."

Bourne gazed down at the alphabet of fish, eluding Laidley's too-clear eyes and trying to be careless and careful at the same time. "My uncle thinks I have some gifts. What I think is that he is the one who wants a mage's power . . . This is the scholar's manuscript, isn't it? Nepenthe told me about the fish. What does she make of them?"

"Merchants' inventories from a caravan."

"So that's the riveting topic that keeps her buried down here, along with her thorns." He realized then that he was lingering, hoping she would hear her name in whatever cranny she had concealed herself and be tempted out. It might work, he thought, so he said it again. "You said you had something to tell Nepenthe about Axis and Kane. What is it?"

"Oh." Laidley straightened, a scholar's eagerness to impart knowledge to the ignorant driving all else from his mind. He picked up a scroll. "It's about the question of Dirxia."

"What?"

"Nepenthe was having a problem naming one of the kingdoms that Axis conquered. Actually, conquered is too precise a word for what he did. You might as accurately talk about a tidal wave conquering a city. The word assumes that someone had time to fight back. Overwhelmed is more like it. Engulfed."

"Yes," Bourne said hazily, feeling overwhelmed by whatever Laidley was babbling about.

"We thought it might be Dirxia, except that Dirxia did not exist when Axis did—"

"Which was when?" Bourne asked, trying for a spar to hold on to in the flood of history.

"When—"

"When did Axis live?"

"Oh. Roughly three thousand years ago, when Eben ruled the world. I haven't narrowed down exactly when he died. With all the poetry written about him through the centuries you'd think he might have lived forever. Anyway, I found another kingdom which did exist about the same time as his kingdom Eben did, and which Axis did conquer. It was called Kirixia; it was west of Eben, across the Baltrean Sea. It was full of goats and olive trees. A trade route ran through it. It was fairly big but not at all wealthy."

"Maybe Axis was practicing."

"Maybe," Laidley said, looking at his frivolous suggestion seriously. "Or maybe it was a kind of poetic device to give status to an otherwise undistinguished land. Axis conquered it, therefore—"

"Therefore it could not be boring," Bourne suggested, stifling a yawn. He added soberly, after a moment, "But it does make you wonder, doesn't it?"

"Does it?"

"Why Nepenthe is so obsessed about all this. It's ancient history. Dust. Tombs. Headless statues that you find sketched in the margins of worm-eaten manuscripts. Where's the magic in it?"

"What magic?"

"What are the thorns really telling her? It's why she won't let us see them, why she clings to them—or they cling to her—as though she got herself buried in a bramble thicket and she can't get out and we can't get in to free her."

"Buried in what?" Laidley asked, struggling.

"That's just it. We don't know. If every thorn is some form of sorcery apart from the word it makes, then who knows what it might be telling Nepenthe to think or do?"

Laidley was looking fish-eyed again. "Is such a thing possible? That the letters themselves—the shapes might be magic in themselves? The words and tale are innocent; the power is in the different alphabet?"

"Look at her," Bourne said helplessly, wishing he could. "She's entranced. Enchanted by ghosts. By a bit of history that would put anyone else to sleep. Something else is speaking to her when she reads, telling her things that we can't see or hear, saying one thing to her eyes and mind, and another to her heart—"

Laidley shivered suddenly. "You're making my skin crawl," he said reproachfully. "I think you're letting your imagination run away with you."

"That's the beginning of magic. Let your imagination run and follow it."

"You're liable to follow it over the cliff and into the sea."

Bourne was silent, contemplating his vision of Nepenthe and her thorns. An odd hollowness touched his heart, as though he had looked down and found the vast nothingness between earth and sea beneath his next step. Fear, the feeling was, he realized suddenly; he had rarely encountered it.

"I'm going to find her," he said restively. "I think those thorns are dangerous and the mages should know about them."

"The mages already saw them," Laidley pointed out, troubled but clinging stubbornly to what he knew. "They sent them to the librarians to translate."

"Then let the librarians translate them. Not Nepenthe."

"She won't thank you if you force her to give them up."

"I don't suppose she will."

"Scholars get obsessed every day over the strangest things. The contents of a caravan, for example. Or the ancient language in which the contents are written."

"Or a conqueror who has been dead for three thousand years? You want her to keep the book. Don't you."

"It's a puzzle," Laidley admitted. "A challenge. And it gives me reasons to find things for her, bring them, speak to her. It seems harmless to me. Well—perhaps not entirely harmless. I'll concede that. But nothing we can't deal with." He raised his head, meeting Bourne's eyes pleadingly. "The three of us. The mage, the scholar, the woman who reveals the magic."

Bourne stared at him, mute again, and oddly touched. "All right," he said tautly, "all right," and saw Laidley's shoulders, hunched under his ears, slide back down into place. "But I want to talk to her. I want her to tell me plainly why she thinks she must hide those thorns from us. Where can she possibly be?"

Laidley stood up. "I'll search, too. I know where many of the ancient epics are kept; she might be there. You look in her chamber. It could be that easy."

"Which way?" Bourne asked, bewildered as ever in the labyrinth. Laidley pointed, moving down the hallway the opposite direction.

"We'll meet here," he suggested, and Bourne nodded.

"Wherever here is," he muttered, winding through the books toward what he thought might be a main corridor. Then he stopped, charmed by an idea. All he had to do was think of her and step . . .

Something flowed between him and his heart's desire. He felt off balance suddenly, uncertain, as though he had stepped into another world entirely. But it was the same, he saw, blinking books and stone into place around him. And there was the woman in front of him.

It was not Nepenthe. He blinked again and recognized that

tall figure with long hair like spun silver and eyes like the sky in winter above the sea. He felt his face blanch before he even knew he had to be afraid.

"Vevay."

She nodded, those eyes holding him rooted to stone. "Bourne of Seale," she said. Her voice sounded as though it could have splintered flint. "I made a journey to the Floating School to find you, but you were here, instead, under the queen's roof without anyone's knowledge."

"Is there something—" he managed.

"Oh, yes. There is something. Your uncle Ermin is plotting to attack the First Crown, and you are under arrest for treason."

# FOURTEEN

Vevay took the young man back to the Floating School. She was too furious to speak again in those brief moments; Bourne of Seale looked too stunned. Once he tried. Vevay saw a face flicker through his thoughts; his eyes grew wide and full of words. But he said nothing until they were in the school, facing Felan in one of the rich, cluttered, comfortable rooms that students rarely saw, full of old books and shy animals. By then Bourne seemed resigned as he gazed helplessly back at Felan.

He said, "That day we spent in the wood."

Felan's shining pate lowered an inch; his own eyes were very calm. "Of course we watched to see what shapes the wood took for you. It shapes your heart; you can hide nothing from it."

"Then why—" Bourne began abruptly, then as abruptly closed his mouth again.

Vevay, who saw the lovely face again in his thoughts, answered grimly, "You have no privacy now. If you did not see that young woman in the wood perhaps it was simply because in that matter your feelings are entirely unambiguous."

"Who is she?" Felan asked.

"Just a transcriptor," Bourne told him. "One of the orphans the librarians raised and trained. She doesn't pay attention to the world beyond the library. Her head is full of ancient languages. She knew nothing about—about—" He shook his head, his mouth tight; his eyes slid away from Felan's. "Whatever," he finished, "my uncle might be doing."

"Do you know?" Vevay demanded.

"I can guess," Bourne answered after a moment. "From comments my uncle made, and from what he wanted me to learn."

"And you never questioned those things."

A dull flush seeped into his face. "It's a family tradition, rebelling against rulers. My great-grandfather was beheaded for it."

"You don't take this seriously!" Vevay exclaimed, exasperated. "You could lose your own head."

"No." He met her eyes, trying hard, she saw, to explain himself to himself as well as to her. "I do take this seriously. It was my uncle Ermin that I never took very seriously. I thought he was mostly talk. He wanted me to come here and study to gain powers to help Seale rebel against Raine. I couldn't imagine actually learning anything that might be useful to anyone. But I found I liked what I was studying. So if he wanted me here, I didn't mind learning."

"And you would have taken all that you learned back to the Second Crown and used your powers to fight against the queen."

"My powers," he repeated incredulously. His eyes moved from her to Felan. "You saw the extent of my powers in the wood. I summoned fire and managed to char some bark on a tree."

"You lifted the Floating School," Felan said.

The blood drained out of Bourne's face again. He stared at Felan; Vevay saw his eyes grow cloudy a moment, almost tranquil, as he remembered his own spell. "I tried," he whispered. "It was just something to do. I thought—I didn't think—It seemed only a dream. A wish. I thought I had only raised it in my head."

"You raised it in your heart."

He blinked, asked with sudden anxiety, "Did I really drop it?"

"Students usually drop it, the first time. I caught it." Vevay saw the golden, dreaming afternoon sky above the dark wood in Felan's own eyes, then. "I made the noise to let you know something had happened."

"My uncle Ermin happened."

"He does get in your way. You should have made your own choices."

"Maybe." He ran fingers through his hair, his face drawn, rueful. "It seems I never took either one of us very seriously. Is that why the wood sent the queen to me later? To show me that I had another choice?"

Felan didn't answer immediately. Vevay, glancing at him, saw the bemusement behind his imperturbable expression. He turned to her for enlightenment. "Was the queen in the wood that day?"

"Of course not. Tessera has never been in the wood. She's afraid of everything."

"Yes," Bourne said, remembering. "She did seem afraid. Whoever I saw. I thought at first she was a student; she talked about things the wood had shown her."

"What things?" Vevay asked tightly.

"An old man she said was a tree; it spoke to her. Deer carrying fire in their antlers. There was something else . . . an armed rider. When I realized that she wasn't a student, I thought the wood had conjured her. After she left, I remembered where I had seen her face before: at her coronation. I understand now, of course too late, why the wood sent her."

"If the queen was in the wood that day," Felan answered, "I did not see her."

"Then I must be mistaken," Bourne said.

But he did not believe that, Vevay saw. "Tell me," she said harshly, "what she looked like. What she wore."

"She had long, very pale hair and a small, pale face. She seemed very shy. And very careful, as though at any moment she might encounter trouble. I remember very clearly what she wore because it seemed odd. Pink satin, under an old dark cloak too big for her, and—"

Vevay made a sound, and he stopped. "Was it real?" she demanded of Felan. "Or a vision of the wood's?"

"I don't know," Felan answered gently. "I didn't see this. But I was watching for magic that affected the students. If the queen was in the wood, then she entered and left so quietly that I was unaware of it. Judging from what Bourne has said, the wood was aware of her and spoke to her. I suggest you ask her."

"I intend to." She was silent a moment, struggling with several inexplicable notions at once: that Tessera might wander off by herself into the wood, that somehow she had eluded Felan's attention but not the wood's; that Bourne, supposedly conspiring with his uncle against the queen, had described her with such kindly perception. "Did she tell you what she was doing in the wood?"

Bourne answered carefully, trying to recall. "No. As I said, at first I thought she was a student, so I thought I knew. When I told her that, she laughed and told me—"

"She laughed? Tessera doesn't laugh."

He hesitated. "Yes. I guessed that she didn't, that she wasn't used to it."

"Go on," Vevay said dourly. "What was she laughing about?"

"That I had thought she was a student, while she had thought I was another apparition of the wood's." He paused again, then closed his eyes a moment, opened them again. He continued wearily, "There was something else she said. Birds that spoke to her told her to beware what she might meet in the wood. She seemed relieved to find that it was only me."

Vevay closed her own eyes, touched them with cold fingers. "You are the most convoluted young man I have ever met.

Find a room for him," she said to Felan. "I will bind him here myself with spells appropriate for someone who does not know his own powers, who might conceivably be capable of anything."

Felan nodded. Bourne stared at the floor. "I'm sorry," he told them, but for what he seemed unsure. "I can't imagine that my uncle would prove much more than a brief annoyance to the queen. The other Crowns would never let him rule."

"He could provide the spark that ignites the whole of Raine," Vevay snapped. "And even that might be only the beginning of trouble."

Bourne lifted his head sharply; even Felan lost some of his composure. But he asked nothing then, just folded the school around them into another of its endless shapes to provide a suitable room for the prisoner. It had little furniture, no windows, and one massive door. While Bourne surveyed it, appalled, Vevay busied herself with some changes. If Bourne managed to astound himself by melting through a wall, he would be impeded by a succession of walls, each a different illusion he would have to understand and unravel. If he managed to open the door, it would lead into whatever fire was burning at the time, or to the terrifying nothingness beyond the edge of the cliff. To escape, he would have to outwit Vevay herself. It was possible, she thought grimly. Anything was, apparently, those days, with Tessera running off alone to talk to trees, and the king who was a queen awakening to warn of the destruction of Raine by brambles.

She left Bourne there, sitting on the hard little bed and contemplating his predicament.

He asked, before she and Felan vanished, "What happens now? To my uncle? To my family still in the queen's palace?"

"I haven't decided yet," Vevay told him. "Troops have been sent to the Second Crown to arrest your uncle. Your family is under guard in the palace."

He sighed soundlessly, already looking harrowed by his vacuous surroundings. "May I have paper at least?" he pleaded. "A pen? A book?"

"No," she said mercilessly. "Sit there and consider what brought you to this place and why. Your great-grandfather lost his head over such things. I suggest you find yours before you become the next headless ghost in your family."

Felan shifted walls and spaces again within the school, brought her back into pleasanter surroundings. She did not sit; he did not wait for her to speak.

"What trouble?"

She told him about Tessera and the dreaming warrior queen, the incomprehensible warning.

"Thorns?" Felan repeated incredulously. "What—"

"I have no idea."

"She said nothing more?"

"No. She warned Tessera of thorns and then retreated back into her moldering bones."

"Perhaps the queen understood it?"

"No."

Felan was silent, unmoored from his tranquillity, his expressions erratic, unfamiliar to Vevay. He scratched his bald head, said finally, "I will tell the other mages, and we will examine the matter with all the power we possess."

"So will I," Vevay promised, "after I examine Tessera. How could the Queen of Raine have been wandering around in that wood without even you noticing?"

"The wood, after all these centuries of magic flowing into it, has a life of its own."

"So apparently does Tessera."

"If it was Tessera."

"It sounded like her. I know that pink gown." She shook her head at her own words. "And as unlike her as anything I would have imagined. Tessera, stopping to chat with a strange young man. Laughing. And of all young men—"

"Ask her," Felan said again, and she did so.


In the palace, she found the queen where she was supposed to be: at a council table with nobles from three different Crowns and half a dozen of her own counselors. They were discussing the border taxes for merchants traveling between Crowns. Tessera, sitting stiffly, was visibly trying to understand the problems. Her attempt was only getting in the way of her thoughts, it seemed to Vevay, judging by the dazed expression in her strained eyes. Taking pity on her, Vevay interrupted and extracted her, leaving her counselors to settle matters, which might soon be moot, anyway, if they were all going to war against thorns.

She drew Tessera past a dozen importunate young nobles, into a private chamber above the sea. As always, Tessera went to the window to watch sea, sky, cloud, anything that did not speak to her in words. This time Vevay joined her instead of talking to her back. She hesitated, wondering how to broach the subject without alarming Tessera.

She gave up, asked baldly, "Were you in the wood recently? Someone said he saw you there."

Tessera looked at her mutely, instantly wary. Vevay waited, trying to emanate nothing beyond friendly curiosity. The queen answered finally, hesitantly. "I went there to get out of the world. A few days ago."

"Did you talk to anyone?"

"A tree. Some birds. A student. I think he was a student."

"He was," Vevay said evenly. "No one knew you were there. None of the mages, I mean. They should have known."

"Do you mean that I should have told them?"

"No. I mean yes. I mean that of course it's dangerous for you to go off on your own without telling anyone, without even a guard with you—"

"I'm sorry."

"But that's not what I meant. You slipped past the combined and very powerful attention of the mages as though you—as though you somehow became part of the wood when you entered it. Or it made you a part of itself."

Tessera was silent again, trying, the mage saw, to figure out if she were in trouble. Trust me, Vevay pleaded, with every calm line of her body, with every quiet breath. The queen's own body relaxed a little finally; her eyes slid again to the sea. "It showed me things," she said softly. "It changes my heart when I walk into it. My heart turns into the smells and shadows, the moss, the flowers and vines, the ancient trees. Sometimes I hear them speak." Vevay's throat closed; she stifled a sound, gazing, dumbfounded, at the bewildering young ruler of Raine. The queen gave a small start then, at a memory. "That's where I first saw her. The first queen of Raine. She was riding through the wood in her armor, with the great sword at her side."

"She was awake and riding around in the wood?" Vevay breathed. "The Dreaming King? Queen?"

"I didn't see her face then, only her long fair hair. She didn't speak, but something told my heart that the warrior was a woman."

"Did she see you?"

"She turned her hidden face toward me and pointed at—" Her own voice died suddenly; her eyes grew wide again, alarmed. But for once she shifted toward Vevay rather than away.

"At what?" Vevay demanded, her voice rising in spite of herself.

"Thorns."

# FIFTEEN

Once Axis had achieved his swift, stunning victory over Kaoldep and, by marriage and war, secured for Eben all the lands from one end to the other of the Serpent, poets began to take note of him in something other than their customary conceits. He had brought magic onto the battlefield in the terrifying form of Kane. His generals were astonished at the powers that roared and spat out of Kane's staff. Kane, fighting for her life with Axis, surprised even herself. Love kindled her fires, forged weapons that scorched the heels of the warriors of Kaoldep as they ran. Kaoldep, hitherto a tranquil realm full of fishers and farmers and rich cities along the delta where merchant ships wandering the Baltrean Sea docked and traded, was ill-prepared for war, especially for one of such ferocity. Axis had only to threaten to burn a city before the king surrendered, pleading for Axis to show mercy to his people. Axis, having got all he wanted, including Kane, declared himself Guardian of the Realm of the Serpent, left one of his generals to restore order to his new lands, and went back home to relax.

He grew restless quickly and summoned his counselors and generals; again Kane listened secretly.

"The river is not enough," he told them. "Eben encompasses the Serpent, but why should I stop there? The world does not end at the boundaries of Eben."

His generals, who had seen for themselves the possibilities in Kane's power, responded with keen interest. One or two of his older counselors, who had lived through his father's wars and had grown fond of the peaceful interim during Telmenon's regency, expressed doubts.

"My lord, the world, as you say, does not end with Eben; it is, in fact, a great deal bigger than your river kingdom. Beware that you don't rouse forces against you that even Kane cannot defeat."

"Who is this Kane, anyway?" another murmured fretfully. "How can you be certain he was not meant to gain your trust and then turn against you and take all of Eben for Ilicia? He came here as a trickster; now he is a sorcerer. What will we find him doing next? Let him show his face."

"I have seen his face," Axis said calmly. "And I have seen into his heart. He will serve me faithfully, as he pledged, all the days of his life."

"My lord, you are young—"

"Yes." He smiled at the aging counselors. "I am the young Lion of Eben and I will fight until I find the one who can stop me. That one will have to kill me. To force Kane to reveal his face would be nothing more than an act of cruelty. If you insist, I will command him. You will only hurt him."

They grumbled more, then left the matter at that for a while; it was obvious that sowing doubts about Kane would not hold the Lion of Eben in his quiet lair. His younger generals, their blood roused by the easy victory, produced maps, suggestions, arguments. Axis listened to them all. Then, later in his secret chamber, he asked Kane what she thought.

They lay tangled in one another's arms, feeding one another almonds and dates, while around them the palace slept.

"You are King of the River," Kane answered simply. "Why not be Emperor of the Sea?"

"The entire sea?" Axis spat out a date pit and raised himself on one elbow to look at her.

"There are many rich port cities all around that inland sea. Why should they not belong to Eben?"

Axis counted kingdoms around the sea, using most of his fingers. "Seven kings would ask me why they should belong to Eben." He looked at her again, his tawny eyes reflecting tears of fire from the candles. "Can you fight seven kingdoms with me?"

Kane nodded. "I will be with you at every battle, as long as I am alive."

She had no idea if she could win seven battles for him; he had not asked her that. They were both testing their powers in those early years; they had no idea then to what lengths they could go. As always, Kane had no real interest in war, only in Axis. If he put himself into danger, she would bring down the moon before she let him be harmed. At odd moments, she found herself missing her lazy afternoons in the courtyard, among the preening peacocks and the laughing children of her cousins, who had begun to marry, and the cheerful, incoherent comments of Axis's toothless daughter as she crowed in wonder at Kane's tricks. His heir, old enough to walk, had watched more soberly, his round plump face a mirror of his young mother's. But while Kane had lost the company of children, she had finally eased the painful hunger in her heart for Axis.

"We are twins," he told her more than once. "Twin thoughts, twin hearts, twin powers. I have more ambition, but you have better ideas."

She had, that day: none of his generals had suggested expanding Eben to include all the kingdoms around the Baltrean Sea. One of them, as his counselors would have hastened to point out, covered as much territory as the six others together. But it was poor and scruffy, an old lion. Its harsh soil and steep, arid mountains made it an unrewarding battlefield; its single port city was its only asset.

"Attack the most dangerous and best fortified first," Kane suggested. "If it falls, the others will be afraid and more easily subdued."

"And Kirixia?"

"Save the largest for last. Your fierce and unconquerable army will close on it around both sides of the Baltrean Sea like a crab-claw. It will not even bother to fight," she promised recklessly.

He laughed, excited by the notion. "Then I shall be the Emperor of Water. And after that? What? The Emperor of Air?"

"The Emperor of Fire," she said, her voice growing husky as she watched the candle fire melting across his golden skin. "The Emperor of Night."

He became her nights, long before he conquered night itself. They did not have many alone in those first busy years. Axis's discretion guarded Kane from suspicion. No one could have connected the masked, scarecrow figure of the sorcerer with a secret lover of the king, especially not after Kane's face was finally exposed.

She had anticipated an assault from the first, out of mistrust, or jealousy, or simple curiosity. But two years at court had lulled her, and Kane's reputation on the battlefield should have been enough to cause any attacker a second thought. So she was prepared, when attack came, but had long forgotten the need to be.

Kane had been summoned to the courtyard gardens by the queen. So she had been told, to her surprise, for the queen had not permitted Kane around her children since the battles of Kaoldep. She felt watched as she made her way beneath an arched trellis of flowering vines toward the inner courtyard. But Kane had always been watched, every moment that the strange, faceless figure moved through the palace. The silence should have warned her. She heard the play of the fountains, the rustle of peacock feathers; she should have heard what she did not: the entwined voices of women and children. As she emerged from the end of the archway, what felt like a brick from the garden wall fell on her head.

She almost cried out, but she was too astonished to make a sound. In that moment she could not imagine what was happening, other than that a star had fallen out of the sky and now her head was pulsing fire. Then someone wrenched the staff from her hands, and she remembered that she was the mute, dangerous Kane. Someone else pulled a cloth tight against her eyes, wrenched her head back to tie it. She gasped with pain and tried to fight; she heard one or two muffled words. Her gauntlet hands were pinioned behind her back. Someone struck her face; she reeled, slumping against the trellis, smelling the sweet, crushed citrus-flowers under her. Big, rough fingers began pulling at the veils around her face.

She struggled, but weakly, only enough to be convincing. A man snapped, "Hold him. Be careful—Don't let him see us. We'll see for ourselves what you truly are beneath that sorcerer's mask."

"The veils are tied around his body, beneath his robes," another man grunted. "I can't pull them up without—"

"Cut them."

Kane felt the blade at her throat and froze. Silk ripped, fluttered away. For the first time in nearly two years she felt sunlight on her mouth.

Kane's mouth. The courtyard was suddenly very quiet, as though even the peacocks were dumb with horror. Then one of them screamed, a distant, fading sound. She heard the men breathing heavily as they stared at the grotesque, deformed face.

They dropped him without a word and ran.

She lay there, waiting to be found rather than picking herself up and going off alone and invisible to care for herself. She had recognized the voice of one of Axis's aging counselors, who was clearly looking for a reason to curtail the king's exhausting impulses for war. He would not expect the sorcerer to remember him from a glimpse or two in the council-chamber. He did not realize that Kane had listened, mute and invisible, to everything he said to the king within that chamber.

A servant found the dazed, bleeding Kane with the veil shredded over his horrifying face. Her shriek brought others. Shocked, babbling, they bore Kane inside, where, unaccountably, as they awaited the physician the patient disappeared. She limped outside to retrieve her staff, which one of her attackers had tossed on top of the trellis. Then she went to Axis's secret chamber, bound up her aching head with her veils, and fell asleep.

Axis found her there later.

She woke to his eyes, wide and golden and unblinking, staring down at her. He leaned down, dropped a kiss as light as a breath on her bruised mouth.

"I will kill whoever did this." She had never heard his voice so devoid of all expression. "Tell me who it was."

"Axis," she said. It hurt to talk, but she had to then, and fast.

"Tell me."

"I will." She touched his shoulder, his wrist, quick, soothing pats. "I will. But you must listen to me."

"Who?"

"They had to—they had to know that Kane is not lying to you. That all his—that all my powers belong to you. They have to trust me. I let them—I let them see my face."

He blinked then, bewildered, and laid the back of his hand against her cheek. "This face?"

"Kane's face. Do you want to see it? I made it for them."

He gave a little, uncertain nod. Then he started as the face he loved rippled into something maimed, distorted, small eyes not quite level, one cheekbone bigger than the other, teeth wandering off in opposite directions beneath lips that could not possibly close over them. He swallowed; expression flowed back into his voice. "That is the ugliest thing I have ever seen."

She smiled, then winced. "That face loves you," she told him. "It is the face of the wedding gift from Ilicia. The face of your power on the battlefield. Now they will all know that Kane is simply Kane, the magician turned sorcerer. Not someone sent to harm you."

"Still." He brushed her familiar face again with his hand. "I will still kill whoever—"

"No." Her fingers found his wrist, tightened. "No. You do not love Kane enough to kill for him."

"Yes, I do."

"Not the Kane the others know. If you kill for me they will

think you are somehow under my power, that you listen to me before you listen to them. Then they will fear me and plot against me. They must think only that I do your bidding because I have pledged my heart to you. That I have no power over you; all the power is truly yours."

His mouth tightened. He coaxed her up, untied the bloody cloth around her head, began to wash it gently until it came free from her hair. She sat quietly, leaning against his chest, her head over his shoulder like a child's. He spoke finally. "What do you want me to do?"

"They did not do this to me. They did this to the Kane they know. What would you do for him?"

He did not answer her then. By the end of the day, the entire palace knew of the attack on Kane. The mystery of his face, which had kept the court guessing since the wedding, was solved. It was every bit as hideous as he had promised. The incident also laid to rest a rumor that had come to Kane's attention recently: that the veiled sorcerer was in truth a beautiful woman who had been in love with Axis, and who had given herself to him as a wedding present. That drifted about as one of the many possible reasons why Axis spent a night now and then in his private chamber, isolated from all and giving no reason why. The glimpse of Kane's face would relieve the queen's mind, Kane knew, as well as her curiosity. The sorcerer was not someone to fear but someone to pity. The reason would be clear, and very simple now, why his love and his power belonged irrevocably to the comely and fearless young king.

Axis said nothing about the incident until Kane was well enough, in a day or two, to come secretly to his council meeting. Then, he discussed Eben's strengths and weaknesses, and the possibilities for war, until one of his older counselors, who had been shifting restively, interrupted him.

"My lord, despite his great powers Kane does seem vulnerable. You cannot depend on him, even though his loyalty to you may be unquestionable."

Axis pondered the counselor's words impassively. Kane, standing in her customary shadow, invisible to all, recognized the voice.

"You advise me to go to battle without him?" the king asked.

"No, my lord—"

"Then with him."

The counselor sighed. "You cannot fight all the kingdoms around the Baltrean Sea without him."

"I agree with you."

"But, my lord, he is not invincible as you have heard. He can be incapacitated with nothing more than a stone."

"Then," Axis said very softly, while the counselor's face grew suddenly waxen beneath his graying beard, "we will make sure that you are never behind him, because only you know what weapon might defeat him." He paused; the room was so quiet that Kane could hear the sobbing coo of mourning doves in the gardens. "Since you seem so reluctant to go to battle," Axis continued, "you give me no choice but to believe that you would be much happier within the peaceful walls of your own home. A pity. We will miss your counsel."

"But, my lord —"

"You will leave tomorrow," Axis said inflexibly. "I'm sure your family will greet your return with great relief."

How his family would have felt no one ever knew, for the counselor never reached his home. He and his entourage were set upon by bandits in the rocky hills north of the palace, and his body returned home without him. Upon receiving the news, Axis proclaimed a day of mourning for the man who had counseled two kings and a regent. He spent most of the day in private with Kane.

Shortly afterward, with Kane at his side, Axis began his great campaign against the Baltrean kingdoms.

> *Seven kingdoms fell*
> *To the Emperor of the Sea.*
> *Seven crowns he took,*
> *Seven pearls of the waters of the Baltrean.*
> *He ringed the sea with the dead*
> *Until the living cried out for mercy.*
> *With the Faceless One beside him*
> *The Emperor walked on water across the Baltrean*
> *Where armies threw down their arms*
> *And his name echoed among the mountains of Kirixia.*

# SIXTEEN

Nepenthe sat hunched over her desk, staring at fish. They were trying to speak, standing on mouths and tails and back-fins to say baskets of grain, slabs of salt, jars of olives and wine. Her eyes saw them, but they could not swim into language through her head. Something blocked their way, a stubborn vision that refused either to make itself real or to go away. It just stayed there, maddeningly silent, refusing to answer questions and refusing to let the fish speak.

Go away, Nepenthe told it coldly, even while she could hear her own heart pleading, Come. Come.

It did neither. She grasped great swaths of her hair in her hands and tugged, rocking her head this way and that. Even that would not dislodge Bourne's face. It was stuck there in her brain like an elusive pebble in a stocking, constantly annoying, impossible to ignore.

Where are you? she pleaded; it did not answer. Bourne. Where have you gone?

"What are you doing?"

She opened her eyes, met the amazed gaze of the scholar, who had wandered down to see how she fared with his fish. "Oh," she said shortly, uninterested in his face. She let go of her hair and picked up her pen. "I'm almost finished."

"Have the fish suddenly become that frustrating?"

"No." She tried to write a perfunctory word; the nib was bone dry.

"Then it must be a two-legged frustration," he suggested shrewdly.

"An earth-dweller," she agreed moodily. Master Croysus straddled a hefty pile of tomes on the floor, looking open to diversion. His face, she saw, had regained a healthier complexion; his eyes looked nearly human again. The coronation celebrations in the world above must be waning.

"Any surprises?" he asked.

"Among the fish? I'm having difficulty with this one with its body full of bubbles. It doesn't appear on any of the other lists."

He leaned forward to study it. "Pearls?" he suggested tentatively. "Coins?"

For a brief moment, she forgot Bourne's face. "Scales?"

They regarded one another with conjecture. "No," the scholar said heavily. "Not scales."

"No," Nepenthe echoed, sighing; they were after all not really fish, and a measuring scale in any language would most likely not resemble a fish scale. She nibbled on the end of her pen, while Bourne's face surfaced again in her head, predictably as sunrise. "I thought," she added, "you would have gone home by now."

"So did I," Master Croysus said. He shifted a tome under one buttock and lowered his voice. "There are rumors of trouble. But no one is talking."

Nepenthe took her pen out of her mouth and wove it into her hair, struggling to understand. "Rumors. How can you hear rumors if nobody—"

"Nobody knows what is going on. Yesterday nobody would go home; today, suddenly, everyone wants to. But it's never convenient; the queen summons the nobles for meetings, then puts them off; they cannot leave. The rulers have been summoned to yet another assembly, but it must wait for the return to the court of Lord Ermin of Seale; the reason for the assembly is vague and keeps changing. The court is uneasy; no one explains. Even the folk on the plain are packing their wagons and drifting away, but the rest of us cannot seem to find an open door."

Nepenthe grunted, her thoughts straying. Perhaps Bourne — But he didn't need a door, open or shut, she reminded herself. All he had to do was —

"Think of me," she whispered. Something pinched the back of her throat; she swallowed.

"What?"

She tossed the pen down. "Nothing."

Master Croysus was still brooding over court matters. "So you see, you do have more time to attend to my fish. You should be able to finish before we leave. Whenever that might be. But don't move them from this place, whatever you do."

"I won't."

"If we must leave quickly for some reason, in the middle of the night for instance, I want to know where to find them."

She looked at him silently; again Bourne melted out of her head, like light in the path of a cloud. "What is happening up there?" she asked softly, suddenly uneasy herself, wondering how an entire library might flee in the dark, and to where. But Master Croysus did not hear her; he was gazing at her again, fixedly, but without seeing her. "I know!" he exclaimed abruptly, and she jumped. "I know where I have seen your face!"

"My face," she repeated blankly.

"I've been trying to remember, since I first saw you."

"You've seen me before?"

"In the margin of a very old book."

"It's not my face, if it's in some old book."

"Yes, it is," he said intractably, and stood up. "I'll find the book and prove it to you."

Bemused, she watched him retreat down the hallway, leaving her to the dead silence of books and stones. She studied the fish full of bubbles again. Bourne's face came between them, filling her eyes, filling her mind with memories, longings, unanswerable questions.

Where are you? she wanted to shout, but only the stones would answer.

She gave up on the fish finally, forgot the scholar, and carried her pens and ink to the secret place where she had hidden the thorns.

They wouldn't stay hidden long, she knew, if Bourne stepped out of nowhere to find her. But after three days without a glimpse of him, she did not care where he found her. The students sometimes had tests, he had told her; entire days when they could not leave the school or the wood until some mysterious thing happened to give them deeper insight into magic. But he had not come that evening when he promised he would. She had waited for him in the refectory until the fire had died and only a taper or two remained alight. Laidley, aware of her unhappiness, had told her that Bourne had appeared earlier that day in the library and had gone to look for her. He had not found her. He had not returned at supper time. Nor the following day, nor the day after that. Nor had he sent any explanation or excuse, in any alphabet. Laidley's silence about the matter grew so pointed that by the third day Nepenthe wanted to throw the meal-gong at him.

"Just say it," she had flared at him finally as they ate their porridge that morning. "Say I told you so."

He could not even be honest. His brows rose owlishly as he swallowed a bite. "I'm surprised," he managed finally.

"He is a hummingbird, quick wings, no thoughts, flitting lightly from heart to heart — I knew that. I knew it before we ever kissed."

"He was worried about you, when you hid the thorns from us. We both went searching for you; we were supposed to meet again, but he vanished. For all I know he might still be wandering around the library, completely lost — "

"He could find me." She stared down at her porridge; his

face was even there, between her and breakfast. She flung her spoon into the bowl and stood up. "He could find me in a step," she whispered. "He could find me with a thought. If he wanted."

She left Laidley making incoherent comments about troublesome times, and went to work on the fish manuscript, where Bourne could find her easily if he wished. He didn't. The scholar did.

And now she consoled herself among her thorns, bewildered and hurt, hiding from Bourne and hoping against hope that he would find her there.

The thorns themselves were becoming pricklier, as though Axis's acquisition of most of the known world around Eben demanded a more complex language. Kingdoms Nepenthe had never heard of fell to his armies. He seemed equally insatiable and invulnerable, collecting more crowns in half a decade than the kings of Raine had in a thousand years. And every ruler, every realm had a name like a bramble bush. She might, Nepenthe decided reluctantly, have to tell Laidley where she had concealed herself, so that he could continue to help her with the historical names. At the same time, while Axis blazed his way across the map of his world and poets celebrated his victories with endless superlatives, Kane's thoughts began to require a larger vocabulary. Puzzling concepts, that might or might not make sense, grew under Nepenthe's pen. Tangled thorns hinted at ideas that connected in some skewed fashion, or possibilities requiring obscure tenses, maybe past or maybe future. Nepenthe, scratching her head over them, forgot about

Bourne for entire minutes as she tried to untangle the canes. She worked all afternoon after the scholar had left her, and into the evening, mesmerized by the new difficulties, and comforted, every time she realized that for a sentence or even half a page, she had not thought about Bourne. She did not think about supper either; the gong rang only distantly beyond the thorns.

She put down her pen finally, yawning, and realized then how dark the library had grown around her. A single candle glowed in the distance, as someone walked down the corridor. She watched it, surprised. She had taken the thorns into a chamber full of antiquities, texts chiseled into slabs of broken sandstone and wax and marble, painted on tanned hides, carved into bone and horn. Only visiting scholars ever came that far down. Perhaps, she thought with a twinge of alarm, Master Croysus was truly fleeing in the middle of the night and had come looking for her.

But it was Laidley.

He sat down among the ruins, letting an armload of books slide to the floor beside him.

"I was worried," he said simply, "when you didn't come to supper. I've been looking for you everywhere."

"Well, you found me," she answered brusquely, for he was not Bourne, and he had invaded her hiding place. Then she relented, for she needed him. "Did I miss supper?"

"By several hours."

"Laidley, was there a kingdom called Auravia?"

He gazed at her a moment expressionlessly before he answered. "Yes. There was. It existed nine hundred years after Axis was born."

"Nine hundred."

"Yes. I told you so. I told you that whoever wrote that was jumbling everything together, regardless of historical order."

But she only nibbled a thumbnail, intrigued. "Maybe. But Kane knows she is doing it. I think she does. That would explain some of the passages."

Laidley ground a fist against one eye, looking aggrieved. "That makes no sense."

"No. But it means my translation does."

Laidley banged his head against the shard of marble behind him. "Now you're making no sense."

"I know."

"Read it to me."

She mulled that over, eyeing him. She had grown into the strange alphabet, she knew; she could recognize more than words. But she did not know what names belonged where in Kane's world, and Laidley would. If he didn't, he would know where to find out. Unlike Bourne, he had no fear of an ancient, harmless language. He would not threaten to take it away from her; he was capable of getting as ensnared as she.

The thought of Bourne blew a dreary mist into the region of her heart. She slumped over her work, lonely for him, wondering where in the night he was, what he was doing, whether he was thinking about her at all. The thorns, she remembered, kept her mind off him. Another long night of wondering waited for her inside her chamber. Better to read to Laidley and keep him awake than be kept awake by the utter silence out of the mages' school.

So she began to read what she had translated since she had disappeared with the thorns.

They both fell asleep, among the dusty, forgotten oddments of language, before she finished.

Nepenthe dreamed that Bourne was calling her over and over. But he could not say her name right because he did not know the language. Every time he called, another word in the form of a bramble came out of him. A wall of thorns began to coil up around him, hiding him from Nepenthe. She could not answer because he could not say her name correctly in thorns; he would not stop calling until she answered. Suddenly terrified, she began to shout her name to him, trying to tell him how to say it. He could not seem to hear her in his prison of thorns; words that did not mean her kept growing until she could only see the top of his golden head.

And then his hair turned into the top of a black hood, just visible above the thorns, and a strange voice said her name.

She woke herself trying to repeat it. Something with a shell in it? Or was it a moth?

"Nepenthe," said the gong, shivering through the silence, and again, in Laidley's voice: "Nepenthe."

"No," she protested, for the name was fading and fading like the sound of the gong. "That wasn't it."

She opened her eyes finally and found it was morning.

She had fallen asleep on the floor with her translation in her lap and her cheek imprinted with a raised wax word of uncertain origin. Laidley, using his armload of books for a pillow, blinked at her sleepily.

"I don't remember," he said hazily, "how much you read and how much I dreamed. In my dreams, Axis went back and forth."

She straightened stiffly, pushing hair out of her eyes. "He was pacing?"

"No. He went back and forth. He didn't care."

"Laidley, what are you talking about?"

"Back and forth," Laidley repeated stubbornly and pulled himself up among the shards. "You'll have to read it to me again. It all seems like a dream."

"Laidley. Say my name."

"Nepenthe," he said, yawning.

She shook her head. "That doesn't sound anything like my name."

"You're an orphan," he reminded her. "You don't know your own name."

"Yes, I do. When I hear it, I know it. I wasn't always an orphan. Someone said my real name in my dream."

"Who?"

About to answer, she stopped, for that answer made no more sense than Laidley's dream. She said it anyway, puzzling over it. "Kane." Laidley only grunted. She sucked a breath then, and whispered, "And Bourne. He was calling me. Again and again."

"Did you answer?"

"No. How could I? He didn't know my name."

Laidley blinked at her. She gathered the pages in her lap and stood up, forgetting why, looking aimlessly around the chamber as though for the wall of thorns.

"Dreams," Laidley murmured. "Wishes."

"Maybe. But someone was calling me, and I heard my name." She felt close to tears, of longing and frustration, for it was another matter entirely, the secret language of dreams. It refused to answer questions except in its own language, and that changed nightly. "I don't know either what is real and what is past," she cried suddenly to Laidley.

He swallowed, said only, gravely, "What can I do to help?"

"If I give you a list of kings and kingdoms, can you find them for me?"

"Yes."

"Then at least we'll know that much."

"What?"

"What was real for Axis and Kane," she said, and in that moment she understood the language of Laidley's dream. "Back and forth," she whispered. "Back and forth." Her fingers went to her mouth, icy with shock. "Oh, Laidley."

"Try not to worry," he said groggily, gathering up his stack of books. "I think he loves you. I wouldn't say that unless I did."

He wandered out to follow the smell of breakfast. Nepenthe, still transfixed, watched him go. She came to life again finally, sank back down among the thorns, and picked up her pen.

# SEVENTEEN

The queen was in the wood, looking for thorns.

If, she reasoned, thorns threatened the Twelve Crowns, then they must be something more than a bramble bush. They would be thorns of great power and magic, like the wood, which was the only source of power Tessera knew. Besides Vevay, that is. But even Vevay seemed uncertain of the origins and capabilities of the mysterious wood. The armed ghost of the first ruler of Raine had appeared there to warn Tessera: even the dead were drawn to it.

The queen was supposed to be somewhere that morning, meeting with someone, while keeping someone else uneasily waiting, and sending a summons throughout the palace for yet another noble, or half a dozen of them; she had lost track. Vevay kept everyone on edge, ruthlessly demanding the guests' constant attendance to the whims of the queen, while refusing to answer any questions. Rumors like mythical beasts stalked

the hallways, colorful, dangerous, and improbable. Only the
family of the Lord of Seale had been allowed to leave, without
fanfare and at some inconvenient hour. At least that was Vevay's explanation of their invisibility. They were actually under guard in the lower chambers of Vevay's tower, where they
had stunning views of the plain and the sea, and no comforts
whatsoever beyond that. Tessera doubted that Vevay would
notice her absence that morning; not even the mage could always remember whom she had told to do what.

"Thorns," Tessera whispered to the wood. "Thorns. Tell me
what they mean. Tell me where they are."

She wandered among the silent trees; nothing spoke. Beyond the wood, spring winds roared over the plain; brilliant,
tattered clouds raced their shadows across the grass. The folk
still on the plain huddled around their fires, or in their wagons. Tessera wondered why they stayed, what they expected.
Perhaps a feeling in their bones kept them lingering close
to what they thought might protect them best. Perhaps they
had tossed their carved pigs' knuckles and read the warnings
in them. On their brightly painted cards the sun fell out of
the sky, or a storm of stars like flaming arrows burned away
the night. Nowhere to go to escape such disasters, so why go
anywhere? The new queen, protecting herself, would protect
them all.

The new queen, questing patiently for thorns, could not
find so much as a raspberry cane. She roamed, hoping for a
talking bird, a wise word dropping from a tree. But everything
seemed half asleep that morning, under patches of shadow

and mist, exuding dreams like the faint breath of warmth out
of a dying ember. Moving like a swimmer underwater through
their dreams, Tessera felt herself fill with scents, obscure
memories, words without sound. Peace, layered in rings of
wood rippling out from the word, was one of the dreams; she
breathed it in, or swallowed it. Now she lumbered like a tree,
heavy with time, her thoughts too slow for words, her outward body a small, unwieldy thing crusted with bark, her hair
doing inexplicable things on top of her head.

In this guise, barely remembering herself, she came upon
the giant in the wood.

She remembered him well enough: his immense, thewed
shoulders, his bald head and broad, expressionless face. The
last time she saw him, he had chased her out of the wood. This
time, she would not run. Like the folk on the plain, she had
nowhere else to go, and he knew the wood better than she.

He did not recognize her, with her thoughts disguised in
tree bark and her hair full of leafing twigs. Around her, she felt
the wood stir out of its dreaming, quicken with interest to listen.

"Giant," she said; how her voice came out of her, she wasn't
sure. "You must help me. You may roar at me and threaten until your teeth fly out of your head, but I will not leave this
wood. You must show me where the thorns are hidden."

A strange expression slid from within the giant's bones,
seeped across his face. He said, "Tessera?"

She felt herself dwindle back into Tessera-shape at the word.
Still she didn't run. The wood was watching; it hid things from
her that she wanted. The armed warrior with her beautiful,

courageous face and her great sword still rode in the queen's heart, ready to battle for her.

She said coldly, "Yes. I am the Queen of Raine, and I need every giant and every bird and every listening leaf in this land to help me before we are all destroyed."

The giant said gravely, "I will help you. Come with me."

He turned; she followed him to his lair.

He led her through a doorway in a great stone wall so high and so wide that its true dimensions were lost within the trees. Once inside, he vanished. Tessera lingered at the threshold, expecting mischief in some startling form. Nothing happened. A long hallway stretched away from her on both sides, lined with many closed doors. All of them were different: dark and square, rounded and painted, carved and oblong, latched with iron, or wood, or gilded metal; one had a window of colored glass; another was fashioned of three rough-hewn planks and wooden nails with heads as wide as the giant's thumbnail. She waited for him to leap out of one door or another. He didn't. He had promised to help her, and had led her to this place with many closed doors. Behind which might be anything, including, she realized suddenly, what she had asked for.

"Thorns," she breathed, and opened the nearest door.

There they were: an enormous, leafless tangled hillock of brambles with wicked spikes of thorns covering the floor. As she stared at them, they began snaking up the walls of the room they had overrun. She felt the door pull out of her hand and turned to see it slam shut, then melt into the stones. Such was the nature of the giant's mischief, she thought grimly: she was trapped in a room full of what she had asked for, and no way out. She could hear them sliding over the stones, scratching like claws. For an instant, she wanted to melt into tears and wail for help like a baby.

But this was nothing, she reminded herself, compared to the imminent disaster that had caused the ancient, sleeping ruler of Raine to sit bolt upright in her tomb. A room full of thorns. Nothing.

They were magic, living things, like the trees in the wood, so she spoke to them.

"I am here," she told them as they began to coil toward her feet. "The Queen of Raine. If you mean to destroy the Twelve Crowns of Raine, then begin the battle with me."

They spoke in her mind then, as they whispered across the stones. The great pile that appeared in her thoughts grew leaves, opened blooms of white and pink and scarlet until the hillock they showed her was green as the grass on the plain, and she couldn't see the thorns for the leaves, nor the leaves for the flowers. She gazed bewilderedly at the bleak, naked canes twining over her boots, and was suddenly illumined.

"Oh!" she cried. "You want light." She looked around her hastily: four walls and a ceiling of solid stone, and not even a door left that they could crawl out of. How could she give them light so that the hungry canes could bud? They were growing importunate, snagging on the hem of her skirt, a great spiky animal wanting to be fed the sun.

"Giant!" she called nervously as a bramble touched her wrist. "Open the door! We can't get out."

The giant, a creature of impulse, had tricked her, it seemed; he did not answer. She gazed desperately at the walls, searching for a chink, a crack in the mortar, a glimpse of day through the ceiling. The canes had wrapped themselves around her ankles now. She couldn't feel the thorns through her boots but she would fall among them if she tried to walk. A memory glanced through her head: the armed, faceless warrior in the wood, pointing her gauntlet hand in warning at the brambles.

"If only I had your sword," she said breathlessly as a thorn tugged on her skirt, "I could knock out a few of these stones—"

She felt the dead weight of it in her hand, and nearly dropped it. She could scarcely see it; it was a silver streak of air and a glimmer of jewel. But it dragged at her hold like all the Twelve Crowns at once, and she dared not drop it lest it vanish again. Her mouth pinched; she felt a crown of sweat bead her brow as she gripped it with both hands, and with more effort than she had put into anything in her life, she found muscles she rarely used and forced the blade of the sword up, then over her shoulder. Shaking, her arms and back aching with the strain, she heaved, spun the blade forward and let it fly at the far wall.

Stones rained down. She shrieked, covering her head, then peered under one elbow at the light pouring from the jagged hole in the wall. Beyond it the wood watched, trees whispering; a bird chuckled. A tide of brambles flowed out of the wall into spring. When they loosed Tessera finally, she followed them, relieved to be leaving the giant's house.

The wall closed behind the last bramble, left her trapped

again within stones. She beat at them; they refused to budge. After a moment, a door formed noiselessly under her fists. It was a simple affair of wood and whitewash, with a brass latch. She glanced behind her; the door through which she had entered the room was still nowhere to be seen.

She sighed and opened the second door.

The giant stood waiting for her.

He said nothing, just blew a great breath at her that slammed the door and pushed her backward into it. She nearly fell over when he ran out of breath. Indignant, she filled her lungs and blew back at him, a feeble breath that stirred a few dust motes in the air between them. He laughed a booming laugh that shook the floorboards. Furious with him for toying with her, she drew breath and blew again, noisily and gracelessly, like a bellows. She thought she saw one eye flutter; his laughter grew a little hollow. The next breath she loosed at him lifted him off his feet.

Obstinately, he was grinning as he got up off the floor. Still he didn't speak. He threw something at her that looked like a little ball of fire. She ducked. It smacked the door and set it on fire.

Gasping, she flung herself away. He had already tossed another ball. She ran; it struck the floor where she had been and set that on fire. She fled across the room, watching him, breathless and astonished, as he pulled another burning ball out of his sleeve, or out of the air. Magic, she thought as she dodged this one. But the fires burning the floorboards and the door were real enough: she felt the painful heat, heard wood sizzle and snap.

The giant formed another ball. This time she did not run; she narrowed her eyes and stood ground grimly, tired of being batted around by this mindless hulk in his confusing house. When he threw, she blew. The ball of fire stopped in midair and bounced back at him.

He caught it, laughing again, and dropped it down his sleeve. "Good," he grunted. "You fought beyond your fear and began to think."

The fires around them vanished at the sound of his voice. She stood panting, staring at him incredulously. An odd feeling spilled through her, filling her like steam fills a pot; when she finally found her voice, it sounded a little like steam blasting the lid off the pot.

"How dare you?" she demanded. Angrier than she had ever been in her life, she did not even know the word for what she felt. "Who are you?"

But he was gone suddenly, and so was the door.

A third door formed in the wall ahead of her.

The strange tempest in her had blown itself out. She gazed wearily at the door, tired of being tormented and teased, and frightened. She was uncomfortably aware that she had misjudged something; she was looking at something askew, not seeing what was in front of her nose. The giant, perhaps, was not a giant? The magical house, perhaps, was not a house?

Perhaps she was not even herself?

She had wielded the sword of the first queen of Raine; she had blown a giant off his feet and outwitted him; she had

brought light to a place with no light; she had understood the magic of the thorns.

"I don't know anymore what I am," she whispered to the door, and put her hand on the latch. It seemed that, opening it, she would understand something she was not sure she wanted to know. There was no other way out. She drew close to the door, still holding its simple wooden latch, and bowed her head against the unseasoned planks.

"I wish," she told it, "that you would just let me back into the wood."

It opened to yet another room; in this one she found Vevay.

Tessera looked at the mage silently, not recognizing the expression on her face at all. She said tentatively, wondering if it were just another teasing bit of magic, "Vevay?"

"Yes," Vevay said simply. She did not move; Tessera took a step toward her.

"You look unfamiliar. What have you been thinking?"

"I was remembering," the mage said. "Things that I had forgotten long ago . . . You reminded me that they are still there, buried away underneath the years." She moved finally, turning, and Tessera saw the door appear in the wall in front of the mage, as though she, too, had been trapped in the giant's house.

But it had not been a giant, and it was not a house . . . Vevay opened the door; Tessera saw the green wood just outside. Vevay stood aside, waiting for the queen to pass.

She took a step then stopped before she crossed the threshold, said without looking at Vevay, "This is the mages' school."

"Yes."

"And the giant. He is a mage."

"Felan. You met him once before, when your father took you with him to visit the school. You were very young; you might have remembered him as a giant."

Tessera nodded. She shifted to take another step but didn't. "And what am I?"

"You tell me," Vevay said.

Tessera looked at her finally. The ancient, beautiful face held many complex things that she had not seen before she began to see herself.

She answered softly, "I will."

"I was searching for you. Felan sent word that you were here. The Lord of Seale did not wait for your messengers to summon him back to court; he is already on his way here." She paused, her smoky eyes hooded, watching something in the distance. "He is bringing his army with him."

Tessera turned her head, gazed blindly at the trees. She moved finally, stepped into the unpredictable world that, like all the rooms in the giant's house, had no way out but through.

# EIGHTEEN

The Emperor of the Sea was not content.

Neither were his armies, which had grown substantially as he made his way around the Baltrean, swollen with warriors from other lands whose heads were stuffed with dreams of glory and plunder. Axis seemed invincible. After Kirixia fell to him, almost without a fight since its ruler had fled before the armies of Eben had even gotten there, he lingered to rest on the sunny Baltrean shores. As always, he left as much unchanged as he could in the lands he conquered. For most, daily life continued much as it had before; only the faces of authority were different. He chose a careful combination of alien conqueror and pragmatic locals to restore peace and preserve order. Aware that an empire begins to crumble the moment the emperor turns his back, he did what he could that was shrewd and prudent to maintain it. Then he turned his back, for his first love was war.

After every campaign, no matter how distant, he returned to Eben. He was most careful with it, since he had almost lost it once. There, while he attended to its affairs, his thoughts would inevitably stray beyond the boundaries of Eben, of his empire, to find his next battlefield. His army, well paid and sheltered between wars, waited patiently for him to decide. It was becoming a fearsome thing, that army of Eben; it was as complicated to handle as an empire. The queen hated it when it took Axis away from Eben, and feared it when he brought it home. It had become a great killing machine, a monster that ate entire kingdoms. If Axis failed to provide for it, it would consume Eben. So she complained to the king, who listened gravely to his wife, and answered simply, "Then I will find it new worlds to conquer, and it will never turn on me."

It was full of strangers, the emperor's army, foreign faces and languages, customs, experiences, warriors who were newly part of the empire and inspired by the young emperor's astonishing victories. Kane, who fought its battles with it, who drifted at night from campfire to campfire, a stray shadow listening to comments, complaints, tales, recognized it as a source for Axis's new worlds. Thus, from a warrior born in Kirixia, whose father had been a trader, she heard of an immense, fabulous kingdom east of the Baltrean, full of exotic beasts, untold wealth, and poetry as old as the world.

When, in Eben, she recognized the signs of restlessness in the Emperor of the Sea, she told him what she had heard.

They lay together, as usual during their most important councils of war, in the placid palace beside the Serpent.

"Does this land have a name?" Axis asked. Around them, the palace was hushed and dark; a single stand of candles showed them one another's face.

"It's called Gilyriad."

"Gilyriad. I've never heard of it." He dropped kisses like warm rain in the crooks of her elbows, in the hollow of her throat. "Does it really exist?"

"I will find out," Kane promised.

She had her ways, which she only explained to Axis if he asked. He rode the twin dragons of empire and war; he had little time to wonder about her sorcery. It existed; she used it for his purposes; it was too complex for him to comprehend, and so he rarely asked. When he did, her answers were frustratingly vague. How could she travel across a battlefield in a breath, so that if he said her name or thought it, there she was beside him?

"I feel you call me," she said. "I take a step." But how? "I make the shortest path to you." How did she find the shortest path? "I eliminate everything that isn't you." How, he asked incredulously, can you eliminate a battlefield? She tried to explain. "It goes elsewhere. Like a pattern on a cloth when you fold it. One end is you, the other end is me. When you lay the cloth flat, we are far apart across the pattern. When you bring one end of the cloth to meet the other, there is no longer any distance between them. The pattern is still there, but no longer between us. It is elsewhere. We are together."

In this fashion she traveled to other places: the docks on the delta where the Serpent flowed into the sea, for instance.

There she listened and questioned until she found a trader who claimed to have traveled to Gilyriad. He showed her seed pods that, crushed, became richly scented spices. He showed her cloth of a strange airy weave dyed unusual colors, and pottery glazed with unfamiliar patterns. He held fine-grained aromatic wood to her nose and opened elegantly wrought chests full of uncut jewels and disks of gold stamped with the faces of rulers she did not recognize.

She brought one of the disks back to Axis.

"A coin," she told him, "from your next conquest."

He studied the face on the disk: a proud, hawk-nosed, disdainful profile. "I will need a map," he murmured, "to show to my generals." He laid the coin in her hand, closed her fingers over it. "When I am Emperor of Gilyriad, spend this in the marketplace on a piece of cloth with a pattern on it that goes elsewhere when we lie together."

She smiled. "I will spend it on a map of the world. Not even that can separate us."

If, she reasoned, the maps of the world she knew showed only the world she knew, then the maps in the world of Gilyriad would show the world as it was known there, which might indeed encompass lands unknown in Eben for the emperor to conquer. She continued her search among traders and sailors, for they roamed farther than the merchants' ships could go in the sheltered Baltrean Sea. She learned of long, arduous trade routes over mountains and plains east of the Baltrean, where tribes of nomads and vast herds of peculiar animals roamed on paths formed over countless centuries by their ancestors. Thus

the world changed its shape in Kane's mind, stunningly and irrevocably. In the mind of the young girl on the bank of the
Serpent, the world had been exactly the size and shape of
Eben. Now it was shifting rapidly into something unimaginably huge and complex. Axis wanted to lead his army across
that complexity and conquer whatever kingdoms he had missed.
He depended upon Kane to show him the way.

She bought maps where she could get them, from sailors
along the shores of the Baltrean. A couple she stole, for the
trade routes leading to rich, exotic cities were the well-kept secrets of wealthy merchants. She laid them side by side in
Axis's secret chamber, where he walked barefoot among them,
studied them silently for a long time. Then he looked at her.
She felt her throat swell at the expression in his eyes. In that
moment they both knew that the world at his feet belonged
to him.

> *Out of the mountains of Kol*
> *The Emperor's army poured like water*
> *Onto the plains of Gilyriad.*
> *Like the stars,*
> *Nameless, countless,*
> *Like the endless drops of rain*
> *Were the masked faces of the warriors of Eben.*
> *The trumpets of Gilyriad sounded,*
> *Bone and brass shouted across the land*
> *Like the battle-cries of fierce beasts*
> *Rushing to meet their doom.*

And doom it was for Gilyriad, after three days, or thirty days, or ninety days and ninety nights of constant battle, depending upon which poet wrote of it. On his march from Eben to Gilyriad, Axis's army had indeed grown like a river, as nomadic warriors and mercenaries streamed into it. Kane fought always at Axis's side through the long battle. Even she lost track of time, for they scarcely slept, and her powers could light up a battlefield even at night. The victory was never in question. But the proud ruler of Gilyriad did not easily give up the land his ancestors had held since the beginnings of language to this masked raider who came out of Nowhere.

*The Lion of Eben*
*Raised the severed head*
*Of the King of Gilyriad by his hair*
*To let him look*
*One last time at his land.*
*A great cry echoed across the plain*
*From the mouth of the dead king to his people:*
*"Bow low, touch your mouths to the dust,*
*For this is the Emperor of the World."*

Actually, the King of Gilyriad was on his feet with his head on his shoulders when he surrendered his army and his kingdom to Axis. He killed himself not long afterward, unable to endure his humiliation. Axis sent his sons to govern remote areas conquered by Gilyriad during its long history. They became minor princelings themselves; Axis had them carefully watched through their lives, for any signs of rebellion and revenge. He himself did not return to Eben for nearly a year. He explored his new acquisition and dealt with its governing bodies. On Kane's advice, when he did return to Eben, he left a great part of the immense swarm that was his army in Gilyriad.

While Axis was putting the realm in order, Kane gave deep and careful thought to their situation. Gilyriad was a sprawling, fertile land, well able to contain the emperor's army. Camped near a wealthy city, it was well fed and kept in order. By then, contrary to the fears of the Queen of Eben, it was fiercely and passionately devoted to the emperor, for he had made it, in a few short years, the matter of legend and epic. Axis's army would have followed him anywhere.

He expected Kane to tell him where.

She traveled through Gilyriad with Axis, staying in the great palaces and cities. While he set his governing bodies in place, she spoke to scholars and explored libraries. For this she used interpreters who had once been sailors or caravan leaders, wanderers who had come to the end of their roads in Gilyriad. Very few people had ever heard of Eben before they suddenly found themselves under its rule. The scholars showed her ancient texts, tried to find ways of explaining them. She demonstrated her powers; illumined, they produced even older words, and took her to meet local witches, sorcerers, and healers. She learned odd, stray things from them. Mostly she offered them gold in return, for they were a wild, scruffy lot underappreciated by those who consulted them.

Sometimes she spent entire days in the sumptuous gardens,

listening while scholars and interpreters read to her. The histories and epics they read were of long-dead heroes, kingdoms with little left of them but their names. They showed her maps of the world according to Gilyriad. A great ocean lay to the east; it had no beginning and no end. No one who ventured forth to find the other side of it had ever returned. Therefore there was no end. Kane nodded solemnly. The ocean went on forever, gradually flowing into the stars, which also went on forever. All that existed lay flat, like a great cloth. All intelligent people had believed, until the emperor had come out of the Gates of Nowhere, that the pattern of the earth on the fabric of existence was roughly the size and shape of Gilyriad.

Now that they realized their error, the scholars asked Kane to change the shape of the world for them. She drew them the world as she knew it, though she made Eben about ten times bigger than it was so that Axis's victory would be more credibly explained. Thoughts washed back and forth in her head, images that their language summoned. The endless sea that flowed into stars. The world lying flat like a cloth. The explorers looking for the end of the world who went out and never returned, presumably still sailing around the stars . . . In her mind she reached out to the flat cloth of existence. She touched it, ruffled it, so that pieces of the pattern that had been an inch apart were now touching. She folded one end against the other; places that had not known of one another's existence were now face-to-face. Stars rained out of the sky, touched the earth. The sea that had no end suddenly found itself a shore.

How? she wondered. How?

And all her explanations to Axis about how she moved across distances resolved themselves into one word: Time.

There, in the tranquil gardens of Gilyriad, as Axis made his peace with his conquered people, she glimpsed the true beginnings of his empire.

> *The Lord of Time*
> *Who opens the Gates of Nowhere*
> *Everywhere at his whim*
> *Knows no boundaries.*
> *No kingdom is safe.*
> *Lock your gates.*
> *Guard your walls.*
> *Bury your gold.*
> *Never sleep.*
> *He will unlock your gates.*
> *He will shatter your towers.*
> *He will take your gold*
> *And give you sleep in return.*
> *That sleep that has no language,*
> *No dream,*
> *No time,*
> *No end.*

# NINETEEN

Bourne sat on the hard, narrow pallet in his prison chamber, flipping a coin. Sometimes the crowned head of the young woman in the wood landed upright, sometimes the twelve linked Crowns of Raine. He would pause to gaze intently at either, as though trying to comprehend the message they were giving him in the alphabet of coins. He had no pen or knife to tally which fell when, so he had decided from the beginning that it didn't matter: he would regard every toss as the first, and every image as a message. The message, which one fall or another of the coin would eventually give him, was how to get himself out of his chamber and into Nepenthe's, so that he could tell her why he had not come to tell her why he had not come.

He had tried. Each time he filled his heart with her, so that longing fashioned the shortest path through time, he would be brought up against a wall. He tried more than once; the second wall looked different. He tried many times, thinking that Vevay could not be shoring up that many spells at once, and somewhere there must be an end to walls. There wasn't. He sank down on the floor and began pitching coins into his shoe, trying to devise a way to outwit the door. It was visible; it functioned; it opened and closed whenever someone from the kitchens brought him food. There seemed no lock on it. He offered money to the servant to show him how to open the door. The servant, who might have been Felan himself for all he knew, only snorted at the idea and went off snickering unpleasantly. Bourne kept his mind on the problem, doggedly throwing the seventeen coins he had in his pocket over and over. An idea grew the way mushrooms seemed to grow, unexpectedly, out of nothing, when no one was watching. There it was: the door in his head and a way to open it. He barely remembered to empty his shoe and put it back on before he went to the door.

He opened it and nearly fell over the cliff.

He closed it again, leaned against it, his heart pounding sickly, still feeling the sudden blast of wind leaping up over the cliff, smelling of sun and salt, pushing against him even as the shock of the long emptiness almost unbalanced him into it. Illusion, he guessed, but was not entirely convinced that, stepping into it, he would not be instantly stripped of every illusion in his young life as he plunged to his death. Nor did he believe that Vevay might bestir herself to rescue him. He—or something—seemed to have tested her patience severely; she didn't look in the mood for mercy.

So he went back to his coins, tossing this time instead of pitching, with the one coin he had that bore the queen's face. It didn't resemble the girl in the wood. The face on the coin belonged to someone older, stronger, tempered. A warrior queen, not the shy woodland creature he had met. That one was magical, talking to trees and birds, and seeing portents in—what had it been?—a bramble bush. Perhaps some of her magic would spark within him at a coin's toss, if her face came up often enough. Queen or Crowns, he threw, again and again. Queen or Crowns. It seemed a question to which he must give his entire attention. If he chose correctly he would find the magic, work the spell, set himself free . . .

This time the spell that stole into his empty mind was not one he had thought to look for. He had no idea how long he had been in the windowless place except by counting meals; already there seemed to have been more than possible. No one came to tell him anything. Even the servant who brought his food and wash-water rarely glanced at him, and refused to acknowledge any remarks. I might as well be invisible, Bourne had thought a hundred times. I might as well be a stone in the wall, without eyes or ears or thoughts. Much longer in this timeless, soundless place, and I will turn into one . . .

Queen or Crowns.

Queen or Crowns.

Queen or Crowns.

"I might as well be," he whispered, flicking the coin with his thumb. "I might as well . . ."

Be invisible.

He heard his breath stop.

Queen.

He picked the coin up as tenderly as if it were a love token, gazing at her face.

Invisible. I might as well be . . .

"Why not?" he asked her. "Why not? No one sees me, anyway. I might as well."

Be invisible.

He sat there for a very long time, holding the face of the young queen, not trying anything, even not to think, just letting himself be what he was, something no one wanted to see, hear, speak to, a stone in the wall, an unlit candle. Something that was nothing. Nowhere. Unnoticed. Invisible.

He placed the coin gently into his pocket and waited.

When the servant brought his next meal, he saw the scattering of coins on the floor where the prisoner had been sitting.

While he straightened, staring incredulously around the room, Bourne walked out of the door into the mages' comfortable library and kept walking as the servant shouted, into the library in his heart.

He appeared in Nepenthe's chamber. Not daring to show his face anywhere in the halls he waited for her there. Sitting on her bed, tossing the coin again to empty his head, he tried to remain invisible. The sky in her tiny window took forever to darken. But it did eventually, and no Vevay came searching for him. He wondered why. He loved an orphan transcriptor in the library; she must know he would go there first. Perhaps because she had caught him there before, that was the last place she expected to find him now. His mouth crooked ruefully. Or she simply thought he would run, since he took so little seriously; she would expect to find him somewhere between the mages' wood and the safety of his uncle's court.

He flipped the coin upward; the door opened.

Nepenthe, staring at the coin falling over her bed, brought both hands over her mouth to stifle a scream.

She tried to scream again when Bourne stumbled off her bed and caught her shoulders. "Nepenthe," he whispered. "It's only me."

She pushed past him into the room, shoved the door closed with her foot. She was trembling; her hands shook badly as she tried to light one taper from another. Bourne took them from her; she gasped sharply, "Don't do that!"

"Do what?"

"Make things float in the air like that."

"Do I?" he asked bewilderedly.

"Bad enough that I couldn't see you when you weren't there—"

"But I'm here, now."

"Where?" she demanded tightly. "Why are you hiding from me? Leave me alone if you can't think of anything better to do than torment me."

He put the taper very carefully in a holder. "Nepenthe." For some reason he was whispering again. "Can't you see me?"

"No!" She was trying, he could tell. Now that he no longer

held anything her eyes searched for him desperately everywhere in the chamber. "I can hear you; I can see things you
hold. But I can't see you at all."

He closed his eyes, slumped against the wall. "Oh," he
breathed, "this is cruel."

"Yes."

"Please." He caught her hand; she tried to pull away, but he
brought her palm to his rough cheek. "Feel that. That's what
grew in however many days I was locked away. How many
days has it been since I should have met you that evening in
the refectory?"

Her wide eyes searched the air her hand cupped. "Five days."

"Five. It felt like half a year."

"Why are you still invisible?"

"Because I don't know how to undo my own spell," he answered raggedly. "I don't know how I managed to turn myself
invisible, but as soon as I knew I was unseen I crept out the
door and came here."

"Where have you been?"

"Somewhere in the mages' school, boxed in by Vevay. She
found me wandering around the library when I was last here
looking for you, and she arrested me for treason."

"Trea—" She tried to stuff the word back into her mouth, as
though saying it would bring down disaster. "Bourne. What
have you been doing?"

He sighed. "Sit with me. You don't have to see me, just feel
my hand in yours, my body beside you. I'll try to explain."

He tried, and watched her trying to understand. What had

seemed a lighthearted venture into the mystery of magic sounded foolish now, fraught with the dangerous ambiguities of history. Her hand grew slack in his hold. Once or twice she tried to interrupt, but he continued doggedly, insisting that he had meant no real harm, that truly he thought himself incapable of—He had actually met the queen in the wood one day and liked her. He had gotten her to smile—

"Bourne." Nepenthe was not smiling. Her eyes were enormous and very dark. His babbling died away; he waited uneasily. "There was a rumor at supper tonight about your uncle. They say he's leading the entire forces of the Second Crown here to attack the queen."

He felt his skin go cold with shock, as though someone had doused him with a bucket of water. At the same time, something was unleashed, a sudden flash of wild magic that he had been holding in place without realizing it. As it dispersed, and the expression in Nepenthe's eyes changed, he knew that he had broken his own spell.

"Bourne!" she cried to his visible face. "Not now!"

"I couldn't help it—" He gripped her hand again; they were both silent, motionless, listening. No irate mages appeared out of nowhere to haul him back into his cage. He loosed her slowly, whispering again, "I didn't know about my uncle. No one has spoken to me for days."

"Can't you turn yourself invisible again? You're in terrible danger."

He looked at her, brushed a strand of hair from her eyes. "You believe me?" he asked wistfully.

"Yes, of course I do; I always knew you had a careless heart," she answered dolefully. "But a transcriptor in the royal library believing in your—well, your foolishness if not your innocence—is not going to matter to anyone else if they find you. What are you going to do? You can't show your face, even down here."

"I don't know." He shifted closer to her, pushed his lips against her hair. "I only came here because I knew I had hurt you. I wanted you to know that I didn't mean to—I've wanted nothing but to come to you for days, explain that maybe I have taken the world too lightly, but never you. For you I work magic. I do things I never knew I could do. Like—" He paused, holding words back, then continued reluctantly. "Like leaving you, now, before I get you into trouble, too."

"No." Her fingers closed on his shoulder, his wrist. "No."

"I can't stay."

"Yes. You can make yourself invisible again. Stay with me. I'll hide you, and feed you—"

"She'll find us both here. You'll be as culpable as I am."

"Then I'll put you where I hide my thorns. No one ever goes there except me. You can practice your invisibility there." She put her arms around him, held him tightly. "Where else can you go? Back to the wood, where the mages will be looking for you? To your uncle's army, to help him fight?" She loosed him as abruptly, to meet his eyes. "Would you do that? Use your mage's powers to fight for the Second Crown?"

"I could," he answered softly. "But what is my uncle going

to do when the warriors of eleven other Crowns converge on this plain around him to rescue their own rulers and protect their powers? The Second Crown is doomed. I'd do better to flee with the gypsies on the plain, go off to a strange city, change my name and do tricks for a living. I don't suppose you would come with me?"

To his surprise, she considered it, her eyes wide, oddly desperate. "Have you got any money?"

"Yes," he said. Then he sighed. "No. I left it all, except for this coin, in the school."

She dropped her face against him, hiding her eyes. "Then we must stay. Anyway, what about your family? You can't run away from them."

"What about them?" he said bitterly. "My uncle is not thinking of them. There won't be much left of it if he continues his march toward the plain."

"Can you stop him?"

"Not with words. The queen and her mages and the other Crowns will put a stop to him soon enough. I won't have a home to go home to."

"Then this must be home for now. Wait with me until it gets late. Then I'll take you to my secret place. I know where the librarians keep spare bedding, and I can bring you food from the refectory kitchens. You'll turn yourself invisible again, and no one will find you."

He saw Vevay's eyes, gray, clear, and winter-cold, knew she could see through any spell he conjured. "For now," he said, and kissed Nepenthe. "I'll stay tonight at least. I won't put you in danger longer than I can help it. But I can't seem to think clearly now."

"Don't think. She'll only find you."


He tried not to, as Nepenthe led him, hours later, through the soundless, shadowy corridors, down every worn stone stair, it seemed, she could find until they must be in the center of the cliff somewhere near the Dreaming King. Was he dreaming now? Bourne wondered. Was Ermin of Seale a nightmare or merely an irritating twitch in the Dreamer's sleep?

Nepenthe deposited him among the broken shards of history, left him with a candle while she went for food and blankets. He studied the old slabs with their incomprehensible letters, shifting the light to see tablets of wax and stiffened hide, all filled with writings that once were urgent and necessary for an orderly world and now were buried away, gathering dust and of no use to anyone.

The little book of thorns caught his eye. It lay closed among Nepenthe's pens and ink jars and papers covered with her careful, miniscule writing. Her translations. He picked one up, scanned it. Kane and Axis, nothing else, nothing but, both names as ancient and dusty as the tablets around him. What, he wondered, not for the first time as he picked up the odd, thorny book, was her obsession?

Thorns.

He blinked, remembering. Something. The queen in the

wood. The warrior that had appeared to her, armed, faceless, pointing, warning silently of—what?

A pile of brambles.

Thorns.

The eerie magic flashed out of him again, sudden fear colliding with sudden power.

"Only the beginning," he heard Vevay say again in memory, talking about his uncle. "Only the beginning of trouble."

# TWENTY

Vevay sat with Felan in the mages' library much later that night, explaining to him where their prisoner had gone.

"Something there is in all this that doesn't meet the eye," she said grimly. "Which is why I left him in the library instead of bringing him back here."

"I don't understand how he freed himself. You put terrible spells on that door."

"Only if he figured out how to open it with magic. Which he shouldn't have done. What have you been teaching the students these days?"

"Nothing very complicated."

"Well, what he actually did wasn't complicated at all. What he actually did was walk out the door after Halvor opened it. Halvor said no one had told him that the prisoner might turn himself invisible."

"No one told me, either," Felan said ruefully. "I had no idea he could do that."

"Neither did he. That's what he told the transcriptor in the library. I could see what drew him back there. She has astonishing eyes, and a face that—well, it reminded me of something; I can't remember what. She took him to a room deep in the cliff, full of old stone tablets and such. She left him there while she went for food and blankets. It didn't look as though he were going anywhere else, so I left him, too, to come here."

"Will he stay there?"

She shrugged slightly. "At least until morning."

"What will he do then?"

"I don't know."

"What will you do?"

"I'll decide then." She paused, her eyes hooded, expressionless, as she tried to piece together events that would not fit. Ermin of Seale's army marching out of the Second Crown to attack the queen; the Dreamer awake and uttering dire warnings not about Ermin but about thorns . . .

"There isn't a bramble bush anywhere on the entire plain," she said impatiently. "There is no danger that I can see beyond Ermin. That's what is so frightening: I can't see!"

"No danger even in Bourne?"

She shook her head helplessly. "I heard everything he said to the young transcriptor he loves. They discussed running off together in a gypsy wagon. The last thing he wanted to do, it seemed, was fight for Ermin of Seale. He said that the Lord of Seale had doomed the Second Crown, and he worried about his family. As well he should. I will have his uncle's head on a platter and his family in a tower on the Outermost Islands for the next five hundred years if the Twelve Crowns gather their forces to fight Ermin and then decide to rebel against the queen while they're at it. Gavin has summoned the queen's warriors. They'll be coming from the north and the south, he said, and they should be able to cut Ermin off before he comes near the plain. And of course the nobles are clamoring to return home and gather their own forces to protect their interests. And to fight for the queen. So they say. You'd think that alone would be reason enough to galvanize a dead warrior's bones. But no. It must be something totally incomprehensible."

"Thorns," Felan murmured.

"Thorns."

"And you think that by leaving Bourne to his own devices, you might learn something about them?"

"His magic is unpredictable, governed by impulse and desire. Pent up here, it may do more harm than good. Let loose, it may unearth something useful." She brooded silently again, then added slowly, "His is not the only wild magic on this plain."

"Tessera."

"Yes." The ominous stillness left her eyes; she looked suddenly bewildered, vulnerable. "I didn't remember."

"What?"

"What power is like when you're that young. If no one names it for you, how can you possibly know what it is? She had no way of telling me. Why she could hear the language of trees. That it might be important. Why should she have told me? Nothing else she could do seemed to please me; why would that? I may be older than I can count, but how could I have not recognized what was under my nose?"

"You were trying to see something else in her," he suggested gently. "You were trying to find her father in her, his strengths and powers. You didn't think of looking for your own."

"No."

"Do you have any idea—"

"No. I don't know how powerful she could be. Or even what branch of her family tree such power came from. That tree is more tangled than the entire wood, and if we couldn't even keep the sex of the first ruler straight, then there's no telling what else has been changed or misplaced or forgotten along the way. There is no time to teach Tessera anything now. She can be trained as a mage later, if she survives her first month as queen. Until then, she will have to rely on us. An aging counselor whose vision is failing, and a handful of schoolmasters who haven't been near a battlefield in decades."

"I could," Felan suggested tranquilly, "drop the Floating School on Ermin's head."

Vevay smiled thinly. "I might ask you to. But the most important thing you can do now is look for—"

"Thorns."

"Thorns." She stirred restively. "I'm trying to find them in the most unlikely places. The transcriptor who is hiding Bourne put him in a secret place where, she said, she kept her thorns.

So of course I followed them there, and looked for anything remotely resembling brambles in the library."

"Was there —"

"I didn't see anything. Just broken stone tablets and a few books and her papers."

"Books." Something quickened in his face; a line disturbed his brow, faint as a dragonfly's wake across water. Vevay gazed at him with wonder. "There was a book that passed among the mages earlier this spring. It was written in a kind of thorny alphabet."

"Was it magic?" Vevay asked quickly.

"It didn't seem so. It seemed just an ancient language that none of us could decipher. A trader gave the book to us; he said he couldn't interest anyone in buying it, and he was tired of carrying it around the Twelve Crowns."

"Is it still here?"

"No. We sent it over to the librarians to see what they would make of it."

Her silvery brows rose. "But you sensed no power in it?"

"Nothing. Nothing beyond the power of a forgotten language to inspire curiosity." He paused. Vevay watched his eyelids descend slowly, tortoise-like, over some thought. He said softly, "Bourne."

"Bourne."

His eyelids lifted again. "I believe that it was Bourne who took the book out of the wood to give to the librarians' messenger. The older students were practicing an exchange of power in the wood that day, and Bourne was the only one of the beginning students not afraid to walk through it."

"Why am I not surprised?" she inquired of the air. "Have the librarians translated it yet?"

"They've said nothing about it."

"Perhaps they gave it to Bourne's friend to translate. That's what she meant by thorns. She kept paper and ink there; she was translating something. I'll go back now and look."

Felan nodded. "Though it's hard to imagine a language powerful enough to rouse the dead of Raine without attracting your attention."

"Well," Vevay said tersely as she rose, "now I'm listening."

But while she heard Bourne's weary snoring in the library chamber as she turned page after page of thorns, nothing spoke behind the letters, within the words, between the lines. She read some of Nepenthe's translation. Axis and Kane, she saw with surprise. She remembered speaking their names not so long ago, telling a story to Gavin to send him to sleep. This was sending her to sleep. She yawned in the middle of Axis's conquest of the ancient kingdom of Gilyriad. Where had that been? she wondered. Far east of the easternmost Crown, the Sixth Crown, she thought, and yawned again.

"Nothing," she told Felan on her return to the mages' library. "Just ancient history."

She slept then, for a few scant hours, until she heard the first bird sing on the tower roof where they nested, and in the darkness before dawn she returned to keep watch over Bourne.

They were together by then, he and the transcriptor Nepenthe, huddled under patched quilts and talking.

"I should leave," he insisted. "Vevay and Felan must be searching for me, and they will find me. That's only a matter of time. I don't want them to find me with you."

"I don't want you to go. You have nowhere to go. Stay with me. The mages will imprison you, if you go back to the school; the queen will arrest you. If you go back to the Second Crown, you'll have to choose which side of a war you'll fight in, and either side might kill you. Stay here."

"And do what? Haunt the library for the rest of my life, never appearing except after dark? I should leave now while I can. Now. Before the sun rises. Come with me. There are books in the world beyond the royal library. I'll find work as an apprentice mage, and you can write and translate."

She hesitated; Vevay heard her draw breath once or twice. Then she whispered something that Vevay heard, but Bourne didn't, for she was turning away from him as she spoke.

"What?"

"I want to. I will go with you. But I have to finish the thorns first."

He pulled her back, catching her shoulders and holding her down, pulling the hair away from her face so she could not hide from him. "I'll finish those thorns for you," he promised grimly. "I'll throw them over the cliff and into the sea."

"And I will go after them," she told him with such chilling calm that Vevay blinked, and Bourne buried his own face in Nepenthe's hair.

"All right," he whispered. "We won't fight over them. I won't take them away from you. I will leave now—"

"No—"

"Listen. I'll ride out of here on one of the traders' wagons; I can do enough magic to convince somebody to hire me as protection against trouble on the road. I'll make my way to a city where I'll be safe, and then I'll write and tell you where I am. You can come to me when you're ready."

"Don't leave," she pleaded. "Isn't there someone you could talk to? One of the mages, or someone in the palace who could tell you what to do? Vevay hasn't found you yet. She would have by now, if she could. Wouldn't she? If you turn yourself invisible again, she wouldn't find you, would she?"

Bourne hesitated. Vevay nodded, encouraging the idea. Bourne, she was convinced, meant no harm to Tessera, but it would not be safe for him to roam freely with all his relatives imprisoned for treason and his uncle leading an army against the palace. Losing Bourne would be a waste of an interesting power that might likely be useful to the queen if they all survived her coronation. Vevay considered making herself visible, then and there, and commanding Bourne to stay. But there were decisions he had to make for himself, if he were to wield a power that could be trusted. All she could do, for the moment, was watch.

"All right," he breathed, dropping his face against Nepenthe's. "I will wait until you're ready. But you must hurry. If war comes to the plain before we leave, we may never get out of here. And if Vevay finds me —"

"Don't say her name."

"She will have no mercy."

"Then you had better remember how you turned yourself invisible in the first place. Can you?"

"I had a coin," he answered, surprising Vevay again. "The queen's face was on it. I think the magic in her inspired me . . ."

"She's magical?"

"You wouldn't notice it, looking at her. I think that's what I used — her ability to hide all that magic, to be unnoticed in the midst of all her power . . . Trees talk to her. She sees birds in the wood. Nobody ever sees birds in the wood."

"Why not?"

"I don't know." He was talking into her hair now, his face nuzzled into her neck; her eyes were closed. "Maybe they're the wood's thoughts, birds are. The trees hide them from the students, or from other humans . . . the way you would hide something precious from clumsy strangers . . . The way you hide the thorns . . ."

Vevay waited until they were both asleep again and took another look at the thorns.

Utterly mystified, she went to attend to the waking queen.

# TWENTY-ONE

"Dirxia," Laidley said. "Auravia. Niscena. Toren. How can you concentrate on this when we are about to be attacked?"

"Go on," Nepenthe said tersely.

"Mordicea. All of these existed centuries after Axis did. Cranoth." He raised his eyes again from the list Nepenthe had given him. "The kingdom of Cranoth still existed when the first king of Raine ruled. How can you possibly believe that Kane wrote this book?"

Nepenthe slid her fingers over her eyes. They were cold and trembled slightly. She couldn't get them warm enough lately; it made writing difficult. "What about Cenele?"

"It's old," Laidley said. "But still at least five centuries later than Eben. Axis could never have conquered it."

"Kane says he did."

"Kane is not Kane."

"What if she is? What if he did?"

Laidley tossed the list down, peered at her. "How?" he asked succinctly, and she sighed.

"It doesn't seem likely, does it?"

"No."

"Nor possible."

"Nepenthe." He hesitated. They were sitting on the bed she had made for Bourne, which Laidley took for hers because he had no idea that Bourne was in the library. Bourne, practicing invisibility, was presumably somewhere in the room; Nepenthe had last seen him sitting on a stack of stone tablets. "Nepenthe," Laidley said again, and stuck.

"What?" she said dolefully.

"Are you—You're not taking all this seriously, are you? I mean: Bourne disappearing isn't causing your mind to—well, to—not to mention Ermin of Seale, which is sufficient reason in itself for Bourne to have vanished out of your life. He's either gone to fight with his uncle, or he's trying to protect you. I know you're extremely disturbed and frightened by all this, but you seem to be wandering off into your imagination."

She nodded, twisting her long hair into a rope and gazing fretfully at the list of kingdoms. "I know. It seems."

"Can't you leave the thorns alone for a while?"

"No."

"What about the fish?"

"What about them?"

"Master Croysus has been looking for you. He has waited for you for the last three mornings beside his fish manuscript, hoping you'll appear. The librarians are beginning to wonder about you. Daimon asked me where you work during the day. Leave the thorns and finish his fish for him. Let the librarians know you're still alive and working."

She nodded again, absently. "All right. Laidley, is there any way that you can imagine, just for a moment, looking at life and time and history from a different angle—"

"No," Laidley said, his face crumpled like a wad of paper with concern. "Not without more evidence than that book."

She looked at him then, wrapped her chilly fingers around his wrist. "Evidence. Yes. That would help, wouldn't it. Laidley, find out when they died."

"Axis and Kane?"

"Yes."

"That should be easy enough. And that would convince you?"

Her fingers eased. "It would help."

"If I do this, will you work on the fish and talk to Master Croysus? And to Daimon?"

"Yes," she said, her eyes straying to the book of thorns beside them. She heard Laidley sigh and met his eyes quickly. "Yes," she said again. "I will. Today. Thank you, Laidley."

The midday gong summoned them; he said, "Come to the refectory with me."

"I'll meet you there."

"Come with me. You missed supper last night."

"No, I—" She stopped. She had indeed; she had slipped out later to pilfer food from the kitchens for herself and Bourne.

Laidley showed no signs of leaving without her. She glanced around covertly between strands of hair. No sign of Bourne. "Laidley—"

"Come," he said, getting to his feet. "If you want me to help you, you can't let those thorns skew your life into something unrecognizable. There's enough in Raine to fear already without adding a dead emperor."

He held out his hand. She took it after a moment, allowed him to hoist her to her feet. His face had flushed shyly at the touch; he glanced at her, then away. I have to tell him, she thought. About Bourne. I have to—

"Your hands are cold," Laidley said.

She folded them into fists, followed him out. "I know. Laidley—"

"What?"

If I tell him, she thought, then two of us will know, and it will be twice as dangerous for the three of us.

"What?" he asked again as they wound through the hallways, following the smells of mutton and hot bread.

"Nothing."

She heard Master Croysus's vigorous voice above all the noise in the refectory before they even reached it.

He was standing between the fire and the librarians' table, eating mutton stew and dispensing news at the same time. His eyes flashed at Nepenthe when she entered; he saluted her with his spoon, chewing and talking at the same time.

"The queen's counselors think that her army will stop the

Lord of Seale long before he reaches the plain. They are gambling on it. If he is not stopped and he reaches the plain, then we will all be trapped here."

"Why doesn't she—"

"Because she doesn't dare. If she lets the rulers summon their own armies, they may not be content with fighting only Ermin of Seale. With her army busy elsewhere, any one of them could attack the First Crown." He swallowed visibly, spooned another bite into his mouth. "All this is making me nervous," he added. "I eat more when I'm nervous."

The librarians queried one another silently. Where would we go? their faces asked. How could we rescue thousands of years of writing collected here from every realm that has ever existed?

"The library has been under siege before," Daimon said calmly. "Several times. We bolt the outer doors and tighten our belts."

"It may not come to that, if Ermin of Seale is stopped quickly enough," Master Croysus said.

"Is there any Crown," someone wondered, "absolutely loyal to the First Crown, whose army the queen could depend on to fight for her?"

Everyone thought; nobody answered. Nepenthe, filling her bowl, tried to warm her fingers against the crockery. She sat down; as always, Laidley sat beside her. Someone gusted to her other side, put down a newly-filled bowl.

"There you are," Master Croysus said. "I've been looking for you."

"Yes," she said. "I'm sorry. I've been distracted. I'll work on the fish this afternoon."

"I wish you would. If the queen changes her mind and lets us go, we'll all be in a graceless scramble to get out. I would hate to abandon the fish. Did you figure out what the pearls meant?"

She had to unscramble that hastily. "Oh. No. But it did occur to me that it might be someone's name."

"Possibly, possibly . . ." He was eyeing her strangely; his thoughts were not on the fish. "This afternoon, you will be at your desk?"

"Yes."

"I'll bring that book to show you, then."

"Yes," she said again, wondering what he was talking about. She ate another bite, then stood up, remembering Bourne. "I have to go."

"You just got here," Laidley protested. "You need to eat."

"I'll be back. I left something—my pens—"

"I'll get them."

"No," she said, so sharply that he froze midway up, and the entire table of librarians turned to stare at her. She gazed back at them wordlessly. Daimon broke the silence.

"Ah. Nepenthe. There you are. We were wondering."

"I'll be back," Nepenthe told him breathlessly.

She ran all the way down to the depths of the library, to the dusty, silent chamber where she had left Bourne and the thorns. It seemed empty when she reached it.

"Bourne?" she said hesitantly, anticipating invisible mages everywhere.

"I'm here," he said with equal caution. "Am I invisible?"

"Yes. Where are you?"

Bedclothes shifted. She went to them, tried to sit and bumped into something. "That's my head," Bourne said. "I'm invisible, not incorporeal." He caught her hand, guided her down. "Did you bring me anything to eat?"

She pulled a bread roll out of her pocket. "That's all I could get. Laidley and Master Croysus were sitting with me."

"Thanks."

Air bit into the bread, rendered it invisible bite by bite. She watched mindlessly a moment, then stirred her thoughts. "I'll get something more for you later. Bourne, should I tell Laidley you're here? He thinks—he doesn't know—"

"He thinks that I abandoned you and you need him."

"I do need him. Just not for that."

"So I heard." Both his breath and what was left of the bread roll hung suspended a moment; she guessed he was gazing at something. "Nepenthe. What did you mean when you asked him if he could look at history and time from a different angle? If he could do that, what might he see?"

She pondered that, glimpsing in brief lightning flashes what she saw. What she thought she saw. She drew back from it impatiently, shaking her head. "It makes no sense—it isn't possible."

"What isn't?"

"Nothing. Just—" She pushed cold fingers against her eyes, continued hollowly, "Laidley must be right. Kane couldn't have written the book. It's nothing but epic and history and poetry all jumbled together, much of it from centuries after Axis died. Axis was a magnificent and terrible figure, someone to fear when there's nothing much else on your mind. Maybe it was just a scribe in a library like this one, surrounded by books and stones, loving words but wanting more life in his life—her life—who invented the mythical alphabet of thorns and became Kane and opened every world for Axis to conquer, so that even the scribe's quiet world would not be safe from him."

The bread roll, half-eaten, was suspended in Bourne's fingers. She looked at him a moment before she realized she was seeing him. Then she jumped, and so did he. "Bourne!" she hissed. "You're visible!"

"I am?"

"Go back—do whatever you do—"

His eyes looked very strange, flat and oddly dark. "Is that what you see in those thorns?"

"I don't know yet what I see! That's why I need Laidley's help. Bourne, you can't keep shifting from visible to invisible and back—won't Vevay notice?"

"Possibly." He put the last of the bread in his mouth and chewed slowly, still gazing at her. "No," he said.

"No, what?"

"No, don't tell Laidley I'm here. Even Laidley, honest as he is, is as human as the rest of us."

"What do you—"

"If he knows I'm here, invisible because Vevay is searching for me, he may decide to help himself by helping her. But let him help you. I'll help you, too. Now."

"Now what?"

"Read me what you've translated since I saw you last."

"I can't now." She rose quickly, hovered over him, troubled. "Laidley will come looking for me here, if I don't go back. He might bring Master Croysus. Bourne, you must learn to vanish and stay vanished."

"How can I when you tell me things like that?"

"It's only that," she explained incoherently. "Nothing more than a tale. That's what I was trying to say. Bourne, please—I must go."

He nodded, his eyes still peculiar, glimpsing, it seemed, what she was trying not to say. "Let me read what you've translated while you're gone. It will give me something to do."

She put the papers in order hastily, thrust them at him. "Don't let Laidley see them move," she warned. "And don't forget to hide yourself."

"I won't," he said absently, coiled on the rumpled pallet and already beginning to read again. She sighed noisily and went back to the refectory.

Neither Laidley nor Master Croysus were there. But she had not met them coming, so she guessed that they had gone their ways to work. She ate a few more bites of stew, while filling her pockets with bread and cheese for Bourne. Then she went back to her desk where she had left the fish, determined to finish her work among them before she admitted one more thorn into her head. She stared at the manuscript for a long time before the fish began to speak again, light glancing off their bright colors, their strange marks, drawing her back with them into their underwater mysteries.

She was pondering the last of them, matching fish-words here with fish-shapes there, coming up with sheep and oats and water bags, when she felt Master Croysus displacing air and exuding smells of mutton and smoke around her. She straightened; he dropped a tome on her desk, nearly upending an ink jar.

"Here you are," he said with satisfaction, letting the broad, heavy parchment pages fall open over the fish.

What looked like a sketch of a very old statue looked imperiously back at her on the page. It was little more than a sculpted head growing out of some oddly coiled leaves. The stone hair was thick and wavy, the eyes wide set above broad, curved cheekbones, the nose and jaw at once delicate and predatory. It was no one, Nepenthe decided, who would ever willingly set foot in a library.

"Who is this?"

"You," Master Croysus repeated.

"It is not."

"It looks exactly like you. Isn't that what you see when you look in a mirror?"

She ruffled her hair, trying to remember. "There aren't many mirrors around here. Anyway, who was she?"

"She is ancient. The book itself is at least six centuries old.

It's a history of the writer's travels through obscure parts of his known world. He had a gift for drawing, as you can see by the odd birds and plants and ruins he sketched as he wrote. This section deals with his journey down what he called the Serpent, a great river flowing into the Baltrean Sea. The head is of a princess of what was in ancient times Great Eben."

Nepenthe looked at him mutely, then down at the sketch again. Her eyes felt dry suddenly, oddly gritty, as though the desert sands of Eben had blown across time into the library.

Master Croysus contemplated the head a moment longer, then shut the book with a crash. "I'm glad I remembered that; it's been haunting me since I saw your face and recognized it. Have you finished with my fish?"

"I think so." She pointed at the last of them; her finger shook slightly. "The pearly fish seems to be the name of the owner of several wagon-loads of skins."

"Ah. Why are you trembling?"

"I'm cold."

"Yes. So am I. It comes of perpetual uncertainty." He opened his leather case, laid the fish manuscripts tenderly back into them. "Thank you, Nepenthe. If I ever come back here, I will gladly bring you whatever language is confounding me at the time. If I ever get out of here, that is . . ."

He dropped a few coins onto the desk where the fish had been. She was still sitting there, staring at the newly-minted queen, not wanting to move, not daring to begin to think again, when she heard her name out of nowhere. She started wildly.

Laidley said, "I'm sorry. I didn't mean to startle you. I've been trying for the past hours to find an answer to your question."

"What question?" she whispered.

"About Axis and Kane. About when they died." He shrugged lightly, trying to look untroubled by anything except the carelessness of history. "Nobody wrote it down, that I can find. No final epic battles, no grievous wounds or illnesses, no sorrowing people, no great funerals, no—nothing. For all anybody seems to know, they might never have died."

# TWENTY-TWO

When the emperor finally returned to Eben after his victory in Gilyriad, he followed his predictable patterns. He rested for a few days; he fathered another child, his fifth by now; he tended to the affairs of Eben; he grew restless; he summoned his generals and counselors to pore over the new shape of the map of the world and talk about war; he withdrew into his private chamber with Kane.

He said, "There are no more worlds to conquer on your maps. Find me another map."

Kane had prepared herself for many months for this demand. She had pulled secrets from the works of the witches and ancient poets of Gilyriad; she had read everything she could borrow or steal from lands between Eben and Gilyriad. She had followed wayward rumors of time and magic into impenetrable forests, harsh crags, and deserts all around the Baltrean. Finally she had penetrated the dangerous and enigmatic mysteries of the Labyrinth of the Serpent, in whom time was supposed to begin and end, and which was guarded by sorcerers from other levels of time. She fought them and saw veils of time part as one fled from her relentless power. She followed him.

And so she answered the Emperor of the World, who, for the first time in his life expected to be disappointed: "My lord, I have found you another world."

He looked at her silently. His face was at the peak of its strength and beauty; it became the mask Kane shaped for him to wear for the rest of his life, in all the worlds he conquered. He knew her better than anyone: the tones of her voice, her expressions, what her postures signified, or the folding of her fingers. She alone called him by name. Now she addressed the ruler of the world as his most trusted counselor, and she expected him to treat her words as carefully as she spoke them.

He asked her, "Where?"

She knew him as well, knew by the utter stillness in his face, as the brazier light molded and illumined it, that he had begun, in thought, to venture beyond the world he knew.

"The name of the kingdom is Cranoth."

"Cranoth." He looked down at her as she sat among cushions beside the brazier. They were still dressed; neither had poured wine, nor tasted the sweets and fruit that servants had left there for the emperor. Unspoken mysteries loomed between them; he sensed them, could not move through them until she showed him what it was she saw. "I haven't heard of Cranoth."

She answered, "It does not yet exist."

For a breath or two he was stone; not an eyelash moved,

only the soft golden light searching the curve of his mouth, the faint lines at the corners of his eyes.

Then he crossed the distance between them, had crossed it before she herself began to breathe. He knelt in front of her, his face shedding decades; he was the child on the banks of the Serpent again, his expression rippling with wonder and joy at something she had done. He took her hands, pressed the backs of her palms against his forehead, against his lips. She felt him trembling as he pressed her hands against his heart.

"You can do this for me," he said incredulously. "You can open time."

"I have done it," she said, and told him about following the warrior-mage of the Serpent's Labyrinth into his own land, the northern kingdom of Cranoth.

"But how did you get back?"

"I forced him to show me the way. He spoke to me freely once he understood that he had no choice and that I already had the power; what I wanted was the knowledge. Every moment, he said, is like a wheel with a hundred spokes in it. We ride always at the hub of the wheel and go forward as it turns. We ignore the array of other moments constantly turning around us. We are surrounded by doorways; we never open them. The sorcerers of the Labyrinth have spent centuries studying the mysteries of time, of past and future. Only one of those dedicated to the Serpent is actually from Eben. All the others are from realms scattered through time, who meet at the hub of the Serpent. Some are from our past; most are from our future. They are all connected to the hub of our moment.

This moment. The next moment becomes a different hub; the spokes will lead to different moments. If every moment is a world, and worlds change with every changing moment then you, my emperor, will never be without a world to conquer, for as long as you desire."

He swallowed, mute again, still trembling at the richness and immensity of the gift she had given him.

"How?" he asked finally, for he was his father's son and liked to see his battles clearly before he fought them.

"I will open each spoke of time and explore the realm it leads me to. That way, I can judge which lands will be worth conquering."

"And my army?"

"Where I can go, so can you, and so will your great army. It will flow through time and appear without warning anywhere you choose. It will be as though you come out of the sky, or the wind. And you can return always to the moment you left. You could conquer fifty realms and come back each time to this fire in the brazier, to the candle burned this far, to this untouched goblet. No one will ever pursue you, you can take whatever you want, keep the land under your rule if you choose, or leave behind only your name for the rulers to quake over and the poets to add to the history of their world."

Axis filled the untouched goblet with a hefty splash of wine, drained it. His face still seemed shaken, vulnerable. But Kane felt his own enormous powers, his strength and fearlessness, his unending ambition to find death and conquer it or become it, which, poets said later, became the same thing in the end.

He set the cup down and took Kane's hands again. "You are the Empress of Time," he breathed, kissing her fingers one by one.

"No, I am Kane. The Hooded One. The faceless sorcerer who does your bidding always, who exists to serve you."

"Yes," he agreed. "Always. Every time I ask, you have already answered. You give me what I want before even my heart has named it."

"I do," she said, watching his bowed head as he crouched in front of her, the Lion of Eben, kissing her knees now, sliding the sandals from her feet.

"Kings reward their servants for a few moments of work," he said, his mouth against one instep. "How can I begin to reward you for every moment you have given me?"

She lifted his face between her hands to find his eyes again. She told him.

Some time after that, she found her way back through time to the northern kingdom of Cranoth.

This time, she did not pursue a mage to get there; she went alone to see for herself. She had learned the most carefully guarded secret of the mages of the Serpent: the pattern of the Labyrinth of Time, which she must follow to find her way out of her own time. She had wrested the pattern from the sorcerer's mind. It burned now like a brand in her own: the path out of the Hub of Time to the infinite spokes in the Wheel. In Axis's private chamber, she walked the pattern and opened the Gates of Nowhere to Cranoth.

She found herself in a prosperous city surrounded on three

sides by rich farmland and on the fourth by a river thick with a flock of gaudy boats and barges. She wandered through the lively city streets, hearing a language that made no sense to her ears, but which she could understand well enough if she listened to its images and feelings with her mind and heart. It was there that she first heard of the land west of Cranoth, the little realm between sea and sky on the edge of the world, hardly worth thinking about then, but the name lingered in her mind. Its queen, Mermion, she heard in passing at a book-stall, liked to collect books. She went on, through the crowded cobbled streets until she found at last the palace of the rulers of Cranoth. She paused among a crowd of idlers at its gates and saw the guards in their elegant armor, the nobles riding fine horses adorned with jeweled bridles and cunningly wrought stirrups. As she stood there, she envisioned the cheerful sky above them rent as by a silent lightning bolt, torn apart to reveal a swarm of faceless riders pouring endlessly into the fields around the city, while those within the walls, busy buying books, selling fruit, riding their haughty steeds, stopped what they were doing, looking puzzled at first, and then incredulous and finally aghast at what had come out of Nowhere into their peaceful afternoon.

Kane walked the Labyrinth back to Eben and told Axis what she had seen.

*The Emperor of Night*
*Stopped the sun, held the moon in the sky*
*Over the King's City in Cranoth.*

*Between the sun and the moon*
*His dark army flowed like water*
*Flooding the fields, climbing the walls,*
*Spilling everywhere into the streets.*
*Those within found nowhere to run.*
*There is nowhere to run from night,*
*Nowhere to hide from time,*
*And the Twins who rule them both.*

Axis returned his army to Gilyriad after overwhelming the
King of Cranoth and razing the walls of his city. His army,
dazed with the sorcery, with the possibilities of fame and
wealth, shouted his name across the plains of Gilyriad from
dusk to dawn until their voices were gone. When he returned
once again to Eben, he brought gifts of jewels and wondrously
embroidered cloth for his wife, and golden spurs for his children. Thus the queen was appeased by his absence. She had
little knowledge of the shape of the world. He told her that he
had conquered Cranoth, and she assumed that it was where
he said it was: west and far north of Eben, a chilly place un-
suitable to raise children in.

The queen spent her days in the courtyard with the fountains
and peacocks, her many children, attendants, courtiers, and a
lover or two among them. Masked, darkly dressed as always,
Kane watched them from a distance and remembered the days
when she conjured doves out of goblets to make the children
laugh. Sometimes, in Axis's private chamber, even in the circle
of his arms, she woke at night and wondered if she could have

led a different life. If she had not wrapped herself up and given herself, body and heart, to Axis on his wedding day. Perhaps by now she might have reclined at ease among her own peacocks, nibbling dates stuffed with almonds and crying to her children not to step on the peacocks' tails. She had spoken to no one but Axis for years. Her own family had grown resigned to her disappearance. Outside of that chamber, she was the mute, faceless, awkward, and formidably powerful sorcerer Kane, who, everyone knew, loved Axis with a helpless, childlike love, and who would have followed him into his tomb.

The second kingdom Axis rode the Labyrinth of the Serpent to conquer was called Gedron. Its nomad king was a fierce marauder himself, like Axis, appearing where he was least expected along the borders of his realm of steppes and plains to slay, plunder, and disappear again, along with herds and flocks, children to be used for slaves, and whatever other wealth his army could carry. Kane was careful to keep herself invisible in his city. It was a city of colorful tents thrown up across a plain; all around it animals pastured on the rich summer grasses. Guards ringed it, watching for trouble and checking the contents of the occasional merchant's caravan that wandered through. Passing one of the caravans, Kane heard again a name she remembered from Cranoth: that of the little northern kingdom whose queen collected books.

It wasn't so small anymore. Now its king ruled five other kingdoms, five Crowns, they were called; the palace perched on the edge of the world had grown huge, and there was a school of magic or sorcery nearby that attracted students from many lands. The merchant from whom Kane overheard all this was haggling for some books that had gotten mixed in with plunder from the latest raid along the Gedron border. Apparently the nobles of Gedron had no use for them. A bargain was struck; books passed from hand to hand, bound for the royal library in the north.

Kane did not mention the kingdom of Five Crowns when she returned to Eben and to Axis. But again, she remembered.

The battle between the Lion of Eben and the Wolf-King of Gedron was swift and bloody. The King of Gedron, furious at being surprised, was equally curious. He wanted such power for himself and made every effort to capture Axis and Kane alive. Of course he had no hope of victory, for the army out of Gilyriad was truly numberless as the stars by then. His tents were flattened, his flocks scattered, his rich plunder taken, before Axis vanished back into Nowhere, leaving the king surrounded by his dead on the plain and wondering what had hit him.

In Gilyriad, as Axis's army shouted and drank and sang the emperor's praises, and the Lion of Eben paced his sumptuous chambers dreaming of more worlds to conquer, Kane looked out a window at the silent, enigmatic moon. She thought of the distant northerly kingdom with its library and its mages' school, its palace overlooking the edge of the world.

Raine.

She knew that night that Axis had given her all that she asked in return for her gifts to him of worlds and time and her life: She was carrying his child.

# TWENTY-THREE

The Queen of Raine sat on the last of the cliff steps, listening. Far beneath her, the gray sea roiled and frothed against the cliffs. Gulls wheeled and cried in winds strong enough to hammer the long zigzag line of steps carved out of the face of the rock a little deeper into the stone. Tessera didn't feel the winds, nor did she hear the breaking waves or birds. Deaf as a barnacle burrowed into its shell, she had made herself. Something enclosed, clinging to the cliff, untroubled by cold or wind; she might have drawn the cliff around her like a cloak. As though testing here, there, for the heartbeat in a stone, she let her mind wander in a timeless, wordless moment, throughout the living thing built into stone that was her palace.

She had stopped searching for thorns some time ago. She had relinquished the word. It got in the way; it did not mean what it said. She listened now for something that did not belong to Raine. Something that did not breathe Raine, whose heart was not steeped, like these ancient stones, in the history of Raine. Occasionally, deep within her solitude, her whole body so intent on Raine that it was scarcely visible except as stone, she sensed the flickering images within the Dreamer's heart, and knew that she had touched even the dead in her search.

When she heard Vevay's summons, she had to remember that she had eyes. She opened them and found she had bones again, and hair, and skin beneath a cloak that had been drenched by a passing squall some time ago. The mage's summons was wordless; it was as though she had opened a window into Tessera's thoughts and peered inside for a moment, looking for her. Tessera stood up, a small living thing now, not part of the immense, stolid pile that grew out of the cliff above her. Some part of her still searched, wandered down chimney stones, drifted through closed doors like air, feeling for something unfamiliar, something amiss. The rest of her, shivering in the damp air, trudged back up the steps to the palace.

She found Vevay in her tower, gazing into a silver bowl of water. Tessera went to her side. Rank after rank of warriors, silent and grim in the rain, marched across the surface of the water. Their tunics bore the linked double circlets of the Second Crown. She couldn't see their faces clearly in the bowl, and what she did see was apt to disappear too soon, leaving headless soldiers moving into the silver.

She raised her eyes after a time to the casement above the

bowl. Vevay's spell, permeating the water, translated itself easily to the glass; the window was broader, and she could see more.

"You have called for an assembly before supper today," Vevay told her, still intent on the images in the bowl. "You will speak to your nobles, tell them that you will permit them to leave as soon as the threat from the Second Crown has been eliminated. You will tell them where Ermin of Seale is now: marching through the Sevine Valley, following the river toward the plain. And you will tell them that the army of the First Crown will come out of the hills west of the valley to stop him before he reaches Dreamer's Plain."

Tessera nodded absently. The mage found Ermin a threat. To Tessera he was insignificant, a problem to occupy the mind when the enormity of the question of thorns became overwhelming. Vevay, not hearing an answer, glanced at her. What, a week earlier, might have caused the mage's voice to tighten with frustration, only elicited a curious question.

"What are you looking at?"

"The army," Tessera said. "You can see more faces in the glass."

"Really?" Vevay watched the movement across the casement. "So you can," she murmured. "Though I find the light distracting. Who taught you to do that?"

"You did."

"I did?"

"I took your spell from the water."

"Oh." She looked back into the bowl, as though expecting to find the spell floating like a paper boat on the water. "What was I saying?"

"My army will stop the army of the Second Crown before it reaches the plain," Tessera said perfunctorily.

"Good. Gavin and Ermin of Seale's uncle and half a dozen nobles rode across the plain to try to negotiate peace with Ermin before he does something irrevocably stupid. You sent them early this morning; I couldn't find you to tell you that."

"Do I tell the assembly that?"

"Yes. It might calm a few nerves. Where have you been all morning?"

"Searching for thorns."

Vevay touched her eyes delicately, as though she felt a sudden twinge. "They do make Ermin moot," she breathed.

"Yes."

"But at least Ermin is a threat everyone can understand. If you told your court to beware of thorns, they would be more likely to beware of you." She brooded at the water, her brows puckered deeply. "You'd think the dead, if they are going to bother to wake after centuries to warn you about something, would be more explicit."

"She dreamed them," Tessera guessed. "Dreams don't speak in words. Maybe the thorns aren't thorns."

"Maybe," Vevay answered grimly, "but it's the only word we've got. There's Ermin of Seale among his generals."

Tessera watched a small group of riders cross the glass: generals, guards, standard-bearers. In the midst of them rode the impetuous leader, a big man with graying yellow hair, his face furrowed and dripping. Following him was a boy who looked scarcely older than Tessera. He carried a trumpet slung on a strap over his shoulder. His calm, secret face, under milky-gold hair, was lowered against the rain. He reminded Tessera of someone.

"Who is that?" she asked curiously.

"Which?"

"The trumpeter. Look, he's carrying something in his pouch."

The leather pouch beneath the boy's trumpet shifted and bulged oddly. He spoke a word, still gazing ahead, and slid a finger into the pouch to stroke whatever was stirring.

"Do you know who he is?" Tessera asked again.

"I believe he is one of Ermin's grandsons. His father is locked up in my tower, below us. I can't believe Ermin would risk him on the battlefield. But then he is risking everything else he has, why not his grandchildren, too?"

"He reminds me of someone . . ." She watched him, wondering what pet he kept in his pouch. He had two fingers burrowed into it now, his light eyes narrowed a little against the rain, watchful but not afraid of what he was riding toward. An unfamiliar feeling grew in Tessera as she stood there. Words ripened in her mind like strange fruit, crowded into her mouth. She wanted, more than anything else, to speak to that boy with the calm, gentle face and the pale eyelashes, ask him what he kept in his pouch that comforted him as he rode toward death. She wanted his eyes to see her; she wanted to hear his voice.

"I remember." Her own voice sounded strange to her ears, but Vevay did not seem to notice anything. "He reminds me of the young man I met in the wood."

"Bourne," Vevay murmured dourly. "Yes. They would be cousins."

"Do you know his name?"

She felt Vevay look at her then, sharply. But the mage only answered equably, "I can't remember it. If Gavin and your nobles manage to negotiate peace, perhaps you can ask him yourself."

Tessera watched the boy cross the window. Peace seemed a meaningless concept, what with the invisible monster roused and turning its eyes toward Raine while Ermin rode obliviously across its battlefield, insisting on his little war. The boy with the pet in his pouch might die like the hare in the wood for his uncle's folly, or he might survive one battle only to face the enormity of the powers that had wakened the warrior-queen of Raine. He rode beyond the window frame toward his fate. Tessera turned restively, thinking, I will never know his name or hear his voice if he dies.

"Where are you going?" Vevay asked as she opened the door.

"To search."

Vevay studied her bowl; the scene in the window shifted. She was watching for Gavin, Tessera guessed. "Don't forget the assembly," the mage murmured. "It may seem unimportant compared to the greater threat, but we can only deal with what we can see. We don't want an insurrection within the

palace as well. Your nobles are very powerful, and if you ab-
dicate your own power over them, they will remove your
crown one way or another. How you deal with Ermin now will
show them how you would deal with them if they attack. It is
vital for you to make these things clear."

"Yes, Vevay," Tessera said absently. The mage sighed.

"Call me if you need me."

Tessera did not go far, only to the tower roof, where she
stood among the snapping pennants and explored the complex, busy world beneath her feet. Her thoughts flowed down-
ward into the stones; she rooted herself there, impervious as a
pennant-pole to the weather. Like the thorns in the giant's
house, she crept everywhere, looking for illumination. In the
wood, the mages searched their accumulated knowledge of
both magic and Raine. The queen roamed as far as she could
within her own boundaries, within the world she knew.

It seemed a small thing when she finally found it. As small
as a thorn. It had hidden itself in the center of the massive cliff:
a bramble growing in the heart of solid stone. A mind like a
dark night-flower bloomed where there was no one to see it. A
poisoned flower in a garden full of flowers. A single deadly
word in the midst of an uncountable number of harmless
words. She did not know what shape it took inside her palace;
she only knew the shape and feel of the dreamlike image in her
heart: a dark star in the center of her world, its power con-
tained now, quiet and secret. It was an unspoken word, an unopened flower, a dream of itself. But it had wakened the dead,
and the living queen sensed if she did not stop it now, it would

explode and blaze in an incandescent fire across the whole of Raine.

She stirred on the rooftop, felt the wind again, her tangled hair. She still sensed the strange power, a seething smudge of dark in her heart. Somewhere in the palace it was, a small unnoticed thing in that immense place, eluding even the mages' acute attention. Tessera, who understood small, unnoticed, powerful things, climbed down the tower steps and went looking for it.

She moved through most of her palace without attracting attention. Only partly visible, preoccupied, and wearing her blandest expression, she persuaded everyone that, if they saw her, she must be there on the most unimportant business and should be ignored. In Vevay's tower room, the mage was busy talking to Gavin's face in the bowl and did not notice the queen at all. There, Tessera felt the troubling power as little more than a slumbering ember. She left without disturbing Vevay, went down again, and down, making her way ever more deeply into stone. As she moved, she sensed the unfamiliar power quickening, burning now, taking its dark fires from the source.

The queen found herself in the library.

She had never been there. If she wanted a book, like everything else it was brought to her. She passed librarians and scholars and scribes, working among what seemed every book or scroll or tablet ever written since the beginning of the world. Language itself might have begun there, she thought; it grew everywhere in those stony burrows, crusting the walls like some kind of ancient life. The dark fire in her heart, the unspoken word, burned unwaveringly down there. She wandered erratically, looking into every book-lined hollow. Are you there? her heart asked. There? No one noticed the queen in their midst; she might have been just another word.

In a chamber far beneath the earth, a stone room full of stone words, she found the thorns.

Her heart recognized them before her eyes realized what they saw: an open book with thorns on every page. She touched them, felt her heart grow confused, desperate, distressed. Beware, they said to her, in the voice of the dreaming warrior. Beware. The room was empty. There was a pallet along one wall, with disheveled blankets. The book lay on a stack of tablets used, apparently, as a desk. Beside the book were pens, jars of ink, a stack of papers. Someone, Tessera guessed, was in the midst of translating the language of thorns. Who? she wondered. Who living in that world within the stones bore so much malice to Raine? Who could work so quietly with such dangerous powers without being harmed by them, and unnoticed by librarians or mages? What formidable enemy did she have living down here in the library, plotting to destroy her realm?

The queen sat down on the stone tablets, picked up the nameless scribe's papers, and read them while she waited.

Hours later she still waited, as silent as one of the old slabs around her and invisible to everyone except the living, luminous eye of history open and watching for the slightest movement from her.

Axis and Kane, she thought numbly. Axis and Kane.

The names were among those that had littered her mind like fallen leaves, learned early in her life and discarded when she achieved enough perspective to realize that they could no longer trouble the world. They were dead, forgotten, harmless as words chiseled on a broken tombstone.

"Axis and Kane," she whispered, and felt the dark wind of their power blowing through her heart.

The tale had ended abruptly at a disturbing shift of pronoun. The pen, lying across the unfinished sentence, had leaked a pool of black instead of the next word. The jar of ink stood open. The transcriptor, startled by something, perhaps her own writing, had gone and not returned. Nothing, not even the assembly she was probably missing, not even Ermin of Seale at her door, could have made Tessera move, not until she saw for herself how the tale would end for Raine.

She recognized the dangerous transcriptor easily, of the two that finally entered with their arms piled with scrolls. "N," the ink jars said, and "Nepenthe" was what the lanky, thin-haired young man called her. His eyes were anxious, but Nepenthe's looked stunned and desperate, in an elegant, unusual face that might have been molded in forgotten eons of history. Tessera, watching her narrowly, saw not the formidable, malicious mage she had expected, but a young woman who, in troubling Raine, had managed to trouble herself beyond all expectation.

"Don't despair, Nepenthe," the young man said softly, even as his own voice shook a little.

"That's not my name," she said tautly, dropping scrolls on

the floor. She sank down to unroll them; the parchment trembled in her fingers.

"It's the only name you know. You should finish it."

"No. They're dead. They must be dead. Laidley, don't stop looking."

"Nep—" He stopped himself, then continued doggedly, "How will you know exactly what you have to fear until you finish the translation? It may reveal something completely unpredictable. It might even explain itself away somehow, tell us that it was not Kane at all who wrote the story, that someone else imagined the whole thing."

Nepenthe, opening one scroll after another, did not seem to be listening. "Laidley, none of these are about Axis at all. They must have been put on the wrong shelves. They're old legal documents dealing with property."

She began to gather them up again with wild haste; Laidley coaxed them out of her hands.

"I'll take them back. I think I know where the ones we want must be. You finish the tale."

"No."

"Nepenthe, we've been searching for hours to find out how they died, and it seems they never did. Maybe the book can tell us what truly happened to them."

"No," she said again, fiercely. "Don't argue with me. I'm right about this."

"What if you're not?" he asked on his way out. His voice floated back down the hall behind him. "And how can you bear not to know how it ends?"

Nepenthe paced as she waited for him. Her path between turns grew shorter and shorter until, Tessera saw with sympathy, she seemed to be turning circles in the middle of the floor.

Finish it, the queen told her silently. Laidley is right. We will not know all there is to fear until you do.

As though Nepenthe heard, she stopped her futile circling to face the open book.

She moved toward it slowly, one soundless step at a time, as though she were trying not to awaken some terrifying monster. She reached out, touched the pen lightly with her fingertips. Just as noiselessly, Tessera moved off the stack of slabs she sat on and went to watch over the transcriptor's shoulder as she finally picked up the pen.

# TWENTY-FOUR

Bourne wended his slow way out of the depths of the library to the top of the highest tower in the palace.

He could think of no other way to find Vevay. Neither desire nor need would fashion a path to her. He had no desire to see her at all, and was not sure which he feared more: the mage or what he needed to tell her. She would feel him looking for her, he thought, and find him first. He only hoped desperately that she would let him speak before she stopped him from wandering in secret under the queen's roof by tossing him over the cliff.

It took hours, it seemed, after he left the library, to find the mage's tower. He was never certain of remaining invisible from one moment to the next. In the library it hardly mattered, since everyone there had their faces in books. But he didn't want to disturb already jittery courtiers and tense guards by appearing out of nowhere in front of them. He measured his invisibility constantly in the eyes and expressions of those he passed. No one seemed to notice him; even if they saw him, he must look like just one more in a place full of weary and perturbed guests who had long exhausted every welcome except the one to leave.

He wandered in the maze of palace expanded through the centuries like a seashell constantly growing new chambers around itself. Finally, by sheer luck, he found the tower as he followed a pair of guards, hoping they would let fall something useful to him as they talked. They led him into what looked like an ancient portion of the palace, with tiny windows and thick, drafty hallways. Then they climbed stairs endlessly up into more recent history, where the stones were carefully cut and mortared and the windows on both sides overlooked sea and plain as well as courtyard walls. At a thick doorway, guarded by another pair, they stopped. Bourne saw stairs spiraling farther upward to one side of the door. Another tower, he guessed, this one not so old as some and promising even giddier views.

The guards saluted one another, the pair at the door moving aside with relief.

"Any trouble?" one of the guards Bourne had followed asked.

"They demand to see the queen. They demand to see Vevay. They demand paper, pens, visitors, and more blankets. They complain that their food is always cold by the time it reaches the tower."

The guard gave an unsympathetic grunt. "So is ours," he said, and took his place beside the door.

"Any news?"

"Ermin of Seale is marching along the Sevine to the plain."

Bourne, feeling his skin constrict, shifted into shadow. My family, he thought numbly. This is where they locked away my brothers and cousins.

He glanced at his hands, wondering if he had shocked himself out of his own spell. He couldn't tell. He took a soundless step into torch light. The guards paid him no attention.

"Is the mage upstairs?"

"Who knows, with mages? But we haven't seen her pass."

They didn't seem to see Bourne either, as he slunk across their vision in the circle of fire and reached the shadowy stairs.

He began to climb.

The mage lived so high that Bourne could practically see into the Sevine Valley across the chain of hills to the east, where his pigheaded uncle was marching. So high that his thoughts seemed to fall dizzyingly away from him, leaving only fear and determination, and a nagging sense of the futility of trying to explain himself. But he had no choice. There was no choice. There was only —

"Thorns," he breathed, as the mage's door flew open at the top of the stairs and he stood face-to-face with Vevay.

She did not look surprised to see him. She gripped his arm, pulled him firmly into her comfortable aerie, and closed the door.

"I've been watching you for hours," she said dourly. "I thought you were searching for the door out of here, or for your family. I didn't expect you to come up here."

"I've been searching for you."

That did surprise her. Her gray eyes grew a shade less frosty, and then began to darken, color seeping up from beneath the melting ice. "What was that you said," she demanded, "when I opened the door?"

"Thorns," he said starkly. "I know what they are."

Her brows leaped upward. Her fingers tightened on his arm. She pushed him backward, guiding him into a chair, looking, he thought as he sat heavily, as though she were swelling visibly with words, and when one finally came out he might be forced to duck.

"That book," she snapped finally. "Isn't it?"

"How do you — how did you — "

"I've been watching you since you came here. What do you think the rulers of Raine keep mages for?"

"But why didn't you come for me?" he asked bewilderedly.

"Because I didn't."

"You have the rest of my family imprisoned in your tower."

"Never mind that," she commanded, so he didn't. She sat opposite him, her hands linked very tightly, keeping herself from flying apart, he guessed. "Watching you," she repeated, "and listening to you."

"In that chamber?" he interrupted, appalled, thinking of Nepenthe.

"It's far past time to hide things, Bourne. Or protect them. When did you sense the power in the book?"

"I didn't. But it had an odd effect on Nepenthe. The young woman who was translating—who—"

"Yes."

"I still don't understand that. And she herself is beginning to be uneasy. But she doesn't understand it either—"

"Neither do I," Vevay said succinctly. "Do you know what you're talking about?"

He nodded. "I think—I think so. I'm talking about Axis and Kane. And about the thorns you told Felan were only the beginning of trouble, and the brambles that the warrior in the wood showed to Tessera." He hesitated, wondering suddenly how in the world to make her believe him, wondering why anybody would.

"Axis and Kane." Her eyes were growing cold again, color-less. "They've been dead for thousands of years."

"Have they?"

"What do you mean?"

"According to Laidley—" he began carefully.

"Who is Laidley?"

"One of the transcriptors. He's been helping Nepenthe. He told her that none of the poets who wrote epics about Axis and Kane ever described how they died."

Vevay closed her eyes, touched them. "It's very odd how those two names, even at a time like this, have such a soporific effect on me."

"Do they?" Bourne said hollowly. "They terrify me."

She looked at him again, silently. "All right," she said. "Axis and Kane. I'm listening."

"They became puzzled—Laidley and Nepenthe—"

"Laidley and—yes."

"About why Kane kept writing about Axis conquering kingdoms that didn't exist when he ruled—or when everyone thinks he ruled."

Her eyes quickened with a touch of interest. "Kane wrote that book?"

"Yes. She was an immensely powerful sorceress—"

"Kane was a man," Vevay protested. "If your Nepenthe could not even translate that much correctly—"

"Kane was a woman," Bourne said steadily. "One of Axis's cousins, who loved Axis and fought beside him all her life. That's why she never permitted anyone to see her face. She became the Masked Sorceress. The Hooded One."

Vevay's face seemed suddenly masklike now. "Go on."

"If you read her book, you get a clear sense of Axis's power. What he wants he conquers. No one ever defeats him. Ever. With Kane, he conquered all the kingdoms he knew about that surrounded his own land. And when he had nothing new to conquer, Kane discovered the enormous kingdom to the east—Gilyriad. His army swarmed over that and he took it. And after Gilyriad, he ran out of lands, so Kane opened time itself to him."

"Opened time."

"Yes. I know it sounds—" He gestured helplessly.

"Go on."

"So that he could take any land he wanted for his empire, even centuries into the future. He would appear out of nowhere—the Gates of Nowhere—with his army as numberless as the stars, and Kane the Hooded One beside him, opening time, turning night into day with her power, and he would utterly overwhelm those who fought him, plunder their wealth, decimate their cities, and vanish again, leaving desolation behind him."

Vevay regarded him fixedly, like an old owl on a stump, giving no hint of which way her thoughts turned. "And you think Axis has his eye on Raine."

"Kane. She chooses; he invades."

"How long has this book been rattling around the Twelve Crowns in the back of a trader's wagon?"

"I don't know."

"No. Nor do you, I suppose, know why an orphaned transcriptor in the depths of the royal library can translate it when none of the mages could."

"It's her profession. She was trained for that."

"The librarians couldn't decipher it either? So they gave it to Nepenthe?"

"No. She—" He swallowed. "I gave it to her to take to the librarians, but she kept it. The librarians never saw it."

The owl blinked; Vevay leaned forward a little in her chair. "So we have one mysterious book in an alphabet of thorns, one young transcriptor who alone can read it, and the threat it portends of a king who conquered his known world three thousand years ago, alive and well and about to attack Raine."

Bourne's hands closed on the arms of his chair. He said tautly, "I know it sounds—"

"Yes. It sounds extremely suspect. I've looked at that book twice, and if there was ever any magic in it, it's about as quiescent as the long-dead magic in the names of Axis and Kane." She raised a hand at Bourne's indrawn breath. "Two things bewilder me. The thorns themselves, which, if we discount the book entirely, still troubled the Dreamer enough to wake and warn us of them."

"The Dreamer—" His voice rose incredulously. "The Dreaming King woke?"

"Queen. She warned Tessera of—" She stopped short at the quick flash of power that echoed Bourne's astonishment. "You really must learn to control that. It reveals you."

"Mermion was a queen?"

"Tessera said the Dreamer was an armed warrior-queen, very tall, with a beautiful face and long pale hair."

"Like the rider she saw in the wood that day."

"Yes."

"Warning her of thorns."

"Yes."

Bourne's hands twisted the chair arms, leaving smudges of light on the wood. "And the second thing?"

"What?"

"You said two things bewilder you."

"Yes. The second thing is: Why would a young woman, inventing a story for herself out of a language nobody else knows how to read, choose to unbury that hoary, antiquated tale? Axis and Kane . . ." Her voice trailed away; she contemplated some memory.

"What is it?" he asked, feeling his own face grow taut with dread.

"I did, too," she answered surprisedly. "I unearthed that tale for Gavin one night before the queen's coronation. Axis and Kane. I couldn't remember how they died, either . . ." She shivered slightly, as at an errant breeze, then looked past memory at Bourne again. "Are you very brave?" she wondered. "Or just very calculating to come to me with this?"

He regarded her silently a moment, and then himself, trying to see through her eyes and marveling at what she found in him. "I'm terrified," he said simply, "that I might be right. And if I am right, then I am terrified of the answer to another question: Why Nepenthe? She is obsessed with this tale. She won't let anyone else study her thorns; she is frightened, too, but she can't stop herself. She wants the ending to this tale. I'm afraid of the ending."

Vevay stood up, paced a step or two. "I've never heard such unlikely nonsense in my life."

"I don't suppose you have."

"And how could we possibly fight a three-thousand-year-old king leading an army as numberless as stars who comes out of nowhere without warning —"

"I don't know."

"And why Nepenthe?" She whirled, paced back to him. "Where is Nepenthe now?"

"Probably with the thorns in the library."

"I looked at those thorns. They were nothing. Shapes. They said nothing to me. There was no warning in them. I felt no power."

"They're just words," Bourne said carefully. "They tell a powerful story."

"To Nepenthe."

"Yes." She was silent again; he watched her as she stood thinking, her face a waning moon's profile within her white hair. "Well," she said finally, "they are the only thorns causing any kind of disturbance anywhere in Raine that I can see. The queen went searching for thorns some hours ago, and I've spent the last hour searching everywhere for her. Perhaps she saw what I couldn't in Nepenthe's book. Let's find out."

# TWENTY-FIVE

The child of Axis and Kane was conceived in the king's secret chamber in Eben, and born in Gilyriad. For several
months before the birth, Kane, who refused to risk her unborn
child on the battlefield, walked the private, scented royal gardens in Gilyriad alone. Axis had left his consort and his army
to return to Eben and attend to affairs of state. If Kane had
asked him, he would have stayed with her. But she did not
ask: it was far more prudent for him to go home for a while,
placate the queen and see to his land. He would soon grow
restless, she knew. But even great lions must wait for their
prey with calm and patience; so he must wait in Eben, until
Kane could give her attention once again to his battles.

In Gilyriad, Kane hid her condition well. She played the
shy and monstrously ugly sorcerer at every moment, so that
the wind breathed never a hint to Axis's army that its Masked
Sorcerer, who led them over the battlements of time itself, was

a young woman and pregnant with their emperor's child. When the time grew close and she wanted help, Kane left the palace. A dark-haired, barefoot woman dressed in patched linens sought aid from the ancient wood-witches. Her accent was peculiar, but the witches were nearly deaf, and anyway didn't need to be told much. They took her into a shadowy hovel, laid her beside a fire scented with herbs and lavender. There her child was born, amid the delighted laughter of snag-toothed witches. The child of a noblewoman of Eben and the Emperor of the World and Time.

Their daughter.

Before the birth, as Kane wandered through the royal gardens, she gave a great deal of thought to the immediate future. The child must remain a secret. There was no room either in Axis's public or private life, or on any battlefield for a child. It could not even be allowed to cry within the royal palace in Gilyriad. Kane could not nurse it there. No one could know about it, for she could trust no one not to gossip. That Kane was not a man but a woman, and had been Axis's lover for years, and now carried his child, was a tale that would lose no time crossing the trade routes out of Gilyriad and finding its way to the emperor's lands around the Baltrean. And from there to the queen's ear in Eben. What she would do, Kane had no idea. The queen assumed that Axis had his lovers. But she had never been faced with the fact that he actually loved anyone. The discovery of such passion and devotion that had taken root long before her marriage and had flourished under her own nose for years after it might inspire such bitterness in the queen as would tear apart Eben, the land Axis loved most. Eben was the foundation stone of his empire. He had already battled to meld Great Eben and Lower Eben into one inseparable state. If the queen inspired her lovers with ambitions and promises to aid them, the foundation stone would crumble. And the emperor would be forced to turn his attention from all the worlds he had not conquered to battle to keep the one he had together.

In the gardens, before the child was born, Kane realized clearly what scant months she and the child would have together before she must leave it and take her customary place at Axis's side. Sitting in the soft green shade, hawks crying in the pellucid blue above her head, she let her thoughts take her here, there, roaming all the kingdoms she had found for Axis, trying to think what would be best for the three of them. She examined every option, including taking the child and disappearing out of Axis's life. But she could not leave him. Nor could she unmask herself and live openly with Axis as his battlesorcerer and consort, and the mother of his child. The emperor's wife would never allow such an interloper to come between Axis and her own heirs to his magnificent empire. It would shatter the peace between them and break their tacit contract: that the queen would be first at his side in the eyes of the world. For that, she had yielded him his heart, never suspecting that he had given it away long before he even knew he had it.

What to do, what to do . . .

The glimmerings of an idea came to her, not whole and

clear, but piece by piece as the slow, tranquil days passed. If she could not raise the child, then someone must . . . in some secret place where the Queen of Eben could never find it, where no one would have the slightest inkling of the circumstances of its birth . . . But under such circumstances that it would find no valuable place in the world while it was raised and educated. It must feel the lack of its proper heritage until Kane returned for it . . . It must be well-educated, exposed even to the magical arts, for it would be the child of a sorceress and an emperor, and in such a mingling of enormous powers, who knew what abilities it might inherit . . . Above all, it must be safe . . .

Alone with her unborn child, these anxious thoughts filling her mind, she faced the uncertainty of their future. She began to write then, both to herself and to the child. Missing Axis, she wrote of him to soothe her longing, and to explain both herself and him to their child. She wrote in the language of their childhood so that no one chancing upon it would be able to read it and expose her. She set her own magic into the letters, so that they would come alive only for her child. Only her child, sensing Kane in every letter, would respond, for the magic would be in its own blood as well. Anyone else would see only a puzzling alphabet and feel no more than curiosity. Her child's heart would recognize the language of Kane.

She carried the little book with her into the woods when her time came, for that language was all she had of Axis to comfort her.

The court at Gilyriad was accustomed to the sorcerer's unpredictable wanderings; no one there questioned his absence. Axis was too far away to know how far she went when she left his world. She took only their daughter, the book, and a few practical gifts from the witches. She wandered through time, staying here for a week, there for a month, her face unmasked, her hair unbound, a passing stranger in every land. She worked small magics, did some healing, performed a few tricks to earn money for food and a bed. At no time did she attract more than a temporary interest in her powers. She had left the Masked Sorcerer in another world. No poets would have noticed the gypsy walking in their midst, the curly-haired child watching the world over her shoulder with great eyes that were sometimes one color, sometimes another, depending on the light. Kane herself did her best to forget her own name. Remembering who she was in her own world meant remembering that she must leave her child.

In her alphabet she could not find a thorn sharp enough to say that. Language would have to turn to thorn in her throat, come out in bloody words for her to say that. So she wandered, trying not to think, until at last she remembered Raine.

There on a cliff, she found the immense palace of the rulers of Raine. What had encompassed five Crowns the last time she looked had now become Twelve Crowns, ruled by a shrewd and vigorous king. With her secret ways, she explored the mages' school in the wood, the palace, and the great royal library within the cliff. There, she learned, the librarians took in orphans and raised them as scribes. They grew up among all the wealth of the accumulated knowledge of the world.

They were well treated, valued for their skills, and encouraged to stay there; if they left the library they must make their own way in the world, for no one else claimed them.

Kane felt the thorns begin to grow in her throat, for it was there, on that plain so high above the sea that she could not hear the waves, that she must do the unthinkable thing. The one tattered, threadbare comfort she took in the deed she contemplated was the powerful and magical kingdom that she had found. This one, she would ask Axis to take for her and for their daughter. In this place, Kane could go unmasked at last, and their daughter would be openly acknowledged; she could freely love both Axis and their child for the rest of her life.

Only that thought gave her the courage to do what she must. She waited until she saw a kindly-looking librarian, dressed in their somber garb and with his packs full of books, riding along the cliff road on his way to the palace. Then she set the child on the high grass at the cliff edge and stood up. The sudden, inexplicable emptiness between them caused them both to cry out: she said her daughter's name, and her daughter wailed the only word she knew. Kane's tears blurred sky and grass and the bright, dancing winds into painful swirls of color. When she threw herself over the cliff under the startled gaze of the librarian, it was because if she had not put such abrupt distance between them, she would have snatched up her child and wandered the worlds with her, nameless and impoverished except in memory, rather than part with her again.

She lingered in Raine just long enough to be sure that her

daughter had indeed found a home among the royal librarians. Then she returned, empty-handed, to Gilyriad, where Axis, sick with dread at her absence, had shut himself in the palace to wait for her.

He stepped into the terrible emptiness she had felt since she had left their daughter on the edge of the plain above the sea. He filled her arms, but not the aching hollow in her heart. She could not cry; she could not speak. She could only cling to him and tremble while he kissed her and murmured incoherent questions. Finally, he drew back a little to see her face.

"Where is our child?"

She wept then, enough to fill the Baltrean Sea and back the Serpent up until it flooded the fields of Eben with saltwater. She told him in their secret language, each thorn tearing her throat as she spoke it.

"There was nothing else I could do," she said again and again. "I did not know what else to do."

He held her, not understanding anything at first, and then finally beginning to see the impossibilities he had not noticed before: the deformed sorcerer nursing a child, or Axis's lover fighting openly beside him on the battlefield, becoming the subject of romance and epic, while his wife smoldered in Eben; the child Kane would not dare leave behind her dragged from battle to battle, dodging arrows as she learned to walk.

"I did not know what else to do."

Finally, when they had both wept all the tears in Gilyriad, their grief blunted with weariness and the comfort of their love, she told him about her plans for Raine.

"I want that land," she said, "for all of us. When the time comes, you will take it. But you will not conquer and vanish. This kingdom that values its scholars and mages you will make part of your empire. Do this for me."

"I will," he answered simply, for he trusted her vision, even if he did not always understand it. "How will we know when the time is right?"

"I have written something for her to read when she is older. I will see that it gets to her. It is her history, her background, her birthright. And our private history, yours and mine. When she understands it, she will tell us. When that time comes, she herself will open the Gates of Time and summon the Emperor of Night. When you take the Twelve Crowns, you will crown her Queen of Raine and she will rule in your name."

The Lion of Eben bent his head to Kane's wishes and raised her hand to his lips.

"And when will the time come?"

"The time is now," I told him.

For so it will be *now* in the future when you read this, my daughter, our daughter, child of Eben and the greatest empire the world will ever know. You are born of the timeless love between the Lion of Eben and the Masked Sorceress, and you are heir to all the open Gates of Time.

Open the Gates.

Summon us.

Remember your name.

# TWENTY-SIX

Nepenthe remembered.

Her name sounded in her head with all the force of the refectory gong, implacable and riveting, reverberating through her. It was the name she had heard in her dreams, the name she must have heard on the cliff's edge before her mother disappeared, and many times before that, in many different places.

"Of course," she breathed, slumping on weakened knees to the stone floor, dragging the open book with her onto her lap. It had always been there, her name, haunting the borderlands of memory, and as familiar, now that she heard it clearly, as morning. "Of course."

Then she froze like a mouse caught in a sudden spill of light in the larder. She did not dare blink. Something enormous had her trapped in its vision, its golden, watching eyes.

Thorns in her head twisted into poetry. *The Lion sees through time*, they reminded her. *Into a different day. Beware if that day is yours . . .*

It can't be true, she thought numbly. It can't be. "Bourne," she called, unable even to tremble. Her voice was no more than a trickle of sound. She felt as exposed as if someone had lifted the palace like a rock to see what lay beneath. "Bourne," she pleaded again in a cricket's chirr, a bat's squeal, unable to wrest any more sound than that out of her petrified self. Caught in a waking nightmare and with no help anywhere, she could not even scream. Bourne must have either been found by Vevay, or run away without Nepenthe. As though that would keep her safe. Or him. Or Laidley, or Master Croysus, or the Queen of Raine herself and her Twelve Crowns, all about to be overrun by an army pouring out of slashed veils of sky whose warriors were numberless as the fish in the sea.

"Bourne," she whispered. "Help me. Laidley. Where are you? I don't know what to do. I don't know what to do."

She became aware then of someone with her in the room, who was sitting on the stack of tablets Nepenthe used for a desk, and staring upward with equal intensity, as though she, too, were waiting for the roof to fall. Nepenthe jumped wildly, her voice freeing itself finally in a scream. The pale-haired stranger slid off the tablets and came to crouch next to Nepenthe, who was trying in vain to place her among the library scribes. She seemed oddly windblown; the pearl pins in her tangled hair had slid askew. By the look of her elegant dress, she must be some highborn young woman who had been amusing herself pretending to be a scholar, and who had gotten herself lost among the antiquities.

"Who are you?" Nepenthe demanded bewilderedly.

The girl gazed at her out of blue-washed eyes that seemed too wary and secretive to belong to a noble's spoiled daughter. She said, "I am the Queen of Raine."

Nepenthe swallowed a lump like a knot of words. The queen, she realized, had been sitting beside Nepenthe's translation of the thorns. If she had found her way this far into the ancient depths of the palace, they must be why.

"Did you—" she managed finally. "Did you read—"

"Yes. All of it. You remembered your name."

"I did." Her voice wobbled badly. "And there is nothing I can do about it. No way I can get us back to the time before I remembered it." She drew breath abruptly, looking askance at the queen. "You were watching me. You were invisible. Like a mage." The queen nodded. Her small, pale face didn't much resemble the face on her coins; it seemed blurred yet, somewhere between child and woman. "Are you a mage?" Nepenthe asked incredulously.

"You aren't what I expected either," the queen answered, responding more to Nepenthe's thoughts, she realized, than to her question. "I received warning of the thorns threatening the Twelve Crowns from the Dreamer." Nepenthe, her lips pinched tightly, gave a muffled squeak of despair. If the Dreamer saw the danger in them, then there could not be a single shard of hope that the tale they told might be only a tale, and the Emperor of Night only the hoary fragment to which poetry clung. "I went searching for the thorns and found them here. I had no idea who, in my own house, held such malice toward my entire realm. So I hid myself while I waited for the terrible sorcerer. It was you."

"I'm an orphaned transcriptor," Nepenthe whispered. "I've been in the library all of my life. There's not a breath of magic in me except for changing fish and thorns into words."

"Not," the queen reminded her, "an orphan. Not now."

Nepenthe closed her eyes, trying to hide again. "I'm sorry," she said through icy fingers. "I'm so sorry. I don't know—I don't know if there is any way to stop them—Axis and Kane—"

"Is that what you would choose? You could see your mother again and know your father. You could be rich and loved and protected. You could go anywhere in time, know anything you want. You could be Queen of Raine."

Nepenthe opened her eyes, stared at the young queen wordlessly. She was trembling now, chilled to her marrow as though all the boisterous winds of plain and sea had seeped through stone into that small chamber. She said finally, haltingly, "I never knew my father. My mother died when I was barely old enough to crawl. The librarians are the only family I have ever had. This library is my home, and the books in it the only places I've ever wanted to go. I've never dreamed of having anything else. Except maybe Bourne. And now a three-thousand-year-old marauding emperor and a sorceress who can travel through time say I am their daughter and they want to put your crown on my head. They're nothing to me! I'd rather keep my familiar world—books and ink pots and languages and Laidley and Bourne—That's what I would choose. If I had a choice. But I don't think we do."

The queen glanced up at the ceiling again, which so far remained unmoved. "I've been here all afternoon waiting for you. I've had some time to think."

"There's nothing anyone can do against Kane." Her throat ached with unshed tears. "You've read her book. You can see that."

A step at the door made her jump again. It evidently startled the queen, who promptly vanished. Laidley, his expression curdled, his mouth taut, came to Nepenthe's side to stare bleakly down at her.

"Laidley," she said without hope. "Did you find—"

"Nothing. I think we're in trouble."

"We are in trouble. The ending of the book of thorns summoned Axis and Kane to Raine."

"No," Laidley breathed, his face turning the color of boiled almonds.

"Yes."

"What does it say? Tell me exactly."

She read it to him, still crouched in the middle of the floor; he sagged down next to her, listening mutely.

He said softly, when she finished the brief passage, "She loved you very much."

"She left me. This is my world."

"She gets what she wants. She wants you back."

"Laidley," she wailed.

"Don't you want to be Queen of Raine?"

"Don't even think that!" she said fiercely, and saw the sudden, dreamy look in his eyes. "Stop seeing me like that! I'm not a desert princess. I am a transcriptor in the royal library of the rulers of Raine."

"Raine is on the verge of war anyway. Does it matter who starts it?"

"Stop," she said sharply, aware of the queen somewhere within the dust motes, but Laidley went off anyway, pursuing his thought.

"Think about it. You'd have your mother beside you to help you rule. You'd see the world instead of dwelling down here like a cave-bat. You could travel to any known kingdom. You could be there at the birth of epic; the point where the stark language of an event becomes colored with imagination."

"Laidley—" she said between her teeth. "Why are you saying these things to me? You can't really want them for me. I might ascend to an unimaginably brilliant life, but where would you be?"

"Still here, from the sound of it. I can't see Kane permitting the destruction of a library, and she does value translators."

Nepenthe's eyes stung drily. "How can you think I would choose such a thing if I had a choice at all?"

"Who would blame you?" Laidley asked simply. "History moves in great, messy shifts of power, in choices made as though by too many people building a house, where one misplaced stone in the foundation slips under the weight of another stone near the roof. Even if the thorns have lost their power and nothing happens to you, Ermin's war may cause enough chaos in the Twelve Crowns to shift power from the First Crown to the Ninth. Or it may pull us all into many squabbling kingdoms, and ten years from now, when we prepare for yet another siege, you may well wish that you had made a different choice today."

"I don't have a choice," she said grimly. She took his hand then, and he turned a rich, winey color she had never seen before. "But I do know this one thing: you have known me and loved me day after day for years. That is more valuable to me than a mother who left me at the edge of the cliff for the librarians to find before I had a tooth in my head."

"Well," he said gruffly, with a trace of his sweet smile, "that's something for me to remember when you're dressed in silk and surrounded by peacocks."

"Don't—"

"I don't understand why you wouldn't want this, if it's remotely possible—"

"Because she only exists in a different language!" she cried. "She's nothing more to me now than thorns. On a page. In a book. Even if she becomes real to me, how could we even talk to each other? And it sounds so lonely. I'll be surrounded by people from all kinds of worlds, and I won't know any of them, and none of them will know me. They won't know my history, since it doesn't exist yet, and theirs is so old it barely exists except in poetry. It will be like living with dreams and ghosts. I'd rather take my chances with the only life I know, and—

"Who is that?" Laidley interrupted bemusedly.

"Our history in the making, and Ermin of Seale at our door instead of—" She became aware of the queen beside her again, listening intently. "Oh. This is the Queen of Raine. She was warned of the thorns and came down here searching for them."

Laidley gawked. "You don't look like the coins."

"I know," said the queen.

He flushed again. "I'm sorry. I don't—I don't know how I should talk to you—and I guess I've said a great deal too much already."

"It seems moot," she answered evenly, "at this point. I may not be queen for long."

"Oh." His hands slid up his arms then, gripped hard. "Oh," he said again, the word wavering as though he had begun to lose his balance. "It's true, then? We really are about to be attacked."

"So it seems."

"Well, should we—what should we—what," he suggested, "about Vevay? Can she stop them?"

"I thought you preferred a different outcome," the queen reminded him.

"That was speculation," he said dazedly. "Scholarly babble. I really prefer a simple world in which I can see Nepenthe every day."

"I see." Her young voice sounded a bit less remote. "I would not like to suspect sedition in my library."

"No. It was more resignation to the inevitable. Is it?" he inquired, his eyes widening nervously. "Inevitable?"

"So it seems," Nepenthe said tightly.

"What about the mages at the school? Can't they do something?"

"I believe so," said the queen.

"And Vevay—She must be as old as Kane—she might think of something."

"We'll ask her," the queen answered, "since she has been here listening for some time."

Laidley closed his eyes, put a hand over them. Nepenthe rose finally from her mouse's crouch on the floor, as a line or two that seemed not Vevay at all sketched themselves in the air. She closed her own eyes, stepping toward what her heart had recognized before it had finished shaping itself.

"Bourne."

She felt his arms around her, melting her ice-locked thoughts, her hoar-frosted bones. "I went to Vevay," she heard him say. "I was so afraid that the thorns might have us all trapped in their tale."

"I think they do. At least you're here with me now. Stay with me," she pleaded. "No matter what happens. Promise—"

His hold tightened around her. "For as long as you want me," he promised blindly into her hair. "I will stay."

"Well," Vevay said, her voice so tart that it drew all their attention as she stood among the dusty remnants of forgotten kingdoms. Her long, silvery hair seemed to spark with anger and frustrated power in the gloom. "Never in my very long life—though not quite so long as you, Laidley, seem to think—have I had to deal with war against Raine from the depths of the royal library. And no, I have not got a single inkling of what to do next."

"I do," said the Queen of Raine. "I know how to hide."

# TWENTY-SEVEN

The queen was in the wood, watching warriors without number pour out of a gash in the sky onto the plain like ink out of a cracked jar, staining the limpid water of the pool that reflected them, the green plain, the sky itself black. They kept coming. Hidden deep within the wood's heart, in the shape of an old crumbling stump or a mossy bank, something half-enchanted, the queen was aware of a terror that did not seem to belong to her. It was distant, detached: a hare trembling under a log, a vole under a leaf. The wide, unblinking eye of the pool was her eye, gazing at the alien magic amassing in her realm. A fine, hidden root work of thought linked her with the familiar powers around her. It was as though she glimpsed others' dreams as they slept: the mages and Vevay and even Bourne weaving illusions of airy nothing around the school, the palace, the folk on the plain, and the nobles and servants within the walls. Even as they watched, their stunned minds trying to comprehend the impossible, they were hidden within the minds of the mages: dreams that did not know they were dreams.

The Emperor of Night appeared clearly in the pool. The crowned figure had ridden into the middle of the plain and waited there while his army flowed on currents of wind, it seemed, down to the grass around him. The tall, slender figure beside him drew Tessera's attention. All the warriors wore cloths over their faces. But the rider wearing black from hair to heel stayed close as a shadow at the emperor's side. Kane, Tessera guessed, and felt the hare's thumping heart as the veiled face turned at the thought of her name. Tessera could not guess what any of them were seeing or thinking. She would not know until Axis finally spoke if the spell she and the mages had cast would hold beyond Kane's first glance at it.

She could see the spell clearly, the magic imposed over the real. Axis's army, still coming, surrounded the little wood like floodwaters. But the spell over the wood made it seem, at first glance, only the lifeless remains of itself, as though Kane had led them all into some far future that not even she had foreseen. All the magic had seeped away and the trees had died. Only stumps and the silvery bones of broken trunks remained of it. In the middle of the dead wood, a crumbling section of wall stood, still guarding the place where the Floating School had once been. It might have taken itself elsewhere sometime in the past centuries; not a hint of it remained.

The tiny pool, Tessera's eye, could see it clearly, cocooned above the wood within an illusion of cloud and sky. Coaxed by

Felan, it had found the center of its own complex labyrinth and hidden itself there, turning its inner empty spaces outward to surround and conceal it. She could not tell if Kane saw it. The dark, silky head of the sorcerer, eyeless as a beetle, turned this way and that, scenting, it seemed, rather than seeing.

The palace of the rulers of Raine still rose from the cliff edge. Once it might have been an intricate, magnificent structure towering above the plain like a small mountain. Now, yawning gates hung by their hinges and slowly splintered. Sagging walls revealed inner rooms choked with grasses and weeds and ceiling stones that had fallen through many floors above. Broken towers had shrugged small hillocks of stone into courtyards and roofless outbuildings. Stairs climbed above cracked walls and ended in space. The palace looked as though it had been decaying for more centuries than Raine had existed; it was being swallowed back into the plain. Along one broad wall gilded with late afternoon sun, a flowering vine grew to what seemed an impossible height, opening great golden trumpet-shaped blossoms to the briny air like a memory within a bitter past of something that had once been good.

The warriors had finally finished coming out of the sky. They covered the entire plain, from the cliff edge to the distant hills beyond which Ermin of Seale so obliviously marched. The pure black that had loosed them was now a gaping, empty seam across the blue. On the plain nothing moved but a horse's flicking tail, a windblown scarf. No one spoke.

Finally the crowned warrior turned his eyes away from the ruined palace to his companion. Tessera could not tell if he spoke. Kane did not look at him. All her attention seemed to be snagged on something in the heart of the ancient stones. She dismounted suddenly. Tessera would have blinked if she could. The pool stayed still, watching. A thought surfaced, the first coherent word in the queen's head for some time.

Thorns.

They were snaking up a shadowy corner between two walls, leafing as they grew, flowering. Tessera watched the spell blooming out of illusion, too mesmerized to be afraid yet. Were they the thorns from the book in the library? she wondered. That magic, Kane's own spell, no one could hide from her. Or were they the thorns that had taken root in Kane's daughter's heart?

As though hearing the wonder from the wood, the Masked Sorceress turned her invisible face toward the trees.

Briefly, Tessera remembered the body that she was hiding. It wanted, in that moment, to spring in panic out of hiding and to run wildly in any direction. But her magic covered it with a crust of moldering wood, moss, bracken. Her hair had rooted itself; her mind seemed to drift like a fish near the bottom of the water. The placid pool, reflecting the two most dangerous faces in the world, remained unruffled when the Emperor of Night pulled apart the black swaths of silk that masked him.

Tessera gazed into the Lion's face.

It seemed hammered out of eons of desert and sun: broad, golden, implacable, and merciless as the harsh sands of Eben. His eyes were wide, tawny gold. Thwarted by the baffling landscape, they remained unreadable. He was looking at his battle-consort, whose invisible face still contemplated the wood. She turned her head, feeling those eyes, and said something to him in a language that Tessera guessed was spoken that day nowhere else in the world.

Then she vanished.

She reappeared so quickly to stand over the pool that she might have seen herself disappear in it. Tessera saw her veiled head again, this time terrifyingly close, peering into the water. The wide, motionless eye of the pool stared unblinkingly back at her.

Again she spoke, very softly. This time Tessera heard, but the word meant nothing to her. The queen, so deeply hidden within the wood, could not even tremble. Whatever word Kane had said did not reveal Tessera; if the sorceress knew the queen was there, she paid no attention. Tessera waited. So did Kane. She sat down on a stump beside the pool. Her hands moved to her veils; for a moment it seemed she would push them aside within the privacy of the trees. But habit stopped her. Tessera could not guess which wood she saw: the dead, gray shards of trees, or the living wood with the queen dispersed through it, eyelashes like blades of grass, fingers like mushrooms, just beneath the surface. She wondered what the sorceress was waiting for.

After what seemed an endless moment, during which even the emperor and his army did nothing, Tessera saw the flowering thorns along the wall across the plain vanish.

They reappeared, too quickly for anyone to have noticed their passage across the plain. And as quickly, they revealed the secret word within the canes: Nepenthe.

She had a few brambles caught in her hair; her fingernails finished shaping themselves out of thorns. She looked half-entranced, half-appalled at the sight of the veiled, featureless head; a sound like a mouse's squeal came out of her. The sorceress lifted her hands quickly, tugged at the silk. Nothing came away easily; she had protected herself too well for too many years. But little by little like a butterfly out of its cocoon, veils loosening and parting, her face appeared.

Nepenthe stared. So did the pool. They looked much alike, the young transcriptor and her three-thousand-year-old mother, with their wide-set eyes and graceful, sculpted bones, their thick, dark hair. Kane's eyes were smoky, opaque; Nepenthe's reflected green within the wood. Her mother's rippling hair was severely braided, while Nepenthe's ran wildly to her waist, with a thorny twig caught here and there, still bound by the frayed spell.

The sorceress said something incomprehensible to her daughter. Nepenthe only looked bewildered, panicked. In that moment Kane seemed to see the vast distance she had put between them when she fell off the cliff into the mists of time. She reached out, gently untangled a stray twig of bramble from her daughter's hair, and held it up. In her fingers it became malleable, twisting to form familiar letters of thorn.

"'I,'" Nepenthe translated, her voice wavering badly. "'Came. For. You.'" She backed a step, shaking her head frantically, hair whipping across her eyes. "No. No. You came to conquer. You came to destroy. You and my father think you can take whatever worlds you want. How could you possibly think I would welcome you here? That I would be grateful to you for coming back after all these years to take away the world I know?"

Kane, interpreting without benefit of language, seemed to hear with her heart her daughter's expressions, the torment and passion in her voice. Her own face suddenly anguished, she held up the little twisting shoot of thorns again.

"'We. Will. Give. You. Every—'" Nepenthe's voice broke on the word; she backed again, her eyes wide, like a cornered animal's. "Nothing here belongs to you! You have nothing here to give! Go away! Leave us alone! You want to give me a kingdom, but you don't know me. You are ancient. Ghosts. Nothing that belongs here. I don't know you—" The thorns spoke again, so quickly they caught at the sorceress's fingers, drawing blood. "'I. Am. Your. Mother. You. Are—' You left me! I learned to live without you. I learned to love without you. You came back too late. Please." She clasped her hands, still stumbling backward. "Please. Just go. It's Axis you love. Stay with him. Forget me and go."

Kane spoke. Nepenthe shook her head fiercely at the word. "No. That's not my name. Nepenthe is my name."

"Nepenthe," the sorceress said. Her own voice trembled. Nepenthe stopped moving and stared at her wordlessly, her hands twisting together. Again the thorns spoke; Nepenthe translated.

"'Do. Not. Leave. Me.'

"You have Axis," Nepenthe whispered. "You have all of time and everything you want—" She paused as the thorns shaped their letters again.

"'Kane. Speaks,'" they said. "'I. Have. No. Name. I. Cannot. Speak.'"

Nepenthe was silent again. The sorceress's face turned briefly away from her as at another summons from the plain. Her eyes glittered oddly as though, Tessera saw, she were about to cry. She said something in her ancient language; the thorns in her hand remained silent.

Nepenthe spoke, her voice nearly soundless in the dead wood. "What is your real name?"

The emperor called again; the sorceress's face twisted as she glanced between wood and plain with desperate indecision.

Then she dropped the thorns without a word, wound the veils again around her head, and vanished.

Nepenthe grew thorns where she stood, out of Kane's spell or out of her own frightened heart, great tangled brambles heavy with leaf and flower, a living anomaly in the dead wood, until no one noticing them with an unmagical eye would see the young woman hiding within the thorns.

Tessera waited for the pulse of numberless hooves pounding across the plain as the sorceress revealed the living realm to the emperor.

She waited. A breeze rippled across the pool. Brambles

stirred, shaped new letters in the air. The great army began to move finally, a vast, unwieldy maelstrom across the entire plain. The eye of the pool grew dark with it, stayed dark for a very long time. Tessera could no longer see the sky, only the endless march of warriors across her realm. She could not tell what direction they were going until the sky began to show a ragged edge of blue. Then she saw the river running back-ward, the army of the night flowing back into the boundless realm of time above the plain.

She did not move for a long time after they vanished. No one did. The old ruins still slumped into themselves on the cliff; the Floating School refused to come down. The green brambles remained brambles, where it was safe. The wood stayed dead. Only the sun moved, dipping slowly behind one of the broken towers above the sea.

Then a bird cried on the plain. So it sounded at first to Tessera, until its strange cry grew more insistent, stronger, and the voice turned suddenly human as the sound it made took shape.

"Nepenthe," it pleaded, the name borne on the sudden wings of wind across the plain. "Nepenthe! Nepenthe!"

The thorns shook. Tessera's eye found the single figure re-maining on the plain: a woman unwrapping veils as she called, loosing them into the wind where they soared like dark birds, tossed from current to current until they rose so high they were recognizable only in memory.

"Nepenthe!"

Nepenthe shook herself free of the thorns. They dwindled and vanished back into her, shedding leaves and flowers behind her as she ran toward her mother on the plain.

Later, hidden deep within the Floating School, surrounded by mages, the sorceress of Eben explained to the Queen of Raine what she had done. She wrote her words in the language of thorn; Nepenthe translated. Tessera watched their faces hovering close together over the paper; alike as sisters, they looked at once timeless and haunted by thousands of years of history.

"I told the emperor that I had led his army by accident too far into the future of Raine," her thorns said in Nepenthe's voice. "I asked him to return to Gilyriad while I searched for the true path to the kingdom where I had left our daughter. He believed me. He trusted me always. He will never see me again." Her pen paused, ink swelling like a tear in the nib. The pen touched paper again before it could fall. "He cannot open the Gates of Time himself. He will remain trapped in his own time, in his world. He may still weave his life into legend and poetry, but he will do it in more predictable ways.

"Of Axis and Kane nothing more will ever be written."

There was a longer silence from the pen, while the sorceress seemed to contemplate past and future in the blank paper beneath the nib. She wrote finally, "It was time. I had nothing of my own, not even my own name." Nepenthe, as though hearing an echo of her own life, stared briefly at her mother. "I had only Axis and our child. I learned today that it is not possible for me to be with them both. I had to choose." Her eyes went to Tessera before she continued. "You do not have to fear me. All I did on the battlefield, I did for Axis. The only thing I ever wanted for myself was him. And our daughter.

"Here in Raine, I can walk with the sunlight on my face. I can speak to anyone who speaks to me. I can learn my daughter's language. I can be called the name I was given when I was born.

"Here I am no longer my own secret.

"Will you let me stay?"

Tessera tested the ring of silence around her as the mages waited for her answer. She sensed calm, astonishment, and very lively curiosity; the air seemed untroubled by mistrust or dissent. Her eyes went to Nepenthe, found nothing ambiguous in her face. She looked still stunned but on the whole quite willing to admit the woman who had emerged out of the pages of a book into her life. Lastly, Tessera consulted Vevay.

You are queen, the mage's eyes told her. You choose.

The queen said to Nepenthe, "You may tell her that she is welcome."

"Thank you," Nepenthe breathed, and took the pen to curl thorns haltingly into words. Her mother did not glance at them. She gazed at Tessera, her eyes limpid, motionless, until with an inner start the queen began to realize what legendary power she had invited into her realm.

The sorceress bowed her head then to the queen, who added dazedly to Nepenthe, "You may stay with her here at the school with the mages while she learns to speak to us."

Nepenthe's glance flicked to Bourne, who was smiling. She said again, "Thank you. You—I caused so much trouble. You're being very generous to us."

"Without your mother's sacrifices, I wouldn't be wearing my crown," Tessera said simply. "I owe her."

"Indeed," Felan said with satisfaction, "she will be an extraordinary asset both to the school and to the library."

"There is still," Tessera said, feeling suddenly weary, wishing to be crusted with moss again and spread thoughtlessly about the wood, "the problem of Ermin of Seale."

"Who ceased being a problem some hours ago," Vevay told her gently. "I spoke to Gavin before Axis appeared and told him to warn the queen's warriors to take cover where they could and to attract no attention until it was no longer possible to avoid battle. Beyond that I didn't explain. I wasn't—I couldn't think exactly how . . . Apparently Ermin reached the eastern foothills beyond the plain this afternoon while Axis and his army were still riding out of the sky. Ermin took one look at what was waiting for him on the plain, and according to Gavin, his army is on its way back to the Second Crown as fast as it can go. Gavin is completely mystified. I still haven't really explained . . . Ermin will probably not stop fleeing until he has put the Twelve Crowns of Raine between him and you. You will have to decide what you want to do with his family. But not today. Everyone here saw what threatened to overwhelm us on Dreamer's Plain. That will cause the rulers of the Crowns to think twice before they weaken the realm with war. And when they hear how you saved Raine—"

"I hid," Tessera interrupted blankly.

"Well, it was more than any of us could think of doing. You found the thorns. You recognized the terrible danger to Raine. You didn't panic. You outwitted your foe. And you performed more feats of magic in one afternoon than all but three rulers of Raine did in their lives. All the Crowns have profound reasons to be grateful for your courage."

Tessera stared at her, astonished by the word. Nepenthe's mother dipped the pen again; all eyes were drawn to its busy scratchings. Nepenthe translated.

"You would have outwitted Axis even without me," the thorns said. "No other ruler in history has ever defeated the Emperor of Night."

The queen felt a tremor within the circle, like a shock of recognition. She found its source in Vevay, who was gazing blankly at the air, her pale eyes filmy with thought.

"I was just remembering," she explained vaguely, hearing Tessera's wordless question, "something a fortune-teller on the plain foresaw in a rainbow of crystals and pigs' knuckles at a time when it seemed your reign was doomed before it even began . . ." Whatever it was, it kindled a sudden confidence in Vevay that Tessera hadn't seen since her father died. "Magic," she murmured, "in the smallest, most unlikely things . . . I needed to be reminded of that."

Nepenthe's mother, her eye on Tessera, smiled faintly as though she had translated without thorns. The queen stood up, tugged toward the confusion and agitation under her roof.

"I'd better go and explain," she said, then blinked at the

enormity of putting a book of thorns, a three-thousand-year-old emperor, an orphaned transcriptor, a pathway through time, and swaths of ancient poetry into simple language. "How do I explain?"

"You'll think of something," Vevay said briskly, rising to accompany her as always into the next complication. "Just begin at the beginning and proceed whichever way you can into hope."